GEORGE MACDONALD FRASER

Captain in Calico

HARPER

Harper
An imprint of HarperCollins*Publishers*
1 London Bridge Street
London SE1 9GF

www.harpercollins.co.uk

First published by HarperCollins*Publishers* 2015

This paperback edition 2016
1

A catalogue record for this book is available from the British Library

ISBN: 978 0 00 810559 4

This novel is entirely a work of fiction. The names, characters and incidents
portrayed in it are the work of the author's imagination. Any resemblance to
actual persons, living or dead, events or localities is entirely coincidental.

Typeset in Janson by Palimpsest Book Production Ltd, Falkirk, Stirlingshire

Printed and bound in Great Britain by Clays Ltd, St Ives plc

MIX
Paper from
responsible sources
FSC
www.fsc.org FSC™ C007454

A Foreword to *Captain in Calico*

The stories we loved best as children were the ones our father used to tell us on Saturday nights, when we would snuggle together under the bedcovers and wait for him to pick up from whatever cliffhanger he'd left us on the week before. The room would be lit only by the glow of a small electric fire, and when the story began, it was like falling into another world. Our father had a warm, dark voice, perfect for story-telling, and invariably the story would be about pirates. He had a special fondness for those outlaws of the sea; their flawed, restless characters captured his imagination more than honourable heroes ever could. It was a lifelong love, and so it was hardly surprising that his first attempt at full-length fiction, *Captain in Calico*, should be a pirate story.

He evidently laboured at it and reworked it over a number of years, presumably in any spare time he had from working long hours as a journalist and bringing up a young family. The book is full of the influences of the writers he had loved as a boy – Sabatini, Wren, Henty, Sir Walter Scott – and the story itself is an old-fashioned yarn of the type he told us as children, but with added sex and violence. The story is based quite closely on real events in the lives of 'Calico' Jack Rackham and Anne Bonney, who were both notorious eighteenth-century pirates (and lovers), reflecting our father's belief that the most compelling stories are those of real events happening to real people. Despite the failure of *Captain in Calico* to find a publisher, his faith in the method of using fiction to bring history to life was borne out by the later success of the Flashman novels, in which he embroidered real historical events with the exploits of his fictional anti-hero. It is interesting to see him trying his hand at a prototype anti-hero in the character of Jack Rackham, and he evidently worked hard to make him a sympathetic rogue with heroic appeal. But it was only when he came to write *Flashman* that he hit upon the perfect device, creating an out-and-out cad who triumphs heroically through a mixture of luck and charm, and in spite of his own cowardice and deceit.

Captain in Calico was rejected by publishers, and in time he came to regard these rejections as justifiable – in the margin of an early typed account of its rejection he has written, apparently years later, the word 'deservedly' – but we believe he retained affection for the story, and the spark of his early and earnest faith in its merits never quite died. We say this because we believe he would have destroyed it otherwise, not left it in a fireproof safe in his old study for us to find after his death. Of course, eventually he hit upon the inspiration of bringing his beloved pirates to life in a quite different way, when he wrote *The Pyrates* – a book of comic genius, and one to which the movie *Pirates of the Caribbean* may owe more than a small debt.

An early reader's report on the manuscript and letters from The Authors' Alliance, which are reprinted here, are direct in their criticisms of the work, seeing it as over-long and derivative. But whatever the novel's flaws, there is no denying that the style is polished, the characters are deftly drawn, and the writing is vivid and powerful.

A book such as *Captain in Calico* would probably be even less likely to find a publisher today than sixty years ago – not because it isn't excellently written, but because ripping yarns are hardly fashionable now – and we do not want readers to be deceived into thinking it is vintage George MacDonald Fraser, and of the standard of the Flashman novels or the McAuslan short stories. Indeed, we thought long and hard before allowing it to be published, and are only doing so because we believe that, as an early work, *Captain in Calico* is a delightful curiosity, one which we hope will provide fans of GMF with a fascinating insight into the inspirations and creative impulses that turned him into such a fine novelist. That he was always a great storyteller was never in doubt. We knew that as children, long ago.

Sie, Caro and Nick Fraser

Contents

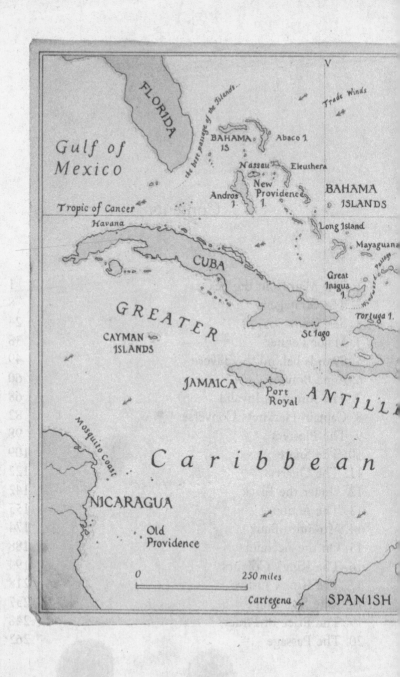

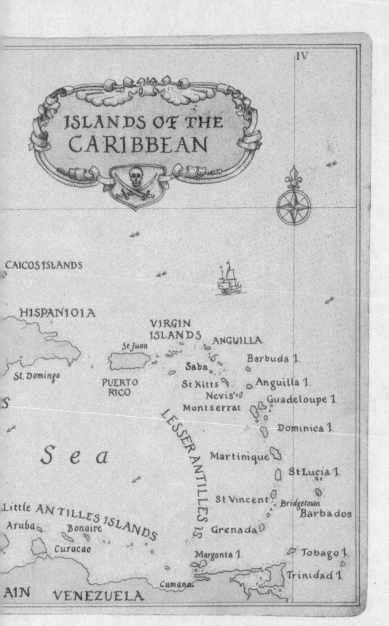

ISLANDS OF THE CARIBBEAN

CAICOS ISLANDS

HISPANIOLA

St Domingo

VIRGIN
ISLANDS

St Juan

PUERTO
RICO

Saba

St Kitts
Nevis
Montserrat

ANGUILLA

Barbuda 1.

Anguilla 1.

Guadeloupe 1.

Dominica 1.

S e a

LESSER ANTILLES IS.

Martinique

St Lucia 1.

Little ANTILLES ISLANDS

Aruba   Bonaire

Curacao

St Vincent

Grenada

Margarita 1.

Bridgetown

Barbados

Tobago 1.

Trinidad 1.

Cumana

AIN   VENEZUELA

1. THE MAN FROM THE SEA

Surveying the distant strand of silver beach washed by the blue Caribbean rollers, Master Tobias Dickey made a mental remark that the view was prodigious fine and life was very good to live. His contentment was born out of a good supper eaten after a hard day's work, and also out of that sense of wellbeing which had possessed him ever since the day on which he had first set foot in this beautiful New Providence of the Bahamas.

He stood at his window in Governor's House, a small, portly man well advanced into middle age, pulling at his pipe of Gibraltar tobacco and comparing its fragrance with that of the bougainvillea with which the garden abounded. Life and the evening were quiet, and Master Dickey never dreamed that he was waiting on the threshold of a high adventure in which he was to be called to play a not unimportant part.

'When I reflect,' he was to write later in his journal, 'on the Peaceful Temper with which I compos'd myself to Rest, suspecting nothing of what was to Befall, I never cease to wonder at the manner in which Providence ever reserv's its

1

most Sudden Strokes for the time when we are least prepar'd, even as the Tempest Breaks when the Tropick Day is most Serene.'

Certainly nothing could have been more placid and contentedly reflective than Master Dickey's mood as he knocked out his pipe, took a last look at the scene on which the sudden Caribbean night would shortly be descending, half closed the broad screen doors and prepared for bed.

It was a far cry, he thought, from a draughty garret in Edinburgh to a Governor's residence, from clerking in an advocate's office to his present post as first secretary, man-of-affairs, and close confidant of the Governor of the Bahamas, Captain Woodes Rogers. Yet it had only been the merest chance that had crossed his path with Woodes Rogers' two years ago when the captain had been renting the Bahama Islands from the Lords Proprietors and obtaining a commission as Governor. Dickey had been a cog in the legal machine which had been engaged on that complex business, but Rogers, the great discoverer and privateer, had noted his diligence and had offered him his present employment. Dickey had accepted with the eagerness of one escaping from slavery, nor, he reflected as he climbed into his comfortable bed and watched the shadows lengthen across his spacious apartment, had he had cause for one moment to regret his step.

Since their landing in New Providence two years ago and the expulsion of those pirates who had used it as a haven there had been much to occupy the new Governor and his assistant. Woodes Rogers saw the Bahamas as an estate of which he was to be steward for twenty-one years, and he set about to make it a model for the Western seas. To a remarkable extent he had succeeded and Master Dickey, at the

Governor's right hand in all things, had been made to feel that he too was doing his share towards making history in the Caribbean.

Thus Master Dickey had ample grounds for satisfaction as he lay musing, and as the shadows deepened in the garden outside he began to doze gently.

He came out of his half-sleep with a sudden start, his thoughts racing back to identify the noise that had disturbed him. Something had moved on the verandah. There had been a quick scraping, as though a foot had brushed over the boards. He listened, straining to catch the sound again, and gradually, as he lay in the warm silence, he became aware of an almost imperceptible but regular rustling just beyond the screen doors. Someone was standing there, and Tobias could hear him breathing.

It was almost dark outside, and he could see nothing but the dim oblong of light between the doors. Slowly he reached out a hand towards the table at the side of his bed, in the drawer of which he kept a loaded pistol as a precaution against nocturnal marauders. His hand closed on the knob and at the same moment a board creaked on the verandah, and a vague shape loomed in the narrow space between the doors.

Sweat broke out on Master Dickey's forehead, but the hand which drew open the drawer and descended on the pistol butt was quite steady. Gently he drew the weapon out and rested it across his body, the barrel pointing towards the window.

'Come in wi' your hands up', he ordered, his finger ready on the trigger in case the intruder should make a sudden move.

To his astonishment the screen doors were pushed gently aside and the figure on the verandah stepped into the room.

3

'If you have a pistol, take care what you're about,' said a deep voice.

'God save us!' exclaimed Master Dickey. He sat bolt upright in bed, the pistol extended in the direction of the stranger. 'Stop you there, my lad. Not a step closer. Guards!' He raised his voice in summons. 'Guards!'

'Why wake the house?' The stranger's voice sounded almost amused to Master Dickey's incredulous ears. 'You've no need for guards. My business is with Governor Rogers.'

'Governor Rogers?' Master Dickey pushed back the bed clothes and stepped out on to the floor, keeping the bed between himself and his mysterious visitor. 'And what the devil d'ye mean by creeping aboot my window, then? Guards!' he shouted again. It seemed that the intruder must be a lunatic.

The heavy tramp of feet and the sound of voices in the passage outside his door heralded the arrival of sentries. Knuckles rapped on the panels.

'Private Nicholas, sir. Is aught the matter?'

'Come in!' called Dickey sharply, and the door opened. 'Light the candle on my side table, sharp, now! There's a mad man in here and I have a pistol pointin' at him.'

'Christ!' exclaimed the startled soldier. Dickey, his eyes still straining against the dark at the dim figure beyond the bed, heard the sentry stumble against the table as he fumbled for the candle.

There was a rasp of flint, and then a yellow spear of flame as the sentry lit the candle. By the candle's faint light the dark shape on which Dickey's pistol was trained came to life as a big man in white shirt and breeches, with a kerchief bound sailor-fashion round his head, who stood calmly surveying the little lawyer and the gaping sentry. In the

4

doorway the light twinkled on the brass buttons of a guard sergeant, and behind him Dickey saw the startled faces of two other soldiers.

The intruder's face, aquiline and brown as a gypsy's, wore an expression of mild amusement. 'You're a game little bantam,' he remarked to Dickey. 'Governor Rogers should sleep easy of nights.'

'Haud your tongue!' snapped Tobias. 'Sergeant, when ye've done gawping d'ye think ye might tak' this thief o' the night under arrest? Bestir yourself, man!'

Hastily the sergeant strode forward and grasped the intruder by the arm. The guards stationed themselves one at each side of the prisoner. With a sigh of relief Master Dickey laid aside his pistol.

'A fine watch ye keep, sergeant,' he observed acidly. 'Hauf the hoose might have been murdered in their beds, and where were you wi' your sentries?'

The sergeant glowered at the prisoner. 'Come on, you,' he began, but Master Dickey cut him short.

'Wait, wait, wait. Sentry, get another light till we see what manner of bird we've caught.' He came round the end of the bed and confronted the prisoner. 'You, now. Who are ye and what are ye after?'

The big man smiled down at him. He was a fine-looking fellow, Dickey admitted, a grand body of a man with those mighty shoulders and that narrow waist. 'You'll grin on the other side of your face, my buckie,' the lawyer added sharply. 'What d'ye mean, keekin' in my door at this hour o' the nicht?'

'I told you,' replied the prisoner mildly. 'I want to see Governor Rogers. Why else would I be here?'

'Tae rob and murder, like enough,' snapped Master

Dickey. 'For why did ye no' come in the light o' day like an honest man?'

'I'll talk to Governor Rogers,' said the other.

Master Dickey stared and shook his head. 'The man's plainly demented,' he observed. 'Here, you, sergeant, tak' him tae the guard-house. Ye'll see the Governor, my lad, have nae fear o' that. And ye'll no' be so glib then, I'm thinking.'

The sergeant tightened his grip on the prisoner's arm, but without apparent effort the big man brushed it away.

'I'll see the Governor,' he said quietly. 'What I have to say won't wait. I've no wish to spend the night in some stinking prison, either. Now, sir,' he addressed Dickey, 'you seem to be a man of some sense; you may be sure Governor Rogers will want to see me, even if he has to leave his bed for it. Will you summon him, or shall I shout for him?'

In spite of the man's cool insolence, Dickey found himself impressed. There might be something in what he said. In these troubled times the Governor had dealings with some queer cattle, and the lawyer had been in New Providence long enough to learn not to judge folk by their appearance. Then too, the fellow had given no trouble; he had not the look of a petty thief, nor was he armed. Master Dickey frowned and pondered and made his decision.

'Call the Governor, sergeant, if ye please.'

The prisoner inclined his head. 'I'm obliged to you, sir.'

Master Dickey's judgement in summoning the Governor proved to be sound. A less active official than Woodes Rogers might have consigned the mysterious visitor to the lock-up for the night and Master Dickey to perdition for ever, but the Governor of the Bahamas was a man who had learned in a hard school the value of prompt investigation. When roused from sleep and informed that a sea-faring man wished to see him on a matter of importance, Rogers said nothing beyond a command that the anonymous intruder should be conducted to the study.

Presently he descended to the hall, wearing a light silk robe over his sleeping clothes, and heard the full tale of Master Dickey's adventure from the lawyer himself. The little Scot was not at his best; he had discovered in returning his pistol to its drawer that it had not been loaded and, in consequence, his report was less calm and ordered than it should have been. Rogers received it without comment and passed on into the long panelled study where the prisoner awaited him.

2. THE STRATAGEM

Dismissing the guard with instructions that sentries be posted in the passage and outside the window, Rogers seated himself behind the long polished table which served him for a desk. Master Dickey took his place unobtrusively at his own smaller table by the window while the Governor considered the tall seaman who stood before him.

Woodes Rogers at this time was slightly past his prime, although still young to have reached the eminence to which his talents had raised him. Discoverer, circumnavigator, sea-fighter and administrator, to his fellow-countrymen in that second decade of the eighteenth century he was comparable with Drake and Raleigh, and not least because of his privateering exploits in the South Sea against the old enemy, Spain. These, incidentally, had made him immensely rich.

Tall, spare and active in spite of the greying hair at his temples, he had the air of one completely masterful and self-possessed. The light from the slender candles threw into relief his prominent nose and high cheek-bones; in spite of an expression which was naturally severe and the puckered scars where a Spanish musket-ball had shattered his jaw he was not unhandsome. His mouth was large and generous and his grey eyes startlingly bright against his weather-beaten skin. They ranged briefly now over the tall figure before him.

'Your name?'

The big man shifted his weight on to his other foot and said easily: 'John Rackham.'

Woodes Rogers' eyes opened a little wider and then he pushed the candlebranch away very deliberately and repeated the name.

'John Rackham. Also known as Calico Jack.'

The big man smiled faintly and nodded. 'So they call me,' he said, with a touch of pride in his voice.

Master Dickey was conscious of a certain coolness on his spine which was not caused by the night air. Of course he knew the name, as he knew the names of 'Blackbeard' Ned Teach and Stede Bonnet and every other freebooter of note in the Caribbean waters. But it was one thing to know the name and quite another to be sitting within a few paces of the man himself and to recall that only a few moments earlier he had been trying conclusions with him in a darkened room with an unloaded pistol.

This Rackham, he recalled, had been one of the pirate brotherhood at New Providence in those fateful days when Woodes Rogers had brought his ships to the island and sent in his proclamation demanding their surrender with the promise of Royal pardon for all who complied. And Rackham had been quartermaster to the pirate Charles Vane who fired on Rogers' ships and fought his way out of the harbour, since when there had been a price on the heads of Vane, Rackham, and the rest of their ship's company. That was two years ago, and in that time Vane's notoriety had spread from end to end of the western seas. There had been his exploit against the Spanish silver fleet in the Florida Gulf and talk of a great treasure taken – the heat with which the Spaniards' protests had been urged at St James' was proof to a knowledgeable world of the blow their pockets must have suffered, and Vane's stock had mounted accordingly.

Of Rackham himself little was known by comparison, and Master Dickey cast back mentally in search of anything he had heard. He thought he recalled the fellow's seamanship being highly spoken of, and he had something of a reputation as a gallant, too. There had been some mention of a woman whom he was to have married in New Providence before he and Vane had fled . . . Master Dickey could not be sure. But for the moment his very presence was sensation enough and Master Dickey felt a not unpleasant excitement once his first surprise had settled.

Woodes Rogers, his voice as level as ever, said:

'I must suppose there is some reason why you should thrust your head into a noose by coming here. For that is what you have done, you realise?'

Rackham's smile faded, but he gave no other sign of apprehension.

'If I'd thought that, I'd not be here. I've no wish to decorate a gibbet yet awhile, though I can understand your Excellency's haste to find one for me. You see me on an errand of mercy, or rather an errand of pardon, which in this case you may think the same thing.'

Woodes Rogers sat back in his chair, staring, and then his brows contracted in an angry frown. 'Pardon? Do I understand that you come here seeking that? You, that for two years have been at large as a pirate, with a price on your head? By God, ye deserve to hang for insolence, if nothing else.' He made a gesture of impatience. 'I must suppose that you are as great a fool as you are a knave if you imagine I'll talk to you of pardons. I have a sharp medicine for pirates, Master Rackham, as you'll find, and it is not compounded of pardons but of hemp. Dickey, call me the guard.'

Rackham stared at him for a second, then shrugged and smiled crookedly. 'As ye please,' he said. 'If ye're bent on losing a fine ship and a hundred prime seamen for the King's service it's your own affair. Call them in and have done.'

'What's this?' Rogers came round the table to confront the pirate. 'What ship's this?' He waved Master Dickey back to his chair.

Rackham answered confidently: 'My brig, the *Kingston*, with my lads aboard. Did ye suppose I swam to Providence?'

There was a moment of dead silence, and Master Dickey watched fascinated the two men facing each other by the table. Somewhere out in the darkness of the sea beyond the rollers washing against Hog Island was a ship manned by desperate men, and Tobias realised that Rogers was faced with a remarkable and difficult situation. Rogers was realising it too.

He put his hands behind him on the edge of the table and leaned against it.

'Where is she?' he asked.

'Offshore.'

Rogers' eyes narrowed. 'I've a mind to squeeze it out of you,' he said.

'You could try,' said Rackham. 'And, as I said, ye could lose a ship to the King's service. To say nothing of the men.'

That was the point. Rogers' commission to suppress piracy was of no greater importance than his duty to maintain a force of privateers for the safety of British possessions and the enrichment of the Treasury. Hence a pardoned pirate enlisted as a privateersman was a double gain to the government. Suddenly the situation was utterly simple: a hundred outlaws seeking pardon on the one hand, and Governor Rogers, holding the power to pardon, and urgently requiring crews for his privateers, on the other. Both stood to gain and there was nothing to lose. It was all so convenient that Rogers distrusted it instinctively. Why, he wondered, this sudden zeal for an honest life on the part of a crew of scoundrels? Rogers had been next door to a pirate himself, he knew the pros and cons of life on 'the great account', and he knew that not since the days of Modyford and Morgan had the filibusters enjoyed such a fruitful harvest as now. With men and ships urgently needed for the fleets in European waters the Caribbean squadrons were stretched to their uttermost, and piracy was as safe as it could ever hope to be. And none would know that better than Calico Jack Rackham. This was not one who would exchange piracy for privateering without some powerful motive, and it was imperative for Rogers to discover what that motive was.

'We'll leave the whereabouts of your brig for the moment. Be sure I shall find it when I desire.' The Governor walked slowly round the table to his seat. 'Of this request for pardon by yourself and your followers – you'll do me the credit to suppose that it is not prompted by sudden reformation. Perhaps you will supply me some reason. Your own, personally.'

Rackham's answer was prompt. 'Two years ago, just before you came to Providence, I was to have married – a lady here, in this town. You'll mind that in those days I was quartermaster to Vane, who then commanded the *Kingston*. He refused the pardon, ye'll remember, and fired on your vessels as they entered harbour. As bad luck had it, I was aboard, and willy-nilly I must sail away with him. I had wanted that pardon – by God I had wanted it.' He leaned forward as he spoke, and his dark face was suddenly grim. 'But there it was. Every man aboard the *Kingston* was outlaw from that day forward, or so we supposed. Myself with the rest. But things have altered over two years. Vane is gone, and Yeates, too – it was Yeates that touched off the first gun against you in the harbour fight. And so, when I heard a few weeks back from a friend who had lately been in Providence that my lady was still unwed – for I'd never heard of her in those two years – the notion took me that perhaps the pardon might not be out of reach after all. I thought that if the law will let bygones be bygones, well, I might pick up where I left off.' He gave a deprecatory shrug. 'Provided she's of the same mind as she was two years gone. When she learns how it fell out, I think she will be.'

Woodes Rogers studied him with interest. 'She must have considerable attractions,' he mused. 'Who is she?'

'Her name is Sampson,' said Rackham. 'Kate Sampson. Her father has plantations –' he broke off at the sudden clatter as Master Tobias's pounce-box fell from his table, dislodged by the little lawyer's uncontrollable start. And in turning in the direction of the interruption, Rackham did not see the colour drain abruptly from Rogers' face at the mention of that name. When he looked back again the Governor had one elbow on the table and his face was shaded by his hand.

'You'll know him,' Rackham concluded. 'An honest little man.'

Woodes Rogers did not reply, but he rose abruptly and walked over towards Dickey's desk. There he stopped, as

13

though undecided, his back to Rackham, looking over Dickey's head towards the windows. The lawyer, glancing at his face from the corner of his eye, saw it strained and ugly, and when the Governor spoke again, his voice was unusually hard.

'That explains your own reason. What of your followers?'

'We put it to a vote; the majority were for coming in. The others had the choice of coming or not, as they pleased, but they fell in with the rest of us.'

'Why?' snapped Rogers. 'Surely some must have preferred to find employment with another pirate captain?'

'With twenty thousand pounds' worth of silver in the *Kingston* to share when they get shore with a Royal pardon under their belts?' Rackham was amused. 'Not they.'

Rogers wheeled on him like lightning. This time he made no attempt to conceal his stupefaction. 'What did you say?' His voice was strained with disbelief.

'Twenty thousand pounds of silver,' Rackham repeated. 'Taken from the Spaniards in the Gulf of Florida. There was more, but it's gone now. Still, they look to what's left to see them snugly provided for ashore.'

Rogers for once was at a loss to preserve his calm. 'Are you mad?' he burst out. 'D'ye suppose for a moment they'll be permitted to keep it? God's light!' He wheeled on Dickey. 'Was there ever such effrontery? They'll have the pardon, will they, and keep their plunder too?'

'Spanish silver,' corrected Rackham. 'Plunder if you will, but the British Crown has no right to it.'

Rogers bridled like an angry cat. 'Will you talk to me of right?' He strode forward, glaring at Rackham. 'Listen, listen but a moment, Master Pirate.' It was all he could do to speak coherently, so great was his rage. 'That silver, or any other

14

loot you may have, is forfeit to the King. That you will understand now. By God, I marvel at you! I do, as I live! Do you know where you stand, or must I inform you? I'll see you and your crew of mangy robbers sunk and damned before you'll have one penny of that silver, aye, and I am Woodes Rogers that say it! You seek the pardon, you say. Then, by heaven, you'll sail your brig into this port, silver and all, and surrender every ounce, or you'll not only see no pardon, I'll have every man-jack of you sun-dried in chains.'

Any normal man's composure would have been shattered by that tirade, but Rackham simply shook his head. 'They'll never agree,' he protested. 'I feared ye might bilk at letting them keep all, but a portion . . .'

'Not a penny.' Rogers' voice was suddenly dreadfully soft. 'And when you tell me they'll refuse and sail away I'll remind you that there is one who will not sail with them, and that one is yourself. You thought my need for privateers so urgent, I suppose, that I should be forced to grant you pardons on your own terms. You learn your error. Not that you'll profit by it. For I intend to do what I proposed at first: I'll have the position of your ship and aught else I need to know wrung from you before the hour is out.'

Master Dickey had never seen him in such a venomous rage, and looked to see the pirate shrink appalled. But although Rackham must have known the danger in which he stood his voice was steady.

'Myself I don't care what becomes of the silver. That's my crew's demand, not mine. I . . .'

'So you say now,' sneered Rogers. 'In effect it does not matter. I have the means at hand to possess myself of your ship, your men, and your silver. For that last the government

15

can afford to forgo your hundred prime seamen. They'll hang very neatly in a row, yourself among them.'

The very confidence in the Governor's voice, its jeering note, stung Rackham as his threats had not been able to do.

'You'll pay a rare price for it, then,' he retorted. 'Aye, you may do as you please with me, but if you think to catch those lads of mine napping you must have forgotten all you learned in the South Sea. Did I come here unprepared, d'ye think? Why, there are men of mine in the town at this moment, and unless I'm back with them within the hour that brig of mine will be hull down and away before you can even force me to tell you where she lies, much less get your bum-boats out of harbour and after her.' His lip curled in a grin of vindictive triumph. 'And if by chance ye closed with her, how many of those precious men of yours would live to bring her to port? You'll find the price of silver marvellously high, supposing you get it.' He laughed contemptuously. 'And ye know ye won't. For they'll fight till she sinks under them, and the dollars will be as far as ever from the King's pocket.'

Now this was the stark truth and Rogers knew it. But for the anger which had possessed him he must have known that the threats he had spoken were empty ones. He should have realised it, but his mind had been further distracted by that name – Kate Sampson – a moment before. That and the sudden revelation of the fortunes which these rascals possessed had upset the normal balance of his reasoning. For a moment he stood, grimly silent, then he paced back to his chair and sat down.

'You would give much for this pardon, would you not?'

'Ye know I'd not be here else.'

'And a moment since you told us that the silver meant nothing to you. As I see it, you would have no need of it,

16

since the lady you intend to marry' – his tone hardened imperceptibly – 'is well provided for.'

'That's not why I seek her, but it's so – yes.'

'Then I see no reason why we should not reach an arrangement that will suit us both,' said Rogers evenly. 'In return for the surrender of your brig and its cargo I shall grant you a pardon.' He paused and Rackham looked at him in bewilderment.

'But the crew . . .'

Rogers' lips moved in what was almost a smile. 'They need not concern us. At least they do not concern me, and I cannot suppose that they concern you.'

'D'ye mean you expect me to betray them?'

Rogers displayed impatience. 'Come, man, you are not a schoolboy. I've seen as much and more of thieves than you, and I never yet found honour enough among them to cover a flea-bite. Are you different from the rest? If so, you can carry your principles higher yet – to the gibbet. For it's there I'll send you – not to-morrow, or the day after, but now, and take my chance of finding your brig.' He paused deliberately. 'So choose. A pardon or a rope.'

Rackham stared at him and suddenly exploded in an exclamation of impatience.

'There's no way it can be done,' he protested. 'Ye cannot have me go back and tell them you've agreed to grant them pardons and they can keep their silver, and then cheat them at the last. Your own credit would be dead for ever, with honest men as well as rogues. And if I was to be the betrayer, and gave you the ship's position now, and ye took them and the treasure, what use would your pardon be to me? It would be a death warrant, for when it was known I'd sold them they'd have a knife in my back before I could wink.'

17

Rogers was contemptuous. 'It would not be known. What I propose would be among the three of us.' He gestured to include Master Dickey. 'Well?'

Rackham considered him through narrowed lids. 'What becomes of my crew?'

'Unless they are extremely rash, no harm at all. Provided, that is, that the plan I have in mind is carried through precisely as I shall direct.' Rogers rose, a lean, commanding figure. 'That will depend on you as much as on any.' He moved round the table, halting face to face with Rackham. 'Can you hesitate?' He laughed shortly. 'If so, you are a greater fool than I take you for, or else you carry scruples to an odd length. Farther than I should carry them myself. For I'd not hang for the sake of a pack of brigands.'

He knew, of course, that there could be only one answer for Rackham, or for anyone in the same position. The pirate hooked his thumbs into his belt and considered the Governor. 'Let me hear,' he said.

It was tantamount to an acceptance, and Rogers propounded his plan as a commander issues instructions.

'It will be very simple. You will return to these men of yours in the town. Tell them my terms were unconditional surrender of themselves and the treasure; tell them that when you refused I would have tortured and hanged you and taken the *Kingston* by force. But you escaped, and now nothing remains but to fly to sea. This should satisfy them. Now, listen. You and your men in town will then return to the *Kingston* this evening, so giving me the day in which to make my preparations, for which I'll need the exact position at which the brig is to take you aboard. I take it you came ashore in a small boat, and the *Kingston* is to stand inshore to take you off.' Without pausing for a reply he swept on.

'When she does, I shall be ready for her. I shall have a cutting-out force at hand – a ship and longboats. It will be so strong that there can be no question of resistance on your part. If perchance there are some hotheads ready to fight you will dissuade them. But I doubt there will be. Then you will surrender, and the terms will be a pardon for those who lay down their arms. In the circumstances your crew should be too relieved to fret over the loss of their plunder.'

He had been pacing up and down as he spoke. Now he stopped and went back to his seat. 'Of course, it will not do for you to leave here to-night as easily as you came. You will escape, and, as I say, take back to your friends a tale of a bloody-minded Governor who would have hanged you and swore to hunt them down. You may think that such a tale will be at variance with the offer of pardon that I shall make you when the *Kingston* is at my mercy to-night. On the contrary it will be seen then that I serve the King's interests by such an offer, since it assures me of the treasure, a ship, and a hundred excellent seamen. They may think me an infernally clever fellow to have found them out, but I enjoy some such reputation already. Certainly they will not suspect you.'

His calm confidence left Rackham in no doubt that he could carry out exactly what he had promised. Yet because the pirate had more of principle than was usual in his kind, he hesitated.

'It's dirty,' he said bluntly, and Rogers was almost amused.

'Pitch defiles those who touch it, but its mark is less permanent than that left by a rope round the neck. That is your choice, and, on my soul, if you can pause over it I swear you're over-nice for your trade.'

Frowning, Rackham considered; then he shrugged. 'It seems there is no choice. I'll do as you say.'

Rogers nodded to Dickey to take up his pen.

'Since we are agreed,' he said, 'where is your ship?'

'Five miles out. She comes in at midnight. There are four of us ashore. Our boat is beached in a cove a mile west of the town, and we meet the *Kingston* a mile offshore, due north.' Master Dickey's pen flew over the paper. 'We carry thirty guns.' He paused. 'What else?'

Rogers had been nodding at each point mentioned. 'Where will you hide to-night?' he asked, adding: 'There must be a hue and cry when you break away from here: it were best if we knew where the patrols must not look for you.'

'We'll be at the Lady of Holland,' said Rackham, and Rogers inwardly approved the choice. It lay on the west of the town, in an unsavoury neighbourhood, convenient to the cove Rackham had mentioned. A few more questions he asked and glanced at the clock.

'Then the sooner we set about it the better,' he said. He looked at Rackham. 'Let me remind you that it will not be to your interest at all to attempt to cross me in this. You walk on a tight-rope, Master Rackham; slip, and I'll see you swing by it.'

With that he turned to Master Dickey. 'There is a guard beyond the window who must be removed. Bid the sergeant bring him round into the house. Wait; not yet a moment. First slip the bar from the shutters so that Master Rackham may have free passage.'

Dickey obeyed, like a man in a trance. This night's work was proving too much for him. Life as he knew it was not like this, with no decent interval between thought and action. It was inconceivable that such a hare-brained scheme, so hastily considered, should be put so abruptly into operation; he had yet to learn that in the Indies prompt decision was

20

not so much a virtue as a necessity, and that to pause for second thoughts was to delay too long.

He removed the bar from the shutters and laid it down. Rogers nodded towards the door. 'Call him now. Perhaps it might be best,' he added to Rackham, 'if you upset my secretary's table as you pass,' and the pirate nodded. Dickey was past being shocked: it was all of a piece with the rest and his only concern, he told himself morbidly, was to do as he was told.

He went to the door and called the sergeant, and as the soldier presented himself Rogers issued his orders.

'This man to the guard-room, sergeant.' He indicated Rackham. 'Bring your sentry from the garden to make an escort with the others. I'll take no chances with this gentleman: he is Calico Jack Rackham, the notorious pirate, so look to him closely.'

The sergeant's eyes bulged at Rackham, and then he was bawling orders in the passage. There was a clatter of running feet and then a voice shouted outside the house. They heard a musket-butt grate on the gravel, followed by the sound of the sentry doubling round in answer to the summons.

The sergeant advanced purposefully on Rackham and was within a few feet of him before the pirate moved: Dickey would not have believed that a man of such size could be so nimble. Two quick strides he took before vaulting over Dickey's table, and then the shutters were flung back and he was away. With a bellow of anger and surprise the sergeant lumbered forward.

'Stop, you! Stop, thief!' He ploughed across to the window. 'You, there, sentry! Damn you, where are you? After him!' He flung one gaitered leg across the sill and tumbled over on to the verandah. 'Shoot, you bloody fool, there's a traitor escaping!'

They heard the sentry's blasphemous exclamation and then a babble of shouts and orders with the sergeant's bellowings providing the central theme. A shot rang out, and then another before the sergeant succeeded in organising the pursuit. Rogers and Dickey stood listening as the noise of that hopeless search grew fainter, and they were still waiting when the sergeant returned and reported that the fugitive was nowhere to be found.

Rogers wasted no time on recriminations. He ordered a general alarm and at his dictation Dickey penned a note to the commander of the Fort to set a company on the hunt. Rogers signed it and handed it to the perspiring sergeant before dismissing him. Then he sat back in his chair.

'So far, very well,' he observed.

But Master Dickey, who had a gift for essentials, was pondering an uncomfortable detail which had been at the back of his mind for the past half hour – a detail which, it seemed to him, should have been causing the Governor much concern. He cleared his throat.

'Ye'll pardon me, sir,' he began, 'if I find a fault – or what seems tae me tae be a fault – in this scheme of yours.'

Rogers looked up. 'Tell me.'

Dickey nodded towards the window. 'This pirate, Rackham, is only lending himself tae your plan for one thing: tae get a pardon and marry. What'll happen when all's done and he finds oot the truth aboot – aboot Mistress Sampson?'

Rogers frowned, then shrugged. 'Why, what should happen? He can do nothing: he will stand in a very tight place, to be sure, for if one breath of what has passed here ever reaches his associates Master Rackham's time will be up. Oh, granted he will conceive himself cheated, but he can attempt nothing against me, for he will know that I have only to drop a word and he'll be a dead man. So he must stew in his anger, I'm afraid.'

Master Dickey pursed his lips. 'You would be a bad enemy.'

'I've known worse. And his hands will be tied. No, I do not think we should fret over Calico Jack. He will have his pardon, which is more than he deserves.'

Master Dickey frowned and sighed in turn. 'I'll be happy to see it by and done wi',' he confessed.

'You shall,' Rogers promised him. 'We hold the cards, from the ace down, and among them is the knave. A Calico Jack.'

3. SEA TRAP

The Lady of Holland enjoyed the doubtful distinction of being the least noisome drinking-shop on the waterfront. Rackham had chosen it because the proprietor was trustworthy – his confidence having been obtained by substantial payment backed by coldly delivered threats – and because it was convenient to the cove where the boat was hidden. Furthermore, the approach of any search party would be heralded by swift warnings running through the alleys like tremors through a web.

He strode through the lanes with elation mounting in his thoughts. He was nearer now to his ambition than he had been at any time in the past two years, and even the knowledge that a hazardous and highly dangerous twenty-four hours lay ahead could not depress him. He had set out for the Governor's house that night with only a vague hope, but now the way seemed clear at last, and barring accidents he could count himself a free and pardoned man. He had no doubt that the Governor's scheme would succeed – he knew something of men and Rogers had impressed him as one who did not permit his plans to go awry.

And then – Kate Sampson: the thought of her could send a thrilling urgency through Rackham's veins. It had been a long time: two years, two ugly, hard years in which he had given her up and come near to forgetting her altogether until that chance meeting with Hedley Archer when he had learned that she was still unmarried. Then, in a few moments, all the old fire had been renewed, all the old memories reawakened, and with them the sudden determination to bridge the years of separation and take up again the course that had been so abruptly broken.

He did not for a moment doubt that he could win her back again, for he chose to see in the fact that she was still unwed an indication that she had found no one to replace him. He was ready to concede that appearances were against him – on the face of it he had deserted her almost on the eve of their marriage – but he was confident that when she realised that he had been forced to leave her against his will and had thereafter supposed himself cut off from her irrevocably, she would understand and forgive him. Nor was this pure egotism on his part: he had truly loved her and knew that his love had been returned. Had it been otherwise their courtship would never have endured as it had done.

Her father, Jonah Sampson, had risen from the poorest beginnings to the control of broad plantations not only in the Bahamas but in Jamaica as well. His wealth was enormous, and in the circumstances it was to have been expected that he would use it to purchase for his only child a brilliant marriage to some nobleman of long pedigree and short purse. But Jonah Sampson was out of the common run of West Indian nabobs; he had spent his early life in the American colonies where ability was preferable to Norman blood, and had learned to put a low value on inherited nobility. Nor

25

was he bound by any sentimental ties to his homeland; his life's work lay in the New World, and it was his dream that the dynasty of commerce which he had founded should continue and expand long after his lifetime.

His first concern was that Kate's husband should be what Master Sampson called a man; and Rackham had passed the test, despite his pirate trade. The second point was that Kate obviously adored him, and Sampson respected her judgement, child of seventeen though she was then.

To a civilised world his decision would have seemed monstrous, but the Bahamas of those days were only half-civilised, and no hard and fast line could be drawn between those who lived within the law and those who lived beyond it. More than one notable fortune had been founded with a cutlass edge wielded within the loose limits of legality in the days of the buccaneers, and because those limits had been tightened of recent years did not, in Master Sampson's view, make those who now lived by plunder one whit worse than their predecessors. At any rate, buccaneer or pirate, Jack Rackham was a likely lad and good enough for him.

So the wooing had prospered until that night of blood and fire when the King's ships had sailed on Providence, and the next dawn had seen Rackham at sea with Vane, a hunted fugitive. But now Vane was dead, and Rackham felt that he was within an ace of completing a circle and coming back to Kate and the life they had planned together.

Three members of his crew awaited him at the Lady of Holland: Bull, the huge, yellow-bearded Yorkshireman, whose strength and courage matched his name; Malloy, a wrinkled old sea-rover, a little simple these days, but of such great experience that his voice was listened to in the *Kingston*'s councils; and Ben, Rackham's lieutenant, steady, dependable, merchantman turned pirate. When Rackham had crossed the darkened common-room of the inn, picking his way among its snoring occupants, and tapped softly on the inner room door, he was admitted with a speed and smoothness that bespoke his comrades' long practice in conspiracy and secret business.

A rush-light flickered, and he saw Ben and Bull on either side of the door and Malloy beyond the table with a taper in his hand. He pushed the latch to behind him.

'What's the word, cap'n?' Malloy came round the table.

Rackham leaned his shoulders on the door and looked round at the three faces. He shook his head, and speaking softly so as not to be overheard in the outer room, told them what had befallen at the Governor's house – told them, that is, all but the plan that Woodes Rogers had concerted. He embroidered, for their benefit, the account of his own escape, and painted a picture of Woodes Rogers which was perhaps more severe than the Governor deserved. They heard him out, Malloy with unconcealed disappointment, Bull with occasional angry rumblings in his throat and muttered imprecations, and Ben with unmoved attention. But there was no question that they believed him.

When he had done Bull flung down on a bench and cursed Woodes Rogers with vicious fury. Malloy sat dejected, and Ben went over to the table and poured out a drink for Rackham. Holding out the pannikin he said: 'You was lucky.'

Rackham took the pannikin. 'Lucky enough. As close to hanging as I ever hope to be.' That at least was true.

'Aye, well, and now what?' Bull's tone challenged him. 'What's to be done?'

Rackham applied himself to his drink before surveying his questioner.

'What else but to go back aboard the *Kingston*? To-night, when Bennett brings her in.'

'Hell, and is that all? And we're to sit here in this poxy kennel all day and wait for the sojers to nab us? Mebbe they'll find our boat, by God, and then we'll be on a lee shore proper.' He swore and slapped the table. 'We should never ha' come: I knew it when there was first talk o' this pardon. Pardon! What bloody hope was there we'd ever smell pardon?'

Ben turned contemptuous eyes on the speaker but said nothing. Rackham answered calmly.

'There was hope until we knew what manner of man this Governor was: others had been pardoned, and so might we if we had not carried such a wealth of silver in the *Kingston*. Now we know where we stand, and ye'll remember it was I who found out, and came near paying for it with my neck while you sat snug here.'

'Snug?' Bull rose in a towering rage. 'Ye'll tell me, perhaps—'

'Be still,' said Rackham coldly. 'The thing's done and there's an end. We're no worse off than we were before, the soldiers won't find us here if they hunt till doomsday, and there's a boat-load of silver out yonder to play with when we're clear away from here. So sleep on that and think yourself lucky.'

Bull was silenced; as Rackham said, they had lost nothing and the risk had been his. While the three others might be disappointed they could accept the situation with the fatalism of their kind. It was the code by which they lived; gentlemen of fortune they styled themselves, and sudden success or failure were no more than tricks won or lost in a game which was unpredictable and in which there was no ultimate goal.

To-morrow was another day, and would find them back at sea again. And they still had the silver. So the three slept soundly enough, while Rackham lay on the hard boards, staring up into the darkness, contemplating his treachery and finding that he felt not the least qualms about what he intended to do. As Rogers had said, his followers would never have hesitated to betray him, if their interests had demanded it. He had only to think of Kate, and the plot he had concerted with Rogers seemed morally right enough. So presently he too slept, while the eastern sky lightened outside, and the patrols which scoured the town left them undisturbed.

They slipped out of a side door of the inn that evening, and made their ways separately to a little alley on the edge of the town. Before them spread the broad silver sweep of the beach, as smooth and dazzling as a snow-field. To the right it was washed gently by the surf; to the left it merged through varied-hued shadows into the inland undergrowth.

The cove where their boat lay concealed was a mile to the westward and their path ran just within the belt of palms and bushes fringing the sand. Here they were hidden and could move swiftly and silently, Ben in the lead, Malloy and Bull together, and Rackham in the rear. Moonlight slanted in ghostly rays between the tangled stems, making little pools of silver in the darkness; it was very still, but there was a hint of wind coming from the sea, and before their journey was over the moon had slid behind the cloud-wrack.

It was as well, Rackham thought. Woodes Rogers' trap would spring all the better in the dark, provided his cutting-out party could find the *Kingston* when she stood in. It would take a good seaman to do that, but Rogers would have a good seaman.

Counting his steps Rackham had reckoned just over sixteen

hundred when a parrot squeaked in the darkness ahead. That was Ben signalling that he had reached the cove, and a few moments later the four of them were crouched in the lee of a little cliff with the water lapping at their feet. Between the two small bluffs at the end of the cove lay the open sea, and close by was their boat, beached beneath the overhang of a great boulder and artfully screened by loose bushes. Since they could hardly hope to float her without some noise they sacrificed silence to speed, flinging aside the branches and running the boat between them over the loose sand to the water's edge.

With Ben and Bull at the oars, Malloy in the bow, and Rackham in the stern, they poled the boat out of the shallows and were soon scudding out between the bluffs to the sea.

With the exception of Malloy, who was to look out for the *Kingston*, they watched the shore receding behind them. The black mouth of the little creek grew smaller, flanked by the vaguely glimmering beach. Then darkness closed in on the little boat, bringing with it a sense of unprotected loneliness: Malloy fidgeted in the bows, casting anxious glances astern until Rackham bade him keep watch in front of him. Ben and Bull, pulling strongly, were sending the boat through the water at a fair speed, and when Rackham calculated that they must be fifteen hundred yards from the shore he ordered them to cease rowing. They rested on their oars, listening while the boat rode the light swell, their ears straining for the tell-tale creak of cord and timber which would herald the presence of the *Kingston*. But no sound came, save the gentle slapping of the waves against the boat and the occasional scrape of the oars in the rowlocks.

Rackham felt the light drift of spray on his cheek. The

wind was freshening and blowing almost dead inshore. Ben noticed it at the same moment.

'It's going to be easier for the *Kingston* to come in than to stand out again,' he muttered.

'What d'ye say?' Bull's head came up. 'Bigod, ye're right!' He strained his eyes into the darkness seaward. 'She's beginning to blow, the windy bitch!'

The little boat was beginning to rock appreciably now, and Rackham gave the order to commence rowing again. They must not drift inshore: if the wind strengthened they might find themselves hard put to it to stand out to the *Kingston*.

'Where the hell are they?' snarled Bull suddenly. He kept turning his head at the end of each stroke to watch for the *Kingston*.

'Wait! In oars!' Malloy, craning over the bow, flung out a hand behind him. 'I hear something.'

They ceased rowing, and Rackham, straining his ears against the noises of the sea, leaned forward between them.

'Listen!' Malloy turned his head towards them. 'D'ye hear nothing?'

Holding their breath, they listened, and sure enough from somewhere in the gloom ahead came the faint but unmistakable creak of a ship. Bull breathed a gusty sigh of relief.

'Wait for the light,' ordered Rackham. He alone knew that there were other vessels than the *Kingston* on the coast that night, and he was taking no chances.

For several minutes they sat motionless, the little boat riding the swell, waiting to catch the flicker of a lantern from the ship. Then Malloy snapped his fingers and pointed, over to starboard. Following his finger they saw it: a single murky glimmer in the darkness which vanished almost as quickly as it had come.

'Pull,' snapped Rackham. 'Those blasted farmers are so far east they'll be in Africa before we can catch 'em!'

But Ben and Bull needed no urging. They swung on the oars like men rowing a race, driving the little boat towards the spot where the light had vanished, and suddenly the great bulk of the ship loomed above them out of the blackness.

''Vast heaving,' said Rackham. 'It's *Kingston*. Give them a hail, Malloy.'

Malloy stood up, one hand braced against the thwart, the other cupped to his mouth.

'*Kingston*, ahoy! It's Cap'n Rackham!'

And pat on the heels of his cry, like the voice of an actor on his cue, came back an answering hail. But it was not from the *Kingston*. Somewhere in the darkness to the eastward, a voice rang out: 'In the King's name!'

Even Rackham, prepared as he was for some intervention, was startled into an oath. That hail had certainly not been more than a quarter of a mile away, which meant that Rogers' ship, somewhere out there in the darkness, had carried out its task to perfection.

Bull heaved himself up with a roar of blasphemous astonishment, stumbled against Malloy and nearly sent him into the sea. The boat swung out of control, with Bull's oar floating away behind it, and then Ben brought her head round to the *Kingston*.

From the sounds that drifted down from the *Kingston*, the ship must have been thrown into utter confusion. A harsh New England voice which Rackham recognised as that of Bennett, his sailing master, was trying to issue orders through the tumult of shouts and fearful questions that had broken the stupified silence following that command from the darkness. And then the noise was stilled as though each man's throat had been choked simultaneously.

A broad blade of flame licked out suddenly in the blackness to the eastward, dwindled, kindled, and blossomed into a great torch that illumined the sea and flung the *Kingston* into sharp silhouette against its crimson glare. While Rackham stared the drift of the boat carried them into the *Kingston*'s shadow and he realised that they were in danger of slipping out of reach of the ship, crippled as they were by the loss of an oar.

'Pull!' he shouted, and Ben flung his weight on the remaining oar. Rackham thrust the tiller over and they edged in towards the *Kingston*'s side.

Bull was shattering the night with his bawling. He was of the slow-witted kind who, when danger appears unheralded, must first of all identify it loudly for their own benefit and that of their fellows.

'It's the King's men!' he roared. 'It's the King's men!'

The nose of the boat thumped the *Kingston*'s side. The arrival of the King's force had been premature, and might have been disastrous with Rackham still in the boat when the success of Rogers' plan demanded that he should be on the *Kingston* to supervise her surrender. Every second counted, for at any moment Bennett might open fire and ruin all. He swung himself on to the rail and took in at a glance the astonishing scene. Beyond the *Kingston* the sea was as bright as day, revealing three fully manned longboats within two cables' lengths of the *Kingston*, and behind them, on the verge of that great circle of light, towering over the scene, a tall ship which could be nothing other than a man-of-war.

Rackham, gaining the deck, saw at once what had produced the dazzling light which illuminated the sea between the Kingston and the Governor's little fleet. Between two of the longboats floated a large raft on which burned a great pile of lumber. Obviously they had towed it between them, and as soon as Malloy's hail had been heard the order had been given to fire the highly combustible mass. Even as Rackham's feet touched the deck another great tongue of flame shot up into the darkness, this time farther out to sea. A second raft had been set alight.

'Stand by to go about!' bawled Rackham. It was a hopeless order but at least it should give the Kingston's crew proof of his intentions. 'Lively, damn you! D'you want to be taken?'

It was Ben, acting promptly, who might have saved the situation for the pirates, and brought Woodes Rogers' plans to nothing. Leaping among the bemused crowd of seamen on the Kingston's deck, he cuffed and kicked them into some semblance of order, driving them aloft to work the ship while Bennett, taking authority upon himself, ran down to take what charge he could of the larboard guns.

Fortunately for Rackham and Rogers, the pirate at the wheel lost his head, and abandoning his charge, ran to take cover below. Rackham, bellowing an oath, scrambled up the ladder towards the poop, slipped intentionally and fell sprawling. He saw Ben coming across the deck, his face contorted with rage, but even as his lieutenant reached his side the boom of a gun rang out across the water and a shot whistled past the Kingston's bows and whined away into the darkness.

Ben pulled up short, glaring over his shoulder towards the longboats.

'Damn the drunk dogs!' he shouted. 'Cowardly bloody scum!' For once his emotions had the better of him, and he raged and stamped, furious at the impotence of the rabble on the *Kingston*'s deck. Some were clustered like sheep about the mainmast, others had run below, while another party were dropping over the side into the boat which Rackham had just left.

'Save your breath, Ben.' Rackham pointed and his lieutenant groaned. The King's ship was gliding across the fire-gleaming water, cutting off the *Kingston*'s escape, while the three long-boats were closing in.

'That's the *Unicorn*,' said Rackham. 'She can blow us out of the water whenever she's a mind to.'

'We can fight her, cap'n!' Ben, having seen one chance slip away, sought desperately to seize another. 'Them flares won't last for ever. See, they're burning down now! If we can hold her off till they go out we can make open sea yet!'

'With those to man the ship and fight her too?' Rackham gestured towards the disordered huddle of men in the waist.

'What odds? It's Execution Dock if we're taken. There's still a chance, for Christ's sake!'

'If you can—' Rackham was beginning, when he was cut short. The voice that had hailed the *Kingston* a few moments before was raised again from the leading longboat, now within pistol shot of the *Kingston*'s side.

'In the King's name! Lay down your arms!'

In the silence that followed Rackham could hear Bennett's muffled voice forward exhorting the gunners. The fool would be letting fly in a moment.

'Go forrard,' he snapped. 'Take command of the guns. Fire when I give the order, but not before.'

To his relief, Ben obeyed. With the lieutenant in charge,

he could be sure that no shot would be fired from the *Kingston* unless he wished it.

'Do you surrender? We have you at our mercy.' The commander of the longboats was hailing again.

Every face on the *Kingston*'s deck was turned aft. Rackham walked over to the rail and shouted: 'Keep your distance! You're under our guns. Come closer and we'll blow you to Florida!'

To his surprise his words brought a ragged cheer from the pirates in the waist. He noticed uneasily that one or two of the hardier spirits were passing arms among their fellows, and some, already armed; were crouching in the shelter of the rail. They might fight after all. And the flares on the rafts were beginning to burn lower. On the other hand, the *Unicorn* was standing in to point-blank range.

'You may trust in His Majesty's mercy,' shouted the voice from the longboat again. 'Governor Woodes Rogers has pledged his word that no harm will come to those who prove themselves loyal by immediate surrender.'

'No harm?' Rackham was echoing the thoughts of his crew. 'What does that mean?'

'Pardon,' was the reply. 'Pardon, on surrender of your ship and yourselves. If you resist, you can expect no mercy.'

'Pardon.' The word was on every tongue. 'The King's pardon!' Gone were the expressions of fear and anger. Their voices were eager now. Rackham turned to meet the surge of men who flocked towards the poop. Leaning on the rail he looked down on them.

'What shall it be?' he shouted. 'Will you fight or surrender to the King?'

With one voice they answered him, their swarthy faces upturned. 'Pardon! We'll take the pardon! Tell him we'll take the pardon!' Their shouts rose in a deafening clamour.

He raised both hands, and the noise subsided. Even as it was dying away and he was preparing to say 'So be it,' a thought occurred to him. He waited until the last murmur had faded. Then he glanced at the shrouds, where the men aloft were already descending, at the main hatchway, where others were crowding up to the deck. Then when every eye was on him, and everyone was silent, he hooked his thumbs into his belt, and looked down at them.

'You cowardly scum,' he said, and turned away. He felt that it was a touch of which Governor Woodes Rogers would approve.

4. MAJOR PENNER

On the following morning, less than twelve hours after their capture, the *Kingston* pirates were admitted to the Royal pardon. It was an impressive ceremony enacted with considerable solemnity on the broad square of the Fort, and New Providence turned out in force to see it. Along one side of the parade awnings had been erected for the most consequential spectators: the planters, merchants, and gentlefolk and their women who constituted the pick of the island's society, and before them, in a canopied chair, sat the Governor, magnificent in lilac taffeta and plumed castor, with Master Dickey at his elbow.

Marshalled in front of the Governor, with Rackham at their head and a hollow square of garrison infantry about them, stood the filibusters of the *Kingston*, none the better for a night in the Fort's wet stone cells. Blinking in the dazzling sunlight they listened as Master Dickey addressed them in the name of the most high and mighty prince, George, of England, Scotland, France, and Ireland, King, and catalogued their misdeeds as form demanded. Elsewhere round the parade ground the area was packed with a throng of townsfolk, intent on the show.

To Rackham the formalities were interminable. He wanted to sign his name and swear his oath and be away to the Sampson house to make his peace with Kate. But he must wait and listen, while the long paragraphs dragged on, watching the well-to-do standing respectfully attentive beneath their awnings while the common folk shuffled and exchanged whispers with their neighbours.

A figure in the ranks of the planters behind the Governor's chair caught Rackham's eye, and he recognised Penner, the former Army officer turned pirate whom he had not seen since his last sojourn in Providence two years ago. It was with a shock of surprise that he identified the bluff, red face and corpulent frame in that company of respectable respected, until he realised that Penner, too, must be a pardoned man; was probably by now a citizen of worth and standing in Providence. It was a heartening thought, and he smiled slowly as Penner inclined his head and half-lifted a hand in token of recognition.

Master Dickey's voice claimed his attention again. The formalities over, the name of King George having been suitably glorified, and that of Governor Rogers likewise praised in its degree, the secretary rolled up his document and presented another, which Woodes Rogers again approved, and Dickey proceeded:

'. . . whereas these several misguided subjects of our Sovereign Lord, having erred from the ways of duty, yet having repented them of their sins, shall, under this solemn oath and contract, be admitted to said Majesty's most gracious and Royal pardon, and to them shall be restored said Majesty's protection, that they may move again in, and be restored to, the proper ways of duty and love to their rightful and most merciful Sovereign.'

Woodes Rogers doffed his castor, an example which every male in the square followed, and prepared to administer the oath. It was a simple document, in contrast to those which had gone before, calling for complete repentance in those who took it, enjoining them to be temperate and truthful, and demanding from them the solemn promise that they would forsake for ever the practice of piracy on the high seas. Finally, it gave assurance that any who broke the oath would be promptly hanged.

'John Rackham, hold up your right hand,' commanded Master Dickey. 'Do you so swear?'

Rackham waited a fraction of a second, savouring the last moment before he should be a free man. 'I do,' he said.

'Benjamin Thorne, do you so swear?'

He was a free man now – as free as Rogers, as Penner, as the King!

'Isaac Nelson, do you so swear?'

Free. And not only a free man but an honest one – his past forgotten, himself absolved by the most regal authority in the world.

One by one the pirates filed forward to sign, or make their marks upon, the heavily sealed document on the Governor's table.

Rackham, in his impatience, scrawled his signature without a glance at the wording of the document. But as he turned from the table he was intercepted by the jovial Major Penner, who had come forward from beneath the awnings.

'John, lad, welcome home!' The burly Penner seized his hand. 'This is the best of fortune. Did ye start to see me in

40

such company, eh?' He jerked a thumb over his shoulder towards the planters. 'It's not to be wondered at. I took the pardon two years ago, when Rogers first arrived. And behold me now!' He laughed resoundingly. 'A man of substance, as you see. And more than that,' – his merry grey eyes twinkled as he dug Rackham in the ribs – ''tis what yourself shall be, and quickly, or I'm no judge. And how has Fate treated you? No need to tell me. None. I heard of your surrender. Plaguey hard, to give up a fortune, but there – what's a few broad pieces beside a Royal pardon?'

'Major, I—' Rackham was impatient to be away, but the burly Major had his arm in a bear-like grip. 'There is someone I must see—'

'All in good time, lad,' Penner reproved him. 'What? There's no guarda costas behind ye now. Time is on our side, and your first hour as a pardoned man ye shall spend in my company. For I've much to tell you. No buts, lad. I'll hear none of them. It would be rank mutiny, no less. Will you deny one of His Majesty's officers?' He released Rackham and stepped back, grinning like a schoolboy.

Rackham was intrigued in spite of himself. 'A King's officer?'

'No less, John. A commissioned privateer, with His Majesty's blessing, the Governor's favour, a stout ship, and a clear conscience.' He dropped his voice confidentially. 'And making more than ever I did on the Account, too. It astonishes me. For years folk like you and I stood outside the law, gentlemen of fortune, as we called ourselves, and lucky we are to be still sound and sane. And what now? I take a Royal pardon, ply the same old trade – or nearly – and sleep sound o' nights. I've a house of my own and half a dozen slaves, and I'm fair on the way to buying a plantation. It's providence, so it is.' And Major Penner complacently shrugged his massive shoulders and looked about him. The Governor and his aides, followed by the gentry, had retired to the Fort to partake of refreshments, and the square was given over to the throng. Penner and Rackham were surrounded by the jostling crowd who had come to congratulate the redeemed pirates and bear them off to celebrate in the New Providence taverns. The dust they raised was irritating, and Penner could hardly make himself heard above the babble of voices.

'Come where we don't have to talk as though we were hailing a main-top,' he said, and taking Rackham by the arm he led him along the edge of the square and through the inner gate of the Fort. A broad stone stairway led up to the parapet upon which the Governor and his company were being regaled: half-way up there was an embrasure in the wall, and it was into this and on to a narrow stone seat that Penner drew him.

'Before we go aloft, I'll tell you what is in my mind,' he confided, settling himself on the stonework. 'It's this way. Since last night, when I heard you were taken, I've been on the watch for you, for fear Burgess of Hornigold would clap their hooks into you. I'm privateering, as I said, and good sailormen aren't too plentiful. I want you, John, as sailing master. In fact, if I had the pick of the coast, I wouldn't take another. You share in the prizes next to me, and in a couple of voyages you're a made man.' He paused. 'Well, what d'ye say? It'll be as easy to you as drawing breath. You're young, you know the life, there's none of the risks of piracy – well, just a few, say – cruises are short and the money's in it.' He waited eagerly for Rackham's answer.

Rackham smiled and shook his head. Counting as he was on marrying an heiress, it was impossible to entertain serious

42

thoughts of the relatively paltry sums that could be picked up privateering. True, he had not a penny to his name, but he had owned little more two years before when he had successfully courted Kate Sampson.

Penner saw his smile and groaned. 'There's a woman in it,' he said. 'I know from the face of ye.'

'You're right, Major,' said Rackham. 'A woman it is. And much as I thank you, I'll want to see more of my wife than I would if I was at sea.'

'A wife, d'ye say?' Penner raised his eyebrows. 'Well, what's a wife? I've one myself – here, in Providence – and to be sure there's another in Galway, but does that stand between me and my livelihood? If it's marriage you're contemplating, amn't I showing you the very way to make the money for it?'

Rackham shook his head. 'I've been away too long. I'd have been with her now, likely, but for you, trying to make my peace again. No offence,' he added. 'But the sea's not for me.'

Penner bit his thumb. 'Well, well, I'll not deny I'm sorry. You'd have been a godsend to me, Johnny lad. But there, I wish ye success with your lady. And if she should refuse you, be sure I won't.' He stood up. 'And now, let's be joining the ladies and gentlemen and wetting our tongues. You'll have a glass to toast you home?'

Rackham glanced uncertainly upwards towards the parapet, and Penner read his thoughts and laughed.

'You're afraid ye're not yet sufficiently pardoned to go abroad among the ladies and gentlemen of Providence society? Man, this pardon isn't a gradual thing, like taking physic or getting drunk. You're a free citizen now. Besides, you're in my company, which is a passport into any society in the Caribbean. Give us your arm.'

43

'But my clothes—'

'Will be as meat and drink to the old women and their daughters,' retorted Penner. 'They'll be agog at the wicked Captain Rackham.' And he led his still unwilling companion up the stairway.

As they mounted the last step Rackham had the presence of mind to pull off his headscarf and so go a little way towards rendering his appearance less piratical. Then Penner was leading him towards the groups about the low tables shaded by gargantuan umbrellas in the hands of slave children. It was hardly a scene of elegance, such as Charles Town might have provided, but it could discomfit Rackham, in spite of his friend's assurances. He saw surprised faces turned towards him, heard the murmur of conversation die away, and wanted to turn and run. But Penner's hand was clasping his arm as in a vice, and then he saw something which stopped him dead, in spite of the Major's efforts. Ten yards away, standing beside a table, in conversation with someone whose back was to him, was Jonah Sampson. And seated on the other side of the table, her face white as she looked at him, was Kate.

For a moment he stood stock-still, powerless to move or heed the Major's tugging at his sleeve, and then Penner found himself brushed aside as Rackham swept impetuously past him and grasped the hands of Mistress Sampson, who had half-risen at his approach.

She cast one anguished look at her father, but it was lost on Rackham. He stood holding her wrists, oblivious of all around him. The scandalised gasp from the company never sounded for him; if he had heard it he would not have heeded. He was momentarily lost in a world which contained only Kate Sampson and himself.

It was the little merchant who broke in upon his idyll.

'Good God! You, sir! Have you lost your senses? D'you know what you do?' Outraged, he thrust himself between them.

Confronted with that empurpling indignation, Rackham was made aware of the scene he had created. He strove to make amends for what he conceived to be a minor breach of good manners.

'Master Sampson, your pardon. I had not thought to see you, or your daughter. I was moved, sir, I –.' He broke off, catching sight of Kate's face. The contempt and mortification he saw there startled him. That he had made a fool of himself was becoming increasingly plain, but that was not an unforgivable sin, so far as he was aware. The events which had followed their last meeting – his apparent flight with Vane, his seeming renunciation of the promises he had made to her – could hardly dispose the Sampsons to welcome his return, but there must be something more than that to account for the white cold fury in Kate's look and the apoplectic surgings of her father.

Bewildered, he looked from one to the other, then at the faces of the other guests. Not one but was regarding him with disgust and indignation. And then a hand descended on his arm and a voice, cold and hard as a sword blade, spoke in his ear.

'You make very free with my betrothed,' it said, and turning he looked into the grim eyes of Woodes Rogers.

A blow in the face would have surprised him less. His bewilderment sought confirmation, and the Governor supplied it.

'My future wife, you dog,' he said, and for once losing control, he struck Rackham across the mouth.

Involuntarily, as he stumbled back, Rackham's hand

45

dropped to his belt, and in a second the gentlemen about the Governor had caught him and held his wrists. But these things were purely physical, and he was still mentally reeling under the first blow that Rogers had dealt him.

Hoarsely, he appealed to Kate. 'Is this true?' She did not answer. Her cheeks were burning, and her eyes were turned away, ignoring him. Her father spoke for her, his face contorted with anger.

'D'ye doubt your ears, you scoundrel?' He was so incensed that it appeared he would follow the Governor's example and strike Rackham, but Rogers intervened. He had recovered his composure, though his eyes still gleamed dangerously.

'That is needless.' It almost suggested that he was ashamed of his own action. 'Major Penner, I'll be obliged if you will remove your companion from this gathering. And I shall have a word to say to you later.'

Dazed and sick, Rackham felt the Major's hand on his arm, and allowed himself to be led away. There was dead silence on the roof, and the Major made haste to get beyond the reach of the company's scandalised regard. But he was not speedy enough to be out of earshot when they caught the Governor's voice attempting, apparently, to resume his conversation with Jonah Sampson.

It was the sound of that voice, level and distinct against the silence, that brought Rackham to a halt. For the moment shock and misery had expelled all other thoughts from his mind; only now, as his numbed brain was beginning to work again, did he realise the full meaning of all that had gone before. It came to him with a staggering impact, and brought him wheeling round, rage and blind hatred in his heart.

Rogers had cheated him – cheated him coldly and deliberately and beyond all chance of retribution. He had known, two nights ago, when he and Rackham had spoken in the Governor's study, that Rackham's only interest in the pardon sprang from his hopes of marrying Kate Sampson. And Rogers had played on that, using Rackham as a pawn to bring him the *Kingston*'s silver. He had placed the pardon temptingly within Rackham's reach on conditions which had not existed, since Rogers himself already possessed the only prize that Rackham hoped to win from the game.

Oh, he had been admirably fooled, made to dance to the puppet-master's bidding and now, like a puppet indeed, unable to stir a finger to avenge himself. To proclaim Rogers a cheat and a liar would have been to assure his own destruction: the whole tale would be round New Providence in an hour and those men whom Rackham had betrayed would ensure that he never saw another sun rise. No, the Governor was safe and snug, his pretty plot concluded to his complete satisfaction, and Rackham was left to swallow the bitter draught of frustrated defeat.

As he swung round now, his face livid, Major Penner thrust out a hand to stop him. 'Why, John, are ye mad? Come away, man—' But Rackham was half-way back from the head of the steps already. The Major saw him stride forward, suddenly stop, hesitate, and then stand, legs apart and arms akimbo, facing the company, who stared at him in disbelief.

'Woodes Rogers.' He had mastered the rage inside him sufficiently to guard his tongue against any slip which might betray the secret which lay between him and the Governor, but there was enough venom in his voice to freeze the company where it sat.

'You played the cheat on me,' he said slowly. 'And I do not forget. We understand each other as pirates, you and I.'

And with that he was gone, leaving them thunderstruck.

Only Woodes Rogers retained complete composure. While those around him expressed themselves in exclamations and oaths, the Governor shrugged his shoulders.

'A fantastic fellow,' he remarked. He was hiding his feelings well. 'But we trouble ourselves about very little. It is no matter.' And by exercising the great powers of persuasion and charm at his command, he steered the conversation into less perturbing channels.

5. SWORDS BEHIND THE TAVERN

Major Penner, having witnessed the strange scene played on the Fort roof, was quick to appreciate that the reasons which had prevented Rackham from accepting an offer to turn privateer did not now exist, for since the lady whom he had hoped to marry was the Governor's property, there could no longer be any ties to hold him ashore. It remained, therefore, for Major Penner to bide patiently until his companion's emotions were less disturbed, and then to repeat his proposal, with every confidence that it would be accepted.

He followed Rackham from the Fort, waiting until his fury should have spent itself somewhat, and then, taking him by the arm, guided him to the nearest tavern, the Cinque Ports.

Plainly Rackham was in no mood for talk. He sat with Penner in a corner of the tap-room, his face set in ugly lines, drinking what was set before him, and staring down at the table in silence. He was not thinking of Kate, as the Major supposed, but of Rogers. He had been hoodwinked, cheated, and there was no hope of redress. Yet the Governor would be made to pay; by God, he would pay.

Half an hour's steady drinking brought him to that stage where his first fury had subsided. He was still silent, but his eyes were bright, and he had begun to whistle a little through his teeth. This disconcerted the Major, who preferred his drunkards to look less lively, and he decided to broach the subject uppermost in his mind.

'Ye'll have wondered, perhaps, why I brought ye here,' he began. Rackham stopped whistling.

'I don't wonder at all. Ye want to remind me that there's a place for me as quartermaster aboard your sloop. I'll take it, never fear. So hold your tongue and let me be.'

So much he had decided. Kate was lost to him, and vengeance on Rogers would have to wait. In the meantime he would be best at sea, away from the temptation of putting a knife in the Governor's stomach some dark night, and away also perhaps from that ill-luck which Providence seemed to hold for him.

But that ill-luck was pursuing him even now, and it came in the shape of a tall, rakish Frenchman named La Bouche who, finding the noon heat oppressive, had turned from the street in search of refreshment.

Apart from the negro waiters and a few idlers Rackham and Penner had the long common-room of the Cinque Ports to themselves until Captain La Bouche and his friends announced their arrival with much boisterous laughter. This La Bouche was one of those adventurers who, two years before, had sailed out of New Providence in defiance of Rogers and the royal proclamation. He had continued sea-roving for a short season but poor fortune had finally driven him to accept the amnesty. Since then, like Penner, he had turned privateer under Government protection, with moderate success.

He hailed Penner effusively and it was evident that he was already a trifle drunk. The Major responded with a curt nod; he had little regard for Captain La Bouche, whom he considered a French fribble. Rackham, looking round and seeing the Frenchman bearing down on them, made no effort to conceal his annoyance; he, too, had no liking for La Bouche, and he was still in the dangerous temper which requires solitude.

La Bouche let out a crow of laughter as he recognised the former pirate.

'Tonerre Dieu!' he exclaimed. 'What have we here? M'sieur le Capitan Rackham! O ho!' He turned to his companions, confiding in a whisper which was plainly audible: 'Once it was the Quartermaster Rackham, then the Capitan, and now it is – eh, what is it? – oui, it is the ci-devant Captain.' Laughing again, he came to stand over the table. 'Oh, my big Jean. An' you have come the way of the rest of us, hein? Well, well. You are wise, Jean. An' I bid you welcome – me, La Bouche.' And in token of that welcome he held out a hand.

Rackham considered it, and the soiled lace at its wrist. La Bouche was as raffish as always, gaudily attired in a taffeta suit which set off his spare figure admirably, and with a plumed hat upon his head. But he was not an attractive picture, with his vulpine features flushed with wine, and his closely set eyes twinkling unpleasantly. Ignoring the hand, Rackham turned back to the table.

'I'm your debtor for that welcome,' he said briefly, but La Bouche was not abashed. Winking broadly at Penner, who was regarding him with distaste, the Frenchman drew up a chair and sat down.

'It is un'erstan'able your frien' has forgot his manners,' he remarked easily to Penner. 'So long at sea, chasing nothing, you know – it makes a man sour. But a big drink, a pretty girl' – he leered salaciously – 'all these things make a man content, like me.' He tapped Rackham on the arm. 'What you say, mon gars – you have a big drink now, with La Bouche, hey? Later we see about the pretty girl.' He slapped his thigh and shouted with laughter, in which his followers, standing about the table, joined.

Rackham looked at him in contempt. 'When I drink, I drink in company of my choosing,' he said. 'You're not of my choosing. Do I make myself plain?'

La Bouche's eyes opened in a stare. 'Hey, what's this? What way is this to speak to me?' He turned to Major Penner. 'Is the big Jean gone more sour than I thought?'

Major Penner, scenting here the beginnings of trouble, made haste to intervene. This La Bouche was something of a bully-duellist, and the last man with whom the Major wanted to see Rackham embroiled. He shook his head in deprecation.

'The lad's had a shock, La Bouche, d'ye see? He means no offence, but he's not entirely himself. It might be best,' he added meaningly, 'to leave him alone to me.'

But La Bouche ignored the hint. He assumed an expression of exaggerated commiseration.

'And is this so? A shock, you say? Poor Jean!' He winked at the Major. 'Perhaps – a lady?' Taking the Major's silence for an affirmative, La Bouche pushed his query further, making no effort to conceal his mockery. 'Perhaps – a Governor's lady?'

Without warning, before the Major could move, Rackham struck the Frenchman across the mouth. Caught off balance, his chair on two legs, La Bouche went pitching over backwards to sprawl on the floor. With a curse, Penner bounded from his seat with a speed surprising in so corpulent a man, and flung his arms round Rackham to prevent him throwing himself at the Frenchman as he lay caught in the ruins of his chair.

'John, ye blind fool! What have ye done?' He exerted all his strength to keep the other from breaking from his grasp. 'Be still man, in God's name!'

'What have I done?' Rackham was glaring over the Major's shoulder at La Bouche, who was making shift to rise with what dignity he could. 'What have I done? Nothing to what I've yet to do, by God! D'ye think I'll be rallied by that French scum?'

'French scum? So?' La Bouche was on his feet now, a very different man from the easy, jesting scoundrel of a moment ago. His face was pale and his mouth tightly set. His eyes gleamed balefully. 'I think this is a little too much. But a little. I have been struck and then insult'. I think, now, we settle this matter.'

'What the hell d'ye mean?' roared Penner in consternation.

'What d'ye suppose he means?' growled Rackham. 'The pimp wants to fight. Well, I'm ready whenever he is.'

Major Penner thrust himself between them in an attempt to compose matters. 'Why, this is folly, John! This . . . this cannot take place. What match are you for this bully-swordsman?' In sudden rage he swung round on La Bouche. 'Ye dirty French rogue! If ye'd kept sober enough to be able to hold your dirty tongue in its place this need never have happened. La Bouche by name and La Bouche by nature! Well, if it's blood ye want ye shall have it – but it's myself will be acting as chirurgeon.'

La Bouche waved him aside. 'No, no, my so gallant Major. My concern is with your friend, not with you. Afterwards, if you will. When I have disposed of this gross piece of English beef. But not yet.' He addressed himself to Rackham. 'Where shall I kill you? We can fight here, if you will.'

Rackham shrugged. 'Wherever ye please.'

La Bouche nodded. He was very much master of himself again. 'Then there is a convenient place behind the house. If you will follow me.' With exaggerated courtesy he led the way.

Seeing that further protest must be futile, Penner attended Rackham in gloomy silence to the waste ground behind the Cinque Ports. He could see but one end to this, and that end would find him without a quartermaster. It was futile to curse the chance that had brought this quarrelsome, swaggering Frenchman to the inn at a moment when Rackham's mood was unusually truculent: the damage was done and Major Penner glumly prepared for the worst.

Rackham, at least, shared none of the soldier's regrets. Here was an outlet for the smouldering rage which had been growing inside him, and La Bouche was a fit object on which to vent it. Nor did he give a second's thought to the possible fatal consequences to himself.

Word of what was forward spread quickly, and as the two principals were taking their ground, a small crowd began to gather behind the tavern. Loafers, seamen and passers-by hurried to the scene – none so common in Providence these days – and made room for themselves about the small clearing. Black, white and brown, they chatted cheerfully as though they were at a play. Others watched from the windows of the Cinque Ports, and a few squatted on the gently sloping roof.

The Frenchman, stripped down to his shirt and breeches, and with his long hair clubbed back in a kerchief, was jovial and confident as he stepped forward into the open space of the duelling-ground; he laughed and flung jests to his supporters in the crowd, and swished his rapier to and fro in the air to loosen his muscles, an extravagant display which brought sycophantic murmurs of approval from his adherents. Tall, supple, and active as a cat, La Bouche was confident of the issue.

Rackham, assisted by the Major, was wrapping a long sash round and round his left forearm to serve him as a shield. This done, he accepted the Major's rapier, and with it the hurried words of advice which his second bestowed on him.

'Be easy, now, Jack,' said the Major for perhaps the twentieth time that day. 'Let him spend his force showing off to his jackals, and watch for a chance.'

It was lame enough counsel, but it reminded Rackham, whose intent had been to allow his temper to guide his sword hand, that he had best go cautiously to work. He nodded, rubbed dirt on his sword hand, and strode forward to face his antagonist.

Le Bouche saluted and slid forward, sinuous as a snake, to the attack. The slim, glittering blades clashed together, La Bouche feinted at his opponent's throat, and as Rackham's guard came up, the Frenchman extended himself in a quick lunge. To his surprise, it was parried neatly with the forte of the blade, and La Bouche slipped back out of danger before the Englishman had time to riposte.

But that quick parry had not been lost on Major Penner. It had been speedy – very speedy for a man of Rackham's build, and the Major took heart. He reminded himself that his principal was an experienced man of his hands, a seasoned practitioner of hand-to-hand fighting. Perhaps he had been wrong to despair.

La Bouche, more cautiously now, came again to the attack, whirling his point in a circle, feeling his opponent out and watching for an opening. Rackham, circling with him, allowed the Frenchman to force the pace, watching his eyes and keeping his point level with the other's waist. Their feet scuffing quickly on the hard earth, they fenced warily, and gradually the smile returned to La Bouche's lips.

He leaped to the attack, his foot stamping, made a double feint, to the stomach and the throat, and with his enemy's blade wavering in wide parade, lunged to take him in the arm. With a despairing swing, like a butcher with a cleaver, Rackham diverted the Frenchman's point, but as La Bouche followed the line of his lunge the bowls of the swords clashed together, and a sudden wrench of La Bouche's wrist sent the Englishman's sword clattering to the ground a dozen paces away.

An involuntary yell from the crowd greeted that sudden disarming; to be followed almost instantly by silence as La Bouche, his evil face agrin, turned to dispose of his weapon-less antagonist. Rackham, his chest heaving with exertion, sweat pouring down his face, watched as the Frenchman, his point raised, advanced to dispatch him. There was no escape; if he turned to run La Bouche's sword would pierce his back in the same moment; if he stayed and faced him death would come with equal certainty. La Bouche made a sudden thrust at his face, and instinctively Rackham leaped back, but it was only a feint. La Bouche stepped back, lowering his point, and mocked him.

'Will you not come for your sword, big Jean? See, it is here.' And the ruffian indicated the fallen rapier at his feet.

A woman's voice, husky and vibrant, spoke from the crowd at Rackham's back.

'Make an end, Pierre. It's over warm for such excitement.' And a ripple of laughter greeted her words.

But the callous mockery of that voice was La Bouche's undoing, for it transformed Rackham's helplessness into violent anger. He tensed for a spring, and in the same moment La Bouche struck. His point ripped out, but even as it did so the Englishman pivoted on his heel and the blade, tearing through his shirt, ploughed a deep furrow along his ribs and driven on by the force of La Bouche's thrust, spent itself on air. La Bouche stumbled, and was in the act of recovering when Rackham's fist crashed against his temple and sent him headlong.

A great shout went up from the spectators, and Rackham, bounding forward, snatched up his sword. La Bouche was on his feet in an instant to meet the Englishman's assault: one mighty back-hand sweep he parried, but he was rattled, and as Rackham's arm went up for another stroke La Bouche lost his head and lunged wildly at his opponent's unguarded front. His point never went home. Rackham swept the blade aside with his left hand, leaving the Frenchman extended and helpless, and before La Bouche could even attempt a recovery Rackham, now inside his guard, had run him through the body. La Bouche's rapier fell from his hand, his mouth opened horribly, and as the sword was withdrawn he collapsed, coughing and retching. For a few seconds Rackham stood looking down at him, then he turned on his heel and walked back to Major Penner.

There was a moment's dead silence, and then the voice of the crowd broke out in noisy confusion. Penner, having shaken Rackham's hand and mastered his delight, went over to join the little group surrounding the fallen Frenchman. La Bouche's face was deadly grey but there was no blood at his lips, and a brief examination enabled the Major to ascertain that the wound was not mortal.

'The more's the pity,' he observed, as he rose from the Frenchman's side. 'He's a dirty hound who would have been better on the road to hell this minute.'

'You dare to mock the dying?' La Bouche's lieutenant, a squat, barrel-chested ruffian, rounded on the Major.

'I wish I had the opportunity,' sighed Penner. 'But he's far from dying. It's a high thrust in the chest' – he indicated the crimson gash of the wound half-hidden by the thick black hair on La Bouche's breast – 'and no one ever died of one of those. Not,' he added hopefully, 'unless ye intend to let him bleed to death.'

Grumbling and cursing, they nevertheless made shift to staunch their captain's bleeding while the Major rejoined Rackham who sat, pale and breathing heavily, on a bench against the tavern wall.

'You're not unscratched yourself,' said Penner, kneeling at his principal's side and making examination of the bloody groove which La Bouche's rapier had cut in his ribs. 'Another inch to the left there and it's yourself would be lying on the sand yonder. And, blast me, what ails your hand?' He swore in disgust at the sight of the crimson stain spreading through the sash which the pirate had swathed on his forearm. 'The graceful art of sword-play! You'll have taken this when you beat his blade aside with your hand. And not the wit to realise that in so turning a point you must touch the blade for an instant only, for fear it has a cutting edge.'

'Talk less and bind it for me,' said Rackham shortly. He lay back, his black head resting against the plaster of the wall, his face grimed with sand and sweat. Reaction had set in, and he was finding it an effort to talk. The Major, having stripped away the bloody sash and sponged the wound, bound a linen cloth tightly about it, remonstrating as he did so, like a mother with an injured child.

'It's thankful we should be you've taken no worse hurt. I was a fool to have let matters go so far. When he disarmed you that time – my God!' The Major shuddered. 'I thought ye were done, and so you would have been, but that ye have the fiend's own luck and a surprising nimbleness on your feet. But, there now, all's well that ends well, as the poet says.'

At that moment they were interrupted by a woman's voice calling them from the roadway, and at the sound of it Rackham spun round so violently that he nearly upset the Major. For it was the voice which had urged La Bouche to run him through when he stood disarmed; the voice which had made him forget his fear in a mad surge of fury, and the recollection of its mockery reawoke his anger against the speaker.

'Major Penner! A moment, Major, if you please.'

The Major, turning with Rackham, swept off his hat and made a clumsy bow towards a carriage which stood at the roadside. He muttered an excuse to Rackham and lumbered towards it.

6. ANNE BONNEY

The woman in the carriage was tall, and quite the most vivid-looking creature Rackham had ever seen. Her hair, beneath a broad-brimmed bonnet, was glossy dark red, and hung to shoulders which in spite of the heat were covered only by a flimsy muslin scarf. Her high-waisted green gown was cut very low on her magnificent bosom, which was bare of ornament; her face was long, with a prominent nose and chin, her brows heavy and dark, and her lips, which were heavily painted, were broad and full, with an odd quirk at the corners that gave her an expression at once wanton and cynical. Massive earrings touched her shoulders, there was a tight choker of black silk round her neck, and the bare forearm which lay along the edge of the carriage was heavily bangled and be-ringed.

'In God's name, Penner, what was the meaning of that moon madness?' She waved a jewelled hand in Rackham's direction. 'D'ye value the hide of your friend so cheap that you'll offer him as meat for a bully-swordsman's chopping?'

'Why, ma'am, I—' Penner shuffled and stammered. 'I was opposed to it, d'ye see – from the outset, but—'

'If that was your opposition, God save us from your encouragement,' observed the woman languidly. She turned her heavy-lidded eyes on Rackham. 'For one who has so narrowly cheated the chaplain your champion is mighty glum,' she observed. 'He has a name, I suppose?'

'Hah, yes,' said Penner. 'My manners are all to pieces, I think. Permit me, ma'am, to present my friend and brother officer, Captain Rackham – Captain John Rackham.' He made a vague gesture of introduction. 'John – er, Captain, – Mistress Bonney.'

Rackham, still resentful of this red-haired Amazon, gave a nod which was the merest apology for a bow. Covered with dust and sweat, he was conscious of the bedraggled figure he must present, and his indignation was not sufficient to make him forget his vanity.

But Mistress Bonney had no thought for his disarray. Her eyes widened at the mention of his name.

'The pirate captain? He that fired on the Governor's fleet and took a fortune in silver from the Spaniards?'

'The same,' said Major Penner, with the proud air of a master exhibiting a prize pupil. 'And now turned privateer with me.'

Mistress Bonney's grey eyes beneath those heavy black brows considered Rackham appreciatively. Her broad lips parted in a smile. 'Faith, it's an honour to meet so distinguished a captain. I had heard you took the pardon this morning. Doubtless you mean to lead a peaceful life ashore.'

She was laughing at him, and he flushed angrily. 'You hear a deal, madam. But it's not all gospel. If they tell you I fired on the King's ships they lie: it was no work of mine but that of a half-drunk fool. Nor did I take any silver from the Spanish. That, too, was another's work.'

'Another half-drunk fool?' she asked, smiling.

'A cold sober traitor,' he answered.

She pursed her lips, her eyes mocking him. 'You keep sound company. And now you are in league with the bold Major. Well, he's neither fool nor traitor, but for the rest he's both drunk and sober, as the mood takes him. Am I right, Major?'

'As always, ma'am,' replied the Major gallantly. 'And never more drunk than in the presence of beauty.'

'A compliment, by God! Put it in verse, Major, and sing it beneath a window.' She turned back to Rackham. 'You, sir, who are a captain, and a pirate, and what not: where did you learn to use a sword so pitifully?'

'Pitifully?' Rackham stared, then laughed. 'Ask La Bouche if my sword-play was pitiful.'

'I've no need to ask. I've eyes in my head. You're a very novice, man. La Bouche might have cut you to shreds.'

'But he didn't, ma'am, as ye'll have observed,' put in the Major hastily, as he saw Rackham's brow growing dark. 'Captain Rackham is not one of your foining rascals; a quick cut and a strong thrust is his way – and very effective, too.'

'It may be. But he can thank God and his good luck that he has a whole skin still,' said Mistress Bonney. 'And where do you take him now?'

'To my house,' said the Major. 'He has a scratch or two that will be the better of bathing and sleep.'

'And what do you know of tending his scratches?' she asked scornfully. Her lazy glance lingered again on Rackham. 'You'd best let me see to him. Climb into the coach, both of you, and we'll take him where he won't be mishandled by some coal-heaver who calls himself a physician. For that's the best he'd have from you, Penner.'

The Major looked uneasily at Rackham. 'If you think it best—' he began. Mistress Bonney waved him aside impatiently.

'Be silent, man. It's for Captain Rackham here to judge.'

Rackham met her bold stare and wondered. His first instinct was to tell this fantastic woman, with her harlot's face and body and mannish tongue, to mind her own business and be gone. She was too bold; too forthright. He could have excused her that if she had been a tavern wench, but she was not. There were the signs of wealth about her, and her voice, for all its oaths and masculinity, was not uneducated. These things, taken with her heavy paint and challenging eyes, made her a queer paradox of a woman; instinct warned him that she was dangerous. But his hand and side were stinging most damnably, and his head throbbed. And so he made the decision which was to change the course of his life, with two words.

'Thank you.' He turned to the Major. 'If Mistress Bonney has anything that will take the ache from these cuts, I'd be a fool to refuse.'

The Major nodded solemnly. He seemed vaguely unwilling, but Rackham was too tired to take notice of him.

They drove up the slight incline through the town, and then the coach wheeled to take the eastern coast road. Lulled by the gentle rocking of the vehicle, Rackham leaned back and allowed his tired body to relax. Soon they were passing through the cane-fields, with their gangs of black slaves working in the blazing sun. Somewhere one of them was chanting in a deep, strong voice, and Rackham closed his eyes and dozed to that slow, haunting melody.

The stopping of the coach shook him out of his half-sleep. They were through the cane-fields now, and were halted on a stretch of road which ran through a quiet palm-grove.

Major Penner had climbed out of the carriage, and looking about for explanation Rackham noticed a small drive winding between the palms to a white, green-shuttered house half-hidden among the trees. Penner was looking uneasy and fidgeting with his hat; he was, apparently, bidding good-bye to Mistress Bonney. Rackham could make nothing of this.

'Is this your house?' he asked her.

'Not yet. I recollected I had a call to make on Mistress Roberts – hers is the house yonder – and Major Penner has gallantly offered to carry a message for me. It is vastly obliging of him. I don't doubt that Fletcher Roberts will bid him to dinner.'

Her explanation was sounding oddly like a series of instructions; the Major could hardly have looked less gallant or obliging.

'I shall look for you again, Major,' she continued, and although she favoured him with her most gracious smile there was finality in her tone. 'In the meantime have no fear for your charge.' And before Rackham could speak the carriage was rolling off and Penner was left standing by the roadside.

Rackham half-turned in his seat to call the driver to halt, but the sudden movement brought a fiery wrench to the wound in his side, and he sank back, gasping with pain. Mistress Bonney, seeing him go suddenly pale, started forward in her seat, only to relax as he lifted his head angrily.

'Why did you leave him there?'

Her generous red lips parted in a slow smile. 'I have good reasons for what I do.'

'It seems so.' He frowned at her. 'You're over-masterful for a woman, mistress.'

She laughed at that. 'It's easy seen you've never called a woman wife, captain. Wait till you're wed and you'll know what mastery is.' She leaned forward again and gently pressed him back into his seat, and he submitted, partly because he doubted his ability to resist, partly because he saw the folly of becoming over-excited.

Mistress Bonney stood up, and despite the rocking of the coach, changed seats gracefully and sat down beside him. Drawing a kerchief from her sleeve she gently wiped the perspiration from his face and brow, and he confessed to himself that her touch was vastly soothing.

'There.' She dropped the kerchief over the side of the coach and sat back from him. 'A little cleaner, and a deal calmer. Give him a few hours' sleep and a bite to eat and he'll be the man he was two hours ago. To set your mind at rest,' she went on, 'I'll show you reasons why we should leave your fiery-faced friend as far behind as possible. One is that I've no mind to have the bungling oaf fussing round you, giving advice about your wounds and likely driving you into a fever. Oh, I've seen a man in these latitudes laid on his back for good with scratches no bigger than yours. You'd be thirsty – show me the man that isn't – and the Major would be slipping in to soothe you with a pannikin of Jamaica, and then another and another, and by morning the cook would be able to roast mutton on your chest. So we leave the gallant Penner where he'll do no harm.' She broke off to find him gazing at her in astonishment. 'What ails thee man?'

He shook his head. 'I never saw a woman like you,' he began. 'You talk like a – like a . . . I never heard a woman to match it.'

'Compliments fly like hail,' she said composedly. 'What you mean is I don't talk like a lady – nor look like one. But since I'm not, it's no odds. I talk as I've a mind, which you may find strange, but it's how I was made. As for how I look, that, too, is how I was made, thank God.' She fixed her grey eyes on him quizzically. 'You could be gallant and say "Amen" surely?'

He looked at her for a moment in silence. 'I could indeed,' he said, and for an instant her lids flickered down over her eyes and her lips parted a trifle.

'But why should you be so concerned for me?' he went on. 'Until an hour ago you had never seen me. What do my wounds matter to you? Penner could have seen to them. What's your reason?'

She shrugged. 'Does it seem so strange? If it does, then I'll tell you gladly. I do it because there are too few tall fellows left in these islands who would stand up to a man who is a better swordsman and fight him with his own weapons. I don't know the cause of your quarrel, nor do I ask. That is your affair. But the only thing I've learned to love and admire in this world is courage. It's what I prize most highly in myself – more even than my body or my face. That's reason enough for what I do.' Then in a moment the grey eyes had resumed their customary languid mockery. 'And if that were not reason enough I'll add another. You must be saved and made well so that someone can teach you the art of weapons. You may be a rare hand with a cutlass, for aught I know, but with a small-sword . . .'

But Rackham was no longer listening. Courage, she said. Yet courage was not a thing he had thought of one way or another; certainly it had nothing to do with his meeting with La Bouche. Courage was not a virtue but a necessity, since without it there could simply be no life as he knew it.

But such abstract contemplation was too much for a man wearied with two wounds and the torpid heat of the afternoon. Easier to lounge in his seat, feeling his stiffened muscles relax, conscious of the somehow comforting presence of this strange woman beside him. He was dreamily surprised when he remembered the dislike with which he had regarded her at first. His resentment had faded: even when he recalled how she had urged La Bouche to kill him he felt only curiosity. And that could wait. With his eyes shut he slumped in his seat, and his last recollection was of an arm about his shoulders and of soft, perfumed flesh pillowing his head.

7. THE AMOROUS INVALID

When Rackham opened his eyes again it was to look upon a high, airy, white-walled room with screen doors overlooking a pleasant garden. He was lying in a huge four-poster bed, marvellously soft, and screened by mosquito curtains. The verandah doors were open, and by turning his head he could see just a little of the foliage in the garden, and the high palisade beyond.

This was her house; she had been bringing him to it when he had fallen asleep. He could not remember arriving, but he had a vague recollection of lying on this very bed while a tall, lean man with heavy jowls bent over him. It had been dusk, with candles in the room, and his last memory was of those little spears of light burning in the dark.

It was a long time since he had lain in a bed like this, and for several minutes he savoured the pleasant drowsiness of his situation. His side was stiff, and his bandaged left hand was aching slightly, but for the rest he was at ease and content to wait until someone should break in upon his rest. So he drowsed gently until a sound in the doorway disturbed him, and he opened his eyes to see Mistress Bonney watching him. He began to struggle into an upright position, but she stopped him with a smile and a raised hand as she came forward. It was the first time he had seen her standing, and it came as a shock to him to realise that she must be nearly as tall as himself. Her figure was in proportion to her height; her shoulders wide and her arms powerful for all their deceptive smoothness. But any impression of masculinity was dispelled by the slimness of her waist, the fullness of the rounded breasts half revealed by her low-cut gown of yellow muslin, and the grace with which she moved.

'And how are my bully-swordsman his wounds to-day?' she asked.

'Stiff,' said Rackham, 'but easier than they were.'

She pouted and sat down on the bed. 'I wish to God it had been La Bouche I had brought home. If I had asked the same question of him he'd have sworn his wounds were nothing to those his heart had suffered when I entered the room. But yours are stiff. Pah!'

'Why, so they are,' said Rackham. He hesitated. 'But I thank you for what you've done. It was – it was very kind, mistress.'

'Why, so it was,' she answered. 'And my name is Anne. A queen's name, you'll remember.' She was smiling at him again. 'Well, doesn't it suggest a compliment? Heavens, man, La Bouche would have given me a score of them.'

'There's a deal too much of La Bouche here,' he said irritably.

'No,' said Anne Bonney. 'A deal too little. Only a big Englishman with an English tongue. But there.' She patted his unwounded hand. 'I like them better, I think.'

He considered her. 'It didn't seem so, yesterday.'

'Yesterday?'

'Finish him off, La Bouche. It's over hot,' he quoted. 'Some such words as those. I don't forget them, mistress.'

'That?' She laughed contemptuously, then looked at him half-smiling. 'Consider, now, and tell me truthfully – did it not anger you?'

'Aye, it did.'

'And you were in such a rage that you half-killed him with your fist and then ran him through?'

He stared at her. 'And you'd have me believe you foresaw all that? You must think me a fool, mistress.'

'I do,' she agreed readily, 'since your wits are so slow that they can't see the obvious. Why else should I do it, but to sting you who were standing there like a pudding, waiting to be killed, and to puff the vanity of that French dung-rooster? If I had wanted to see La Bouche pay you, should I have brought you here?'

'How do I know? You're a woman, and have reasons no man can understand.' But he was half-convinced. 'It may be as you say. God knows I've enough to be grateful to you for.'

She turned and leaned across towards him. 'Grateful?'

'Aye, of course,' he said, a little shame-faced.

She leaned closer, until she was so near that he could feel her breath on his face, and inhale the heavy sweetness of her perfume. He put up his hand and caressed her shoulder gently, then the red lips parted and she was in his arms, her mouth pressed fiercely against his. he fondled her shoulders and neck, and felt her shudder. For a moment they clung together, and then she drew away, her moist lips trembling. 'And you supposed to be a sick man,' she sighed. 'God help us when you're well.'

He stretched out a hand towards her, but she rose quickly.

'No, no, my lad. The weather's warm enough. Fevers mount too easily in this heat.'

'I'm in no danger of fever,' he exclaimed impatiently. 'Anne—'

'Who said you were? Anyway there's work to do for us who can't stay abed.' She went to the door. 'You're best lying still until the doctor sees you again.' Then she winked and smiled at him. 'Later, perhaps.' The door closed behind her and he was alone again.

For several minutes he lay quite still. So there was more to Mistress Bonney after all than the mannish talk and the banter. Only for a few seconds had the mask dropped, but in that brief space she had been all woman, and a very beautiful and passionate woman besides. Compared with her, the lately adored Kate Sampson seemed a pale, insignificant creature – attractive enough, but only a pretty miss beside this splendid red-headed Hebe. This was the kind of woman a man could meet on equal terms – and yet be a woman for all that.

He did not see her again that day, but he thought of little else, which may have had something to do with the slight feverishness which the doctor – who visited him in the evening – detected when he made his examination. However, he pronounced himself generally satisfied and suggested that the patient might get up next morning. Rackham would have questioned him, for apart from the negro slaves who brought him his meals he had seen no one, and there was much which he wanted to know about his mysterious hostess, but the doctor was not communicative. So, still wondering, the pardoned pirate spent a second night beneath Mistress Bonney's hospitable roof, and in the morning, feeling considerably more energetic than on the previous day, got out of bed as soon as the slaves had given him his breakfast.

His wounds seemed to have mended swiftly, and he dressed unaided. His own clothes had gone, but in a cupboard he found a clean shirt and breeches which fitted him tolerably well, linen stockings, and shoes. Since the day was warm he sauntered out on to the verandah. Steps at one end led down into the garden, and soon he was wandering along the path which ran round the house.

Whoever Anne Bonney might be, she obviously had money. The gardens were spacious and well kept, and while Rackham was no naturalist, he could make the mercenary's subconscious computation of what all this splendour would be worth if translated into coin.

The sudden dry crack of a pistol shot broke the morning quiet, and Rackham wheeled abruptly. He was at one side of the house, and the shot had been fired behind the building, somewhere among a cluster of low, thatched sheds just inside the palisade, fifty yards away.

He was walking towards them when a second shot sounded, and this time he caught sight of a tiny blue smoke-puff rising behind a wicker wall adjoining one of the huts. To reach it he had to cross a hard-beaten open space behind the house, and separated from it by a stout wooden stockade. Evidently these sheds housed the plantation slaves. He reached the end of the wicker screen and walked round it.

A tall man, dressed in a close-fitting suit of black, and wearing long riding boots, stood with his back to Rackham. His right hand held a pistol, and he was aiming at an orange set on a post some twenty paces distant. Behind the target a pile of spongy palmetto logs ensured safety from the pistol balls.

The pistol cracked and Rackham saw the orange move slightly, but it did not fall. The tall man gave an exclamation of disgust and picked up another pistol from a bench in front of him. Again he aimed, but the broad-brimmed hat he wore interfered with his vision and he swept it off impatiently. To Rackham's amazement a cascade of red hair fell to the black-clad shoulders as the hat was removed, and at his exclamation Anne Bonney turned abruptly.

'My pirate!' she cried gaily, and dropped the pistol on to the bench. As she advanced on him Rackham found himself thinking how admirably her masculine clothing became her: if she had been gracefully feminine in her accustomed dress, she was even more beautifully lithe in her new habit.

'You see me at practice,' she announced. And without giving him a moment to reply: 'Are you better indeed? Do your wounds pain you yet?'

Rackham smiled. 'I live,' he said. 'Do you go on with your shooting.'

'Nay, I've done enough. There are better things to do, now that I have my pirate on his feet again.'

'But the orange is still whole,' he pointed out.

'Bah, now I shall never hit it,' she pouted, but she turned back to the bench and picked up her pistol. She fired again, hardly taking aim, and the orange was spattered against the log screen.

'There,' she said, tossing her head. 'Now let me see the prowler who sets foot in this plantation.'

'What if you have no pistol?' jested Rackham, but she took him seriously. 'Come and see,' she said, and led him into a shed which flanked her pistol range. It was a long, airless place, with a plank floor, and in one corner a pile of what appeared to be long cushions. Anne Bonney crossed to a cupboard beside the pile, and opening it, took out a flat slim case. To Rackham's surprise it contained two slender rapiers, deadly Spanish tools with three razor edges and needle-fine points.

'These will serve if I have no pistols,' said Anne, and she swished one of the blades in the air with evident familiarity.

While he watched she stooped to the pile of cushions, and lifting one, suspended it from a hook in the main rafter. Then, stepping back, she came on guard. Fascinated, Rackham watched her point flicker in and out as she went through the various guards. With quick, smooth steps, always academically upright, advancing and retreating, she made play with an imaginary opponent before extending herself in a lunge which sent the blade in and out through the target in one lightning movement. Again and again she thrust, her point finding the same spot with unvarying accuracy.

At last she turned towards him. 'Would you care to prowl, sir?' she asked, with mock demureness.

'Not I, by God,' said Rackham. 'Ye've seen the sorry showing I make with a sword. I'll not pretend. I never was a fencer.'

She chuckled and was about to turn away to restore her weapon to is case, but his hand on her wrist detained her. For a moment she resisted and then she allowed herself to be drawn into his arms, and opened her mouth on his. Her arms went about his neck and he pulled her down on to the pile of cushions. His arms tightened about her, pressing her so close that she began to feel dizzy, but it was a wholly delightful dizziness, and she made no attempt to draw away. And at that moment a foot scraped behind them.

Involuntarily she started away from him, looking round. There were three men in the doorway. One was a stout, yellow-faced person of middle height, richly dressed in biscuit-coloured taffeta, who was watching them with twinkling little eyes that were close set on either side of his broad snub nose. He was leaning on a long cane, and his face, under his broad-brimmed hat, was twisted into a peculiar, ugly smile. Beside him stood a huge, bearded fellow bearing a coiled whip; obviously a plantation overseer. He was grinning broadly as he surveyed them. The third man, who stood slightly behind, was a negro.

Astonished and angry, Rackham was on the point of asking what the devil they wanted; was, in fact, already weighing up the burly overseer as an adversary; but Anne Bonney was there before him. He might have expected her to spring to her feet, angrily to order them away or – although it was hard to imagine – she might have shown signs of guilt or confusion. But she did none of these. Instead, she surveyed the three coldly, leaned back into Rackham's arms, and said softly, almost lazily: 'Get out.'

The stout man's smile grew a trifle broader, and definitely uglier. With his free hand he made an odd fluttering movement, and inclined his head in a conciliatory gesture. His shifty eyes looked everywhere but at her.

'Of course, of course, my dear,' he said in a thin, piping voice. 'But you forget, I have not yet been presented.' His eyes rested for a moment on Rackham's face, then dropped again.

'Get out,' said Anne Bonney, in the same quiet voice.

The expression on the man's face never altered, but the bearded overseer let out a rumble of laughter. Without bothering to glance at him the stout man said: 'Be off, Kane. I'll see you at the house.'

The overseer turned away, still grinning, and the slave went with him, but his master remained in the doorway. For a few seconds Anne Bonney looked at him dispassionately, then she stretched her arm behind Rackham's neck, and without apparent exertion, pulled his face down to hers and kissed him. He would have shaken her off, but her grip was uncommonly strong, and she held him for a few seconds before he broke away, flushing with embarrassment.

The man in the doorway continued to smile his ugly smile.

'I regret the intrusion, mistress,' he said. 'But I must convey my felicitations to the captain on his recovery. My congratulations, sir.' He bowed in Rackham's direction. 'We shall do all in our power to make your stay here an enjoyable one. Please regard this estate, and everything on it, as your own.'

His irony was obvious, and Rackham was about to spring up with an angry retort when Anne Bonney forestalled him.

'Get out,' she said for the third time, and the stout man, with a bow and a last smirk, obeyed.

'Of course, my own. My service to you, captain. Remember, what we have is here for your pleasure.' He bowed again and they heard his steps retreating across the yard.

Rackham started to get to his feet, but Anne Bonney, reclining across his knees, laid a hand on his arm.

'Let him be,' she said.

'But who the devil is he?'

She glanced up at him. 'My husband. Did you not know?'

'Your husband?' He stared at her in dismay.

'It was apparent, surely.' She sat up and smoothed her close-fitting black shirt. 'Ye didn't think he was my father, I hope.'

'Good God,' said Rackham. 'And you sat here with me—'

'Be still,' she chided him. 'What's to concern you? You had designs on me yourself, and they're no more dishonourable because I'm married.'

76

She stood up and patted her hair into place. If she was troubled that her husband had found her in Rackham's arms, she showed no signs of it. But for Rackham it was a blow: the thought that she might be married had never entered his head; perhaps he had not wanted to think of it. Since it was so, then the sooner he turned his back on the Bonneys, man and wife, and got him to sea with Penner, the better.

But he did not want to turn his back on Anne Bonney. The past few hours he had spent in an idyll, and he wanted it to continue. He wanted this woman, and not only in a physical sense. He wanted to be with her, to hear her voice, to watch her, to listen to her deep, soft laugh and to catch the bright, inviting glance of her grey eyes. But a husband – that was an obstacle not to be overcome. She might despise and detest the man, but she was bound to him and he to her. There was no escaping it.

While he sat there, silent, she paced to the door and stood looking into the sunlight.

'What will you do?' she asked at length.

'I?' Rackham grimaced. 'What is there to be done? I can change into my own clothes again, and thank you for your kindness to me. What else?'

'Because of him?'

'Because he is your husband.'

She gave a bitter little smile and came to sit down beside him again. 'Strange,' she said. 'Because of a man I hate, I must lose a man—' Deliberately she left the end of the sentence unspoken, and as she expected, he turned on her, eager to hear it.

'Because of the man – Go on!' His hands were on her shoulders, turning her towards him, and then he saw that her eyes were full of tears. For a moment he looked at her,

77

and then, with a little sob, she was clinging to him, her lips on his. Fiercely he drew her to him, feeling the pressure of her breasts against him; then she went limp in his arms.

For a long moment they clung together, then he gently pushed her a little away, holding her by the shoulders and looking down into her face.

'Do you – would you leave him and come away with me?' he asked.

She did not answer for a moment. 'Come away?' she repeated. 'Come away?' She smiled gently at him. 'To come away is not so easy.'

'Why not?' He was all eagerness. 'Wherever you will – Charles Town, New York, England even. Say the word and it's done, lass.'

She shook her head. 'Castles in the air. This is the King's land, and there is a law, reckless John, that commands obedience from wives, even to husbands like mine. Would you put yourself beyond pardon for nothing? Husband-robbing is an ill venture for a reformed buccaneer.'

He had no answer to this, and for a moment she sat, her eyes weighing and searching him. At last he said: 'What use to talk, then? I'd best be gone, I think.'

But at this she seemed surprised. 'So soon? Where's the need, at least for a day or so until your wounds are quite healed?'

'But you said—'

'I said "no" to some foolish talk of flying with you. But that's no reason for you to stamp away in the sulks. Is it not pleasant here?'

'Oh, aye, with your husband lurking at corners, mighty pleasant—'

'You are his guest,' she interrupted, and her voice was

suddenly hard. 'Himself he said so. Oh, I know the dirty grin on his face. Well, give him poor jest for poor jest. Take him at his word. What's to hinder you?'

He knew there were several reasons, but it would have taken a more cold-blooded man than Rackham to enunciate them. He hesitated, and then: 'As you will,' he said, and she seemed well pleased.

They went out of the shed, and as they paced together across the compound, Rackham asked: 'If you hate the man so much, how did you come to wed him in the first place?'

Anne Bonney shrugged. 'He bought me. It is his way. He found me in Charles Town, when I was seventeen, a maid in a tavern where my mother was linen-mistress. I was virtuous, too, if you'll believe it, and he found he could not have me as he pleased. I wondered at the time that he was foolish enough to offer marriage to a lass of no account, but he did.' She laughed. 'He might have had a score of women, ladies of some consequence, for he is a wealthy man. But he wanted me. At least, he wanted my body, and no other would do. So he bought it. He made me the mistress of this' – she gestured around her – 'and gave my mother a pension. I have wanted for nothing since, and I kept my part of the bargain, which was to be his bed-mate. At first I was afraid he would tire of me. Child as I was, I had seen something of men. But he did not tire.' Her voice sounded flat and hopeless.

'What then?'

'Then? Some months ago I told him I would remain his wife, but I would be his mistress no longer. God knows I was no cheat. I had made a bargain and was ready to keep it, although I shuddered every time he touched me. But there were some things I would not do; things he tried to force me to do, in the name of our marriage. Things that only the mind of a beast could imagine.' Her voice was trembling with anger. 'It was then I told him I would kill him if he tried to touch me again. He said nothing at the time just looked at me with his foul smile and said 'As you wish, my dear. It is very well.' He knew I meant what I had said. And so he hates me; not only because I refused him, but because I know what a vile soul he has. And yet, I know from the way he looks at me that he still wants me. I can feel his eyes on me whenever we are in a room together, or when I pass him in the house, shifting and watching, but never meeting mine.' The words were coming in a torrent now; in a moment she would break down. 'He will drive me mad! Every day I feel I cannot bear it any longer!' She was sobbing, but without tears, and Rackham was moved to put his arm about her shoulders.

'Easy, now, easy,' he told her. 'He'll do you no harm, that I promise.' The discovery that she had a woman's weakness despite her assumed worldliness gave him confidence, as she intended it should. 'But can you not leave him, go into the town, say, and live there? You're no defenceless female; you could fend for yourself.'

Some of her wonted defiance crept back into her voice. 'I promised to be his wife, and that I'll remain. But it shall be in name only. Besides, I manage his house to his satisfaction and my own; sometimes it is very pleasant here. I'm not so great a fool that I can't see the advantages of being Mistress Bonney. Only – only, when these black moods come on me, when I have to talk to him, or see him, I could wish I were back in Charles Town. But I know I would never go back to that. I've known poverty and hardship, and I know that a woman needs a man to protect her, even such a man as James Bonney.'

'Poor lass,' said Rackham.

'Poor lass be damned,' said Anne Bonney. 'He bids you stay here so that I may give him cause to go whining to the Governor that I'm a faithless wife. Well, you'll stay, and if I catch his dirty eye on me I'll spit in it.'

They had reached the garden in front of the house by now, and Rackham was about to mount the steps, but she detained him, her hand on his wrist. He turned to find that the whimsical smile that the events of the last hour had driven from her face had returned.

'Are all pirates so gallant and kindly?' she asked.

Rackham dissembled his confusion with a laugh. 'Gallant and kindly?' he echoed. And he added, a little puzzled: 'No one has ever said such a thing to me before.'

'Perhaps no one has known you so well,' she replied. 'Now be off to your own room. My patient has been too long in the sun.'

When he had taken leave of her she stood looking after him for a moment, thoughtfully tapping her full lower lip with a ringed finger. Then she smiled a slow smile which at length broke into a soft laugh, much to the astonishment of a passing black slave who saw his eccentric mistress, dressed in her man's clothes, apparently laughing at nothing. Under his startled eyes Anne Bonney tossed her red head and strode off, humming a catch as she went.

8. CAPTAIN HARKNESS
CONVERSES

In what had passed between her and Rackham since their chance meeting outside the Cinque Ports, Anne Bonney had been something less than honest. That she was strongly attracted to him is certain, but she was not deeply in love with him, and would not have scrupled to discard him had he not provided her with a means whereby she believed she could realise an ambition she had long cherished.

This was an ambition born in those early days when she had been a tavern-servant in Charles Town. Young Anne had realised then the probable fate of a woman of her station – a lifetime of drudgery and poverty if she remained single, or an almost equally miserable existence if she married, as the wife of some lowly paid, overworked member of her own class. Either way there would be none of the luxuries which she saw enjoyed by the wealthy ladies of the colony, and it was on those luxuries that she had set her heart. Money, ease and power formed the triple goal for the tavern girl. James Bonney had supplied her with all three – up to a point, but Mistress Anne was not content with what, she soon realised, was a fairly modest rung on the ladder. She wanted more, much more, than a Bahaman plantation and a fairly rich husband whom she detested. She had advanced far enough in the social scale to begin thinking of the gay capitals of Europe which she had never seen, and of the kind of money that existed there, and it seemed, with the entry of Rackham into her life, that perhaps she had found the bridge on which she might cross to her heart's desire.

On the day after she had brought him to her home – and at that time her interest in him was still purely feminine – she had driven into Providence on some errand connected with the household. It was during this visit to the town that a chance remark opened the gate to what she believed would be her destiny.

She had called at Mullen's the draper's, in Well Street, where she had encountered Captain Harkness, of the military, with two other officers. Gallantly the captain had exchanged pleasantries with her, and had commented, reprovingly, on the news that she had extended her hospitality to the notorious ex-pirate, Captain Rackham.

'For look you, ma'am, he's a dangerous rogue,' he admonished her. 'As ruthless and wanton a knave as ever sailed under canvas. In these outposts, and in these times, it is true that social barriers are not so . . . so, ah . . . rigid as would be the case elsewhere, and one must come and go very often in odd company. Duty demands it, and circumstances make strange bedfellows.'

'Captain Harkness, you've been spying, by God,' said Anne Bonney.

The Captain coloured and made haste to explain. 'You

83

mistake my meaning, ma'am,' said he, greatly shocked. 'I vow you do. Good God, no, ma'am, I had not meant . . .'

'And what did you mean, sir?' asked Anne Bonney, enjoying his discomfiture.

'Why, this, ma'am: it is not fitting that you should harbour this scoundrel,' said the blunt soldier.

'But the King has made him as good a citizen as you or I, Captain. He is pardoned, you remember.'

Captain Harkness shook his head. 'So is many another traitor, and that proves nothing.' Aptly he quoted Holy Writ: 'Can the Ethiopian change his skin, or the leopard his spots?'

'Or Calico Jack his shirt?' suggested Mistress Bonney, and thereby convulsed the Captain's friends.

'Captain, you are too stern, too severe,' she chided him, and he melted under the languorous twinkle of her grey eyes.

'Perhaps I am, ma'am, perhaps so. But here it is only of concern for you. For he is a pirate, remember. And you are a woman. I tremble' – a thing Captain Harkness had never done in his life – 'for your safety, and shall continue so until that hardened, penniless robber is out from under your roof.'

'Nay, now, not penniless,' said Anne Bonney. 'Or if he is, blame Governor Rogers. They tell me Captain Rackham had treasure when she was taken.'

'Why, so he had,' agreed one of the officers. 'But he must whistle for it now, the rogue. Next week will see it on its way to England. Friend Harkness will be glad to see it go.'

'And so I shall,' sighed Harkness. He explained: 'While it remains at the Fort I am responsible for it, ma'am. Oh, it's safe enough, but I own I'll be happier when I see it shipped for England. Then it will be another's care.'

'Aye, and a greater burden than I'd care to carry,' put in

one of his companions. 'Half a million would be too much for me. I hope Captain Bankier sleeps sound of nights.'

Anne Bonney turned wide eyes on the speaker. 'Half a million, sir? Did the pirates' treasure amount to so much? I thought such sums belonged only in the stories that old sailors tell of Morgan and Montbars.'

Captain Harkness explained. 'No, no, ma'am. The silver taken from the *Kingston* is only a small part of what is to be shipped home.' He grew confidential, flattered by her interest. 'As ye'll perhaps know, the privateers have been active these many months past, and what they have brought back from their cruises amounts now to this considerable sum. This last treasure from the *Kingston* decided His Excellency. He now has more plunder bestowed in the Fort than he dares to keep, and I don't blame him. So he has determined it must go home. God knows it was no easy decision, for the privateers are sloops, and too small for such a task, and he has few larger vessels to spare. But there it is: better to send it home and deplete his little fleet than to have it here where a Spanish raid might carry it off.'

'But surely there is small likelihood of such a raid.'

The Captain solemnly wagged his head. 'Who can say, ma'am? They've tried it before. Given wind of what we have here, there's no saying they won't try it again. No, no. His Excellency is wise, I think. Better the slight risk a brig will run bearing it across the Atlantic than the greater risk of keeping it even a month longer here, ill-defended as we are.'

The draper's presence at their elbows reminded Captain Harkness that perhaps he had exceeded the bounds of prudence in speaking so freely; the shipment of treasure to be made the following week was, after all, a highly secret matter.

'Ye'll understand, of course, that no word of what I've told you must get about,' he enjoined, but Mistress Bonney seemed not to hear him. She picked a piece of scarlet material from the draper's tray, considered it, spread it along the outrageously low-cut bosom of her black taffeta gown, and invited his opinion.

'Does it flatter me, Captain Harkness, this shade?'

Her inattention was a reassurance in itself. Fascinated by the full charms which her question required him to inspect, he gallantly corrected her.

'Nothing, ma'am, could flatter you,' he protested, and with that their talk turned to lighter topics. Presently she took her leave, and drove home unusually thoughtful, pondering what Harkness had told her. And in that brief drive she saw that the whim which had prompted her to take Rackham to her home had provided her with an undreamed of opportunity.

The idea which came to her as she drove back to the plantation was as wild and preposterous as any that ever passed through a woman's mind. To the ordinary female, however daring or ambitious, it could never even have suggested itself, but Anne Bonney was no ordinary woman, which is why she has a unique place in British maritime history.

Here, at a stroke, was a way to realise her dream of wealth unbounded. Half a million of money would shortly be on its way to England. Under her hand she had a filibuster captain, a man noted for his skill in seamanship as well as his courage and resource, wise in the ways of sea-robbery, an experienced practitioner in his trade. True, he had taken a Royal pardon, and might be reluctant to return to his old life. But he could be coaxed or constrained, she had no doubts of that. It must be done carefully and artfully, but it must be done.

So that day and the next she went to work in her own way, and on that morning when they parted after their conversation in the plantation yard, Anne Bonney saw that the time was near when she could account the first part of her plan, the winning of Captain Rackham, completed.

Yet she hesitated, fearing that in spite of the hold which she was obtaining over him, he would reject her plan for the appallingly risky venture it was. So another day passed, and it was only a visit from Major Penner on the following morning, anxious for news of his quartermaster-elect, that provided her with the spur she needed.

The burly privateer brought with him a remarkable piece of tavern gossip which, he confided to Mistress Bonney, had best be kept from Rackham's ears. What it amounted to was the suggestion that Woodes Rogers, obsessed by jealousy, had paid La Bouche to put a quarrel on Rackham and kill him. The grog-shops, declared the Major, were full of it, and he was fearful that if Rackham got wind of the tale he might be stung into some rash attempt at vengeance on the Governor. Whatever the outcome, Penner pointed out glumly, he would certainly be left without a quartermaster.

Anne Bonney scoffed his rumour out of court, but when the Major had gone his way somewhat reassured, she paced about the verandah deep in thought. It seemed that this piece of nonsense might be turned to account: she knew the story of Rackham and Kate Sampson: he would be ready, she reasoned, to believe anything to the discredit of Woodes Rogers.

She sought him out, and found him strolling on the dirt road through the coffee plantation. She had changed into her masculine riding habit, and her hair was held in place by a folded black silk kerchief run through a gold ring and looped on her shoulder. Being quick to notice his undisguised admiration of her, she asked herself why she had ever doubted that she could mould his will to hers.

Seeing no profit in mincing words, she went straight to the point.

'Do you know that you go in danger of your life?' was her somewhat dramatic opening, and to her surprise he only seemed amused.

'That is nothing new. Nor is this the first time I've been told so. What danger is it?' Idly he flicked a pebble aside with his foot, and Anne Bonney smiled grimly to herself as she prepared to shatter his composure.

'No ordinary danger. One very highly placed, and powerful. He seeks your life, and already he has hired one assassin to kill you.'

'Who?'

'Governor Woodes Rogers,' she said, and Rackham swung round as though he had been stung. She misunderstood, and laid a hand on his arm.

'Wait, John, wait. There's no doubt of it. I have it from a sure source—'

'Doubt it! Why should I doubt it?' he cried. 'It's what I might have expected, by God!'

'Then you believe me?' She had expected him to scoff at her, make demands for proof.

'Aye, I believe you. It's not enough that he should cheat me, aye, and steal from me, too. I should have foreseen how that filibuster mind of his would work. He knew he had wronged me, and he looked to me to deal with him as a pirate would deal. And so I would have dealt when the time came. But he will forestall me, will he?' He laughed almost in delight.

Anne Bonney found this beyond her. He was actually standing there grinning at her.

'I don't understand you,' she said.

'How should you?' He took her by the hand. 'Listen, Anne. This great gentleman of a Governor, this Woodes Rogers, did me a great wrong. No matter what. But it was such a wrong that I had no way to pay it back to him. Now, if what you tell me is true, I see a way. Tell me, who was the assassin you spoke of?'

But this was not at all to Mistress Bonney's liking. It should have been for her to point the way. 'What will you do?' she asked uneasily.

'Never fear, it'll be a safe way. Tell me the name of this murderer, and I'll squeeze a confession out of him that will have his dirty excellency squirming to find a way out of his own snare.'

'And who would believe it?' She smiled cynically.

His face darkened. 'Then there are other ways. The assassin's knife always has two edges. There are more men than one in Providence willing to open a throat.'

'Aye, to open yours, perhaps, but not the Governor's.'

He considered her through narrowed eyes. 'And if I were to slit his throat myself, then? God knows, I'm not unwilling, and it's the surest way of protecting myself.'

She shook her head. 'How many people saw him strike you on the Fort roof?' she asked. 'They would remember, and the law would require no evidence beyond that. Pirates are gone out of fashion these days.'

'Then what the hell am I to do?' he demanded. 'Wait till that bloody King's monkey gets me first?'

Anne Bonney felt her heart beat a little faster. She looked round, over the fields of coffee plants, where the slaves mumbled and laughed as they worked. This was the time, she told herself. Never if not now. She would provide him with a weapon to strike Woodes Rogers and enrich himself at the same time.

Only she must weigh her words, and use every trick in her power to convince him.

'Come back to the house,' she said. 'I think I know of a way.'

They walked back to the house, and Rackham followed her through the cool, silent hall and down a passage to a small retiring room off her own bedchamber, richly furnished with a polished table, embroidered chairs and couch, and a carpet of heavy pile.

Removing her headscarf before a small mirror in the panelling, Anne Bonney smoothed out her red hair and turned towards Rackham, who was visibly restraining his impatience.

'Come, then, lass,' he said, his dark face eager. 'Let's hear this way of yours.'

'It would be a way,' she began, 'for both of us. It would pay your score with the Governor; it would free me from – from this. And it would mean that you and I could – could be together, Jack.' She raised her eyes to his appealingly. For once she was not acting: she was hoping desperately for success. 'Don't laugh at me. Hear me out. And then tell me, not in a word "aye" or "no", but just tell me . . . if it could be done.'

Intrigued, he seated himself at the table. 'Go on.'

'Next week a ship sails from Providence for England. It will carry the treasure which was taken from your own ship, the *Kingston*, and other money as well, most of it in silver. The whole amounts to half a million pieces. I want to take it. By piracy, for there's no other way.' She stopped and faced him resolutely. 'Can it be done?'

He looked at her appalled. Then he shook his head in amazement. 'You're mad to think of it,' was all he could say.

'Can it be done? Could it be done?' she insisted.

'The thing's an idiot's dream,' he protested. 'Guarded as she would be . . .'

'Not guarded,' she contradicted. 'One ship alone. Only Woodes Rogers and a few of his officers know what is intended. He is as short of shipping as every other Governor in the Caribbean, but he dare not keep such a huge sum here. It has been piling up at the Fort there this two years past: now it's so great he can't risk keeping it where the Spaniards might get wind of it and make a raid. It must go soon – surely you understand?'

'Even so, if what you say is true—' he was beginning, when she interrupted him with her question: 'Could it be done?'

He covered his face with one hand, kneading his brow between thumb and fingers. Her insistence demanded an answer, so he pondered it, and made a reply as to a hypothetical question.

'Men said Morgan could never take Panama. They would have said he could never escape from Maracaibo. But he took Panama; he escaped from Maracaibo. So I say all things are possible, given the brain to plan and the courage to enact. And the skill, and the luck. Given all these, and a crew of lunatics led by another of the same: who knows?' He shrugged. 'Perhaps it could be done, but—'

'Never heed the "buts". Enough that you admit it's possible. Now, listen to me. I can find out everything that is to be found – time of sailing, the crew, the captain, the armaments, even the course. Things you could never find, but simple to a woman. I can—'

'Wait, wait, wait!' he cried. 'For God's sake, this is folly. Believe me. I know something of these things. I know the difficulties, and the dangers. I know a thousand and one things to spike this madness dead.' He slapped his palm on the table. Then he went on more quietly. 'I'm a pardoned man, you'll remember. This would be the kind of enterprise that would most likely end in speedy death or capture. And that would mean Ketch's Hornpipe for me and every man aboard.' He shook his head. 'I'm not so out of love with life that I'll throw it away for nothing.'

She found her resolution wavering before that firm refusal, but she was not the woman to give in at a few words.

'I said there were things I could find out,' she reminded him. 'But there are things I already know. Tell me, could you raise a crew for such an enterprise as this?'

'I've no intent to try.'

'But if you had. Oh, bear with me a little, Jack, please. You promised to hear me out. Could you raise a crew?'

He shrugged impatiently. 'Aye, I suppose so.'

'Within a week?'

'Yes, in two days. Perhaps one day. I flatter myself I know where to look. But I tell you I'm not looking.'

In spite of this she took fresh heart. 'How many?' she asked.

'Enough to sail the *Kingston*. Perhaps more. Say a hundred and twenty. But if you're thinking that would suffice to tackle a treasure-ship carrying half a million pieces – Jesus! what a pile – you can forget it.'

She leaned forward over the table, her voice eager. 'Now I'll tell you something, Captain Rackham. It's one of the few things I know already about this treasure-ship. She carries eighty seamen; eighty, I tell you. No more.' She was rewarded by the sight of his incredulously dropping jaw.

'Eighty! Never in this world!'

'Then ask yourself,' she continued, 'where can Woodes Rogers come by any more? Those eighty are half the crew of the *Unicorn*, the only naval ship he has – and they're as many as he can take from her. Could he trust men from the privateers? Aye, you can smile. Don't you see he has no more men in the Bahamas than those he can get from that one King's ship? He daren't risk the honesty of a single man who isn't in the royal service.'

He scratched his chin reflectively. 'You're well informed, I'll say that. But there's a snag in it. There must be. Why, the man is begging and praying for trouble if he lets all that money loose in one bottom with only eighty men to sail and fight his ship.'

'There will be soldiers, too,' she added. 'Perhaps fifty.' She watched him uneasily, and he shook his head.

'That's still too few for him. Far too few. But too many for me,' he added warningly. 'There's something rotten about it somewhere, which would make me extra cautious even if I was considering it, which I'm not.'

'But he depends on secrecy,' explained Anne Bonney. 'He intends that the ship shall sail without a soul knowing what she carries or where.'

'Secrecy? And what's his secrecy worth?' He leaned back in his chair and eyed her sardonically. 'When you know of it, and I, and my Lord Jack Dandy and Tim the bumboatman and God knows who else beside. Why, half the Fort must know it now, and half Providence to-morrow. The thing's unchancy; I can smell it already.'

His scorn, so confidently expressed, did more to quench

her hopes even than his earlier refusals. But seeing that he had wavered, too, and that she had only to convince him that the Governor's plan was not a trap, she persisted.

'I tell you it is secret. Only a chance remark from that ogling booby Harkness, who thinks that no woman has a mind that can hold a fact longer than she can hold a breath, gave me first wind of it. Then I set to work to find out all. Surely you can understand that I can question where others dare not; that I have weapons will open any door and loose any tongue?'

'Aye, aye, I don't doubt it.' He smiled wryly. 'Ye've a powerful way with the men, I grant you. I've noticed myself.'

'But it can be done.' Her voice was vibrant. 'You know it can be done. Yourself admitted it, given luck and planning, and the courage. And we shall have those. You can find a crew, I can get the information we still need. There is a ship, too, that we must have, and you must see to it. It would have to be stolen.'

'Stolen?' Rackham tried to stifle his irritation. 'D'ye think it's like plucking an apple, then, to steal a ship?'

'Has it never been done?'

'Aye, but—'

'Aye, but, be damned to you! Do I have to teach a pirate that piracy isn't easy? D'ye think half a million pieces will fall into your lap for nothing?' She stood with her booted feet planted apart, hands on hips, like a swashing captain, a militant Hebe. 'Of course there is a risk, and there will be danger—'

'I need no woman to teach me my trade,' he began angrily.

'It's not your trade,' she taunted. 'Your trade is lying in bed and bumbling and mumbling about risks you're afraid to take.'

'Afraid?' He stared at her incredulously. 'Afraid? I'll take that from no one—'

'Aye, will you not?' She curled a lip. 'What holds you, then? Is a fortune not lure enough for you? A fortune – and me?'

It checked his angry outburst for the few seconds she needed. Then her scorn vanished as suddenly as it had come. Her tone became pleading again. 'Oh, Jack, it is the only way. It would mean so much for us both – release from this, happiness, as much money as we'd need to live a thousand lives. And it can be done – you know it can.'

He hesitated, and it is possible in that moment he took stock of past, present, and future, and weighed what was to lose against what was to gain, and resolved. He had never acquired the habit of lingering over decisions. On the one hand there was nothing to keep him in Providence; in fact there appeared to be every reason why he should place himself beyond the Governor's reach as quickly as possible; on the other there was the chance of a fortune and Mistress Bonney besides. Both were tempting, but the risk was appalling. And yet, was it more desperate than enterprises to which he had set his hand in the past?

'Give me a moment to think,' he said slowly, and she knew that she had won.

'As you please.' She kept her voice level in spite of her exultation. 'I'll leave you a moment.' And without another word she withdrew, closing the door of her bedroom softly behind her.

For a moment she stood listening at the panels. Then she crossed swiftly to her dressing table and began to strip off her riding habit. Under her breath she hummed a jig tune, and in her light-heartedness she scattered the garments about the room. When she had undressed she stood in front of her long gilt-framed mirror and examined herself critically, turning this way and that, and smiling with some satisfaction at her reflection. She shook her long red mane of hair from side to side, gathered it up in her hands, considered the various ways in which she might arrange it, and eventually decided it looked best as it was.

She slipped into a heavy green brocade gown before seating herself and beginning a close inspection of her complexion with a hand mirror. She had a few more minutes, she decided, before Rackham announced the acceptance which she now accounted foregone: she must spend them preparing to look her best.

Presently she heard him call. She rose unhesitatingly, took one last quick look at herself in the long mirror, tapped her cheek-bone with her rabbit's-foot, and walking across to the door, opened it. He was standing with his back to her, at the table, but he turned at the sound of the latch. She saw his brows contract and his eyes glint as he caught sight of her, and felt well pleased with herself.

She smiled at him. 'And has he held his council of war?'

'He has,' said Rackham, and smiled wryly in return.

'And the answer, then?'

'The answer,' he said, pacing slowly up to her, 'is "aye" – if you'll find time, date, and course as you promised. But I warn you again, it's a deadly risk, and only an even chance – if that – of success. I think myself I must be mad to listen to you.'

She moved a little closer to him, and for all her height she had to look up into the lean dark face. She put up her hands to his cheeks and caressed them gently.

'Not mad at all, captain. It's the hot weather. It turns

men's heads.' She ran the tip of one finger along his lips. 'Even great hardy sea-faring men.'

He caught her closer, and she shivered in his grip, writhing against his hard strong body. He stooped towards her face, but she turned it swiftly away with a gasping little laugh and made as though to try to break from his embrace.

'Great hardy sea-faring men most of all,' she whispered. His lips quested down her cheek and neck and on to her plump shoulder as he pushed away the loose gown that covered it. For a moment longer she resisted him, and then his lips met her mouth, sweet and loose and moist, her nails dug convulsively into his shoulders, and the robe fell with a soft rustle about their feet.

9. THE PLOTTERS

Next day Rackham left the Bonney plantation and went into Providence to lodge at the Cinque Ports. He was not a sensitive man, and was ready to cuckold Bonney whenever the opportunity arose, but he felt a reluctance to do it under the man's own roof, or to meet Bonney's shifty eye and guess that the planter knew what was happening and was content for some warped purpose of his own to smirk and say nothing.

But this apart, having fallen in with Anne Bonney's plan, Rackham was now faced with the enormous task of obtaining a crew and a ship, all in secrecy, and of plotting a course of action to ensure that when the argosy sailed for England he and his companions would be hard on her heels.

As a first step he decided to enrol Ben, his former lieutenant, whom he found at breakfast in one of the wine-shops on Fish Street. Rackham had no hesitation in approaching one who, like himself, was a pardoned man, for he knew Ben and trusted him, although he told him no more than was necessary – that there was an opportunity of taking a treasure as valuable as any carried in a single bottom within living memory, that Rackham had weighed the risks and found the project dangerous but not impossible, and that a hundred and fifty men would be required.

Ben picked his teeth with a fish-bone and knitted his brows.

'Time's the thing,' he observed. 'I can find the men, but once found they want to be safe aboard before they can start blabbing. 'Tisn't as if we were in a free port any more. Afore the Government came ye could call for volunteers from the cross, but this bloody Rogers has an eye in every bottle and an ear in every jug. Soon as we start scoutin' for men the buzz'll go round, an' they'll know more about it at Governor's House than we do ourselves.'

Rackham soon dispelled his anxiety. 'I'm not asking you to find the whole crew. Most of them you can leave to me. I want you to seek out thirty at most – men who sailed in the *Kingston*, or any others you can trust. But you must be able to trust them, mind that. Get Malloy and Bull, if you can. The others I'll manage.'

He had no clear idea how he would recruit them but Ben unconsciously pointed the way.

'Bull's signed wi' Penner,' he said, 'but I can lay hold of Malloy. Kemp the gunner, too.'

'Bull? With Penner, is he?' Rackham was thoughtful. 'By God, it would be a crew ready found if we could bring in Penner himself. And his men wouldn't need to know it till we were at sea.'

'Aye.' Ben was dubious. 'Mind that all his crew won't be pardoned brothers like us. God knows what sort of hymn-singers and gentlemen-adventurers he's got aboard. Whitehall pimps and youngest sons whose fathers left 'em nowt. They might not take kindly to sailing under the black.'

'They'll take kindly,' said Rackham, 'when there's money

in it.' The more he thought of Penner the better he liked the notion. He got up from the table. 'Find me those thirty men, Ben, and look for me at the Cinque Ports.'

'Aye.' Ben rose with him. 'But Jacky,' he added, frowning, 'if as you go seeking Penner and his crew, mind what I said about the gentlemen-'venturers. There's queer cattle on privateers these days, and honest men can work mischief among a crew of rogues.'

It was advice that Rackham was one day to remember, but at present he was too preoccupied with the realisation of how much the Major's participation would mean to their venture. Penner was a former pirate and seasoned sea-fighter. He had a crew, most of whom, in spite of Ben's fears, would be unlikely to scruple at piracy. Furthermore, he was ready to sail – only the hope of signing Rackham as quartermaster detained him in Providence – and he could have his men aboard his sloop and ready when Rackham wanted them. Thus, the hazardous business of raising a crew would be safely accomplished, and Penner could lie offshore if need be while Rackham and the thirty rascals whom Ben would recruit could attend to the final details. These would include gathering the last scraps of information about Rogers' argosy – here Anne Bonney would prove invaluable – and, when the treasure-ship had sailed, the stealing of a brig for the enterprise.

This last was the major problem, for Penner's sloop would be a hopeless proposition against a ship of war, but it was by no means insurmountable. The *Kingston* lay in Providence harbour, with an anchor watch; it might not be easy to cut her out with thirty men and put to sea all in half an hour, but Rackham had known riskier ventures safely accomplished. Then, with Penner's crew transferred to the *Kingston* they could be off on the heels of Rogers' argosy.

So he reasoned, recklessly perhaps, but aware that to be less than bold would be to invite failure. Thus, in a few minutes, his plan took general shape, and since Penner's participation was vital Rackham straightway sought him out, sounded him carefully, and laid the proposal before him. In this, as in Ben's case, he did not hesitate; he had to trust someone, and if piracy had taught him nothing else it had made him a tolerable judge of men.

After the Major's initial outburst of alarm and astonishment, their argument followed closely on the lines of that which had taken place between Anne Bonney and Rackham the previous day. But with this difference, that Rackham was a better advocate for the enterprise than she had been, since he understood better what it involved, and Penner, once his first fears had been overcome, proved a willing listener.

At length he sat back, surveying Rackham with thoughtful eyes. 'No question of its being a hanging job, is there? And saucy Anne thought it out for herself, ye say? A remarkable woman, that. Remarkable. Though I'd not trust her overfar. However, that's by the way. I like it, John; I think I like it well. A captain's share; let's see, that could see a man rolling in the best of Paris or Rome for the rest of his days. Aye, or snug under a sandbank in the Windward Passage. You're sure of your information?'

'Certain,' said Rackham. He was conscious of a great relief. Penner's acceptance meant more than the Major knew, for to Rackham it was another professional opinion pronouncing in favour of the enterprise. 'It's settled, then?'

'Settled,' said Penner, and they shook hands. The Major sighed. 'Perhaps I'll live to regret it. God knows, I grow greedy as I grow old.' But he said it with some satisfaction.

It was a satisfaction that Anne Bonney was at first slow to

share when, booted, breeched, and cloaked in black, with a broad-brimmed hat pulled down over her face, she joined Rackham in the Cinque Ports that night and found the Major with him above stairs.

'Aye, well, ye might have chosen worse,' she conceded after Rackham had urged the advantages of the Major's participation. 'It'll be one more sprightly young gallant to bear me company on the voyage.'

'On the voyage?' Rackham stared. 'But you cannot come on the voyage.'

'Can't I, by God! And why not?'

'Why, because—' Rackham began enumerating reasons, but she cut him short.

'I expected this. You'd have me wait behind until all was over, I suppose. Let me tell you that where you go I go, and that only on those terms will you go at all.' She swung one booted leg over the other and smiled grimly. 'For only I know the argosy's date of sailing, and without that you're done.'

They protested, but there was no answer to her. She had the whip hand, and perforce they must agree. And with that question settled to Mistress Bonney's satisfaction they proceeded to discussion of details.

Rackham announced that he had marked the *Kingston* for the voyage. He knew her qualities, and he had learned only that evening that she was soon to be towed out beyond Hog Island to careen. This point had decided him, for it would be far simpler to seize a ship anchored outside the harbour. Her actual capture would be made the night after the argosy had sailed, and it would be effected by Rackham's thirty men. They would sail her out to Salt Cay, where Penner's sloop would be waiting, and his crew – who would be in ignorance of what was forward – would supplement the *Kingston*'s manpower. Then they would pursue the argosy, whose probable course they would have learned from the information that Anne Bonney was to supply.

Since they could plan no further for the moment that concluded their business, and Penner bade them good-night. It was another hour, however, before Anne Bonney took her leave with a promise that she would keep in touch with Rackham through her slave-boy Nicodemus, and visit him with information when opportunity offered.

'And not just with information,' she murmured as she kissed him good-night.

'Have a care, lass.' He tightened his embrace. 'That husband of yours . . . if he finds out that you visit me it could go ill for you.'

She mocked him for his fears, and slipped away into the night, leaving him with an uneasiness he could not define.

It said little for Woodes Rogers' intelligence system that the plot was hatched and Rackham's thirty men recruited without so much as a breath of it reaching the authorities. By the week's end Rackham had learned through Anne Bonney, who had aids to investigation denied the Governor, that the argosy would be the brig *Star*, of thirty guns, and carrying a hundred and eighty seamen and marines. Since the *Kingston* had twenty-four pieces and his crew and Penner's men would total two hundred, Rackham was well satisfied. And on the Monday night Anne Bonney came to the Cinque Ports again with the news that the *Star* would sail on the Wednesday.

Rackham sighed with a relief not unmixed with caution. 'It's going smooth. Too smooth, perhaps. I'll be glad to get a deck beneath my feet again.'

But Anne Bonney had no reservations. 'Why, what should go amiss? You'll take the *Kingston*, and we'll take the *Star*, and then we'll be far away, and richer than we ever dreamed.'

Thereafter they forgot the *Kingston* for a while, but before she left him they agreed that she would return on the Wednesday evening at nine o'clock so that Penner could take her aboard the sloop while Rackham and his men prepared for their attempt on the brig now riding out beyond Hog Island.

Exultant as she was, it was not to be expected that Anne Bonney should notice as she slipped out of Rackham's room that farther down the passage a door which had been slightly ajar closed softly as she passed. Beyond that door stood Kane, Bonney's overseer, an unpleasant smile on his bearded features as he listened to her footsteps receding on the stairs. So his master had been right, and Mistress Anne was caught tripping. He drew a coin from his pocket and tossed it in the direction of the buxom negress who drowsed on the bed, then, pulling down his hat, he in his turn made his way from the inn by the back way.

Bonney was in bed when Kane returned to the plantation, so the overseer's report had to wait until morning. He presented it to his master while the latter sat alone at break-fast, and Bonney's little eyes narrowed as he listened. When Kane had finished his recital, garnished as it was by his own obscene speculations, the planter pushed aside the plate on which his food lay untasted.

'So. Then I must know when she intends to see him again. Find out, Kane.'

The grin on Kane's heavy features vanished. 'Am I to ask her?'

Bonney gestured in annoyance, but his eyes were everywhere

but on his overseer's face. 'Fool! Would she be like to tell you? Her slave-boy, man. He must know. It is obvious she must have been out at his contrivance. Question him.' For a brief second he looked Kane in the face. 'Find out within the hour. I hold you responsible, Kane.'

Kane's face split in an evil smile. 'Aye, sir, you'll know within the hour.' Then a thought struck him, and he paused, fingering his scrubby chin. 'Though the brat's mighty staunch to her, at that. Ye could skin some o' these blacks alive and they'd never tell if they'd no mind to.'

'Then skin him alive if need be,' said Bonney softly. 'Never tell me you've no means to make a man speak, let alone a child.'

Kane considered. 'Aye, it might be. Wait, though. The little bastard's got a grandfather in the plantation. An old rogue that minds the water-butt. How would it be to ask him – in front of the boy?' His smirk left Bonney in no doubt of what was implied.

'Do what you please. Only find out. And see, too, that Mistress Bonney, who is in her room, is kept there. Meanwhile, no word to a soul.'

Kane left him with the joyous satisfaction of a man who has before him a pleasant task which he can easily accomplish. He was in no doubt of this, and having issued his orders he took his way to a shed at some distance from the house, there to wait until little Nicodemus and his grandfather should be brought. Presently, when they arrived, escorted by the negro guards employed on the plantation, where Bonney and Kane himself were the only white men, the overseer addressed his question to the slave-boy.

Terrified, the child rolled his eyes towards his grandfather, but the old negro, who had barely understood the question, since he knew nothing of the matter behind it, could give him no assistance. So Nicodemus stood dumb and frightened, and Kane snapped an order.

In panic Nicodemus watched while his grandfather was spreadeagled to four stakes in the earth floor of the hut. The old negro lay face down, but kept trying to turn his head to see what was happening above him. He did not speak, but they could hear his teeth chattering in his head.

Kane licked his lips and picked up his whip from the table. It was a hideous thong of plaited leather, and as every slave on the plantation knew, Kane could make it cut to the bone. He snaked out the lash so that its tip lay within a few inches of the old man's face. Then he repeated his question.

Wild with terror, and faced with the agonising choice of seeing his grandfather flogged – probably to death – or betraying the mistress he worshipped (for a betrayal Nicodemus realised it would be), the boy stared in horrified fascination. Then he shook his head and Kane grinned and swung his arm.

A minute later the child was kneeling by his grandfather's body, crying piteously, and in an almost incoherent torrent of words trying to explain that what they asked him was something he must not tell. The old slave smiled at him out of a face grey with agony, and when Nicodemus, sobbing, asked him a question, he shook his grizzled head and laid it in the dust again.

Kane swore and kicked the boy aside. Nicodemus crouched with his hands over his face, but he could still hear the sickening crack of Kane's whip as it cut the life out of his grandfather's body.

Presently the whipping stopped, and he was wrenched to his feet again. Kane jerked his thumb at the inert figure on the floor.

'Must I flog him to death? It's all one to me. Or will you come to your senses?' He shook the child to and fro. 'When does she go again, ye little swine?'

Nicodemus looked past him at the body of the old man, and then blurted out: 'To-morrow.'

Kane held him at arm's length, and grinned into the little dark face that was darker now with hatred. 'I could ha' burned you to death afore you'd ha' told me,' he said. 'Just as well ye did, for the old bastard's dead.' He let the boy go. 'Pity ye didn't know, eh?' He turned on his heel. 'Keep that brat in the roundhouse,' he instructed the guards, and strode back to the house to report his success.

'Very well,' said Bonney, when Kane told him. He sat in silence for some minutes, his plump fingers playing with a quill, and when he spoke he kept glancing shiftily about the room as though he suspected unseen listeners.

'This was the evidence we needed,' he reflected aloud. 'You must have your tale pat, Kane, when the time comes to tell it to the Governor.'

Kane was taken aback. 'The Governor?'

'But of course.' Bonney's eyes were bright with malicious pleasure. 'Who else? We must have all in train. She is a wife, and adultery is a serious matter, you know. If she prefers a gallant to myself she must be prepared to pay the price.' It was the measure of the man that he could discuss his own cuckoldry in front of his servant. 'Yes, we shall to His Excellency, and Mistress Bonney shall be dealt with for what she is. Do you know what that means, Kane?' Bonney rose from the table, and the only sign of excitement about him was the quill twisting nervously in his fingers. 'I shall tell you. She shall go to the cart-tail. I shall see her lashed through the streets by the public hangman. Oh, she'll not hold her head so high once she's had the whip about her body, I'll warrant. And it may be that she'll come home again a more dutiful wife.'

Kane was a hardy rascal, but even he was shaken by the venom of the other's tone and the outrageousness of his suggestion. He stood dumb while Bonney slowly paced the room.

'And for her pirate lover,' Bonney went on, 'I think we can contrive without Governor Rogers' assistance. Yes, he shall be our first concern: a grace before meat.' He chuckled softly. 'But that you may leave to me. I think I can promise Captain Rackham even livelier entertainment than he had on his first visit, and Mistress Anne shall share it with us before we take her to the Governor.'

10. THE SNARE

From a small knoll overlooking the promontory of Dick Point, and conveniently screened on its landward sides by scrub, Rackham and Penner watched the brig *Star* dip her stately way across the sapphire bay beneath them. Her canvas gleamed in the bright sunshine, and across the half mile of water came the squeal of the bosun's pipe and the creak of tackle as she swung on to her south-easterly course and glided down the coast.

Rackham watched with a glass to his eye while Penner, his coat laid by and his close-cropped head swathed in a handkerchief, lay with his chin in his hands and blinked contentedly on the beauty of the scene.

In the glass Rackham could see quite plainly the features of the officers on the poop, and the scarlet-coated sentries at the ladder. When he trained the lens on the rigging he could even make out the knife at the waist of a half-naked sailor swinging his way up the futtock shrouds and into the main-top.

'I could wish she carried more rubbish on her timbers,'

he observed to Penner. 'There's a good greasy keel under that water. Set her running before the wind and she'll lead the *Kingston* a fine dance. Still, she'll need all her speed and more if she's ever to see Port Royal.'

Penner screwed up his eyes against the sunlight. 'Why is Rogers sending her to Jamaica at all?' he wondered. 'She might have made a straight trip to England without danger, or if he wants to find an escort for her, what ails him that he doesn't send her north to Charles Town? He's risking his treasure in the lousiest, most dangerous stretch of ocean between Campeche and Carlisle Bay. It's most plaguily odd.'

'Not when you think of the other risks,' said Rackham. 'It had to go quickly, but he daren't send it to Charles Town, with the Florida Channel so thick with Dons there's hardly room for the fish. A straight run to England's too risky for a single ship, he reckons, so he looks to Port Royal and there he sends the *Star*. He'll let the Jamaica Squadron worry about her. Anyway, what does he have to fear?' He pointed down at the brig, which now had them directly on her starboard beam. 'She's nimble enough to outsail most vessels: Rogers is a seaman, and ye can wager he picked her himself. She'll not outsail the *Kingston*, though, unless I've forgotten my trade.'

'But could he not have sent to Jamaica for an escort, and then made the ocean crossing in safety?' Penner persisted.

'And how long would it have taken to get one of the Jamaica Squadron up here? Every night Rogers would have been prowling down to his cellars to see the Spaniards weren't pinching his dollars. He wanted it out of his hands, so he couldn't be blamed for losing it. It's safer at sea than ever it was here. I had some of it aboard long enough to know. I ran the bloody stuff from Cuba to St Kitts looking for a safe place, and the longer I sailed the surer I was it was safest of all right under my feet.' He shook his head at the recollection. 'I know what's been in Rogers' mind, how he's been lying awake of nights, sweating.'

The Major sighed. 'Aye, it's some consolation, now, when you lose a thing, knowing that him that stole it is having the horrors wondering what to do with it. Can ye picture the dirty looks there's going to be aboard the *Kingston* when we've taken the booty and everyone's ready to cut his neighbour's throat?'

'I've seen it before,' said Rackham. He stood up and shook the sand from his clothing. 'I'll know how to deal with it.'

The Major rose and donned his coat. Together they watched the *Star* as she stood down from the point, the Union flag stirring gently at her peak.

'South over Tongue of the Ocean,' said Rackham. 'Then south-westerly through the Old Channel for the Windward Passage. If she ever rounds Cape Maysi it'll be our own fault.' He smiled. 'One way or the other, we can say good-bye to the sea for good.'

Separately they returned to town, Penner to make his last preparations aboard his sloop which lay in the harbour ready to sail, Rackham to take a last look by daylight at the *Kingston*, lying now beyond Hog Island, the flat bank that protected the harbour from the open sea. Standing in a doorway out of the hustle of the waterfront he could look across the channel and see the *Kingston*'s masts above the scrub which dotted Hog Island: not until to-morrow or the day after did the port authorities intend to beach her for careening, and by then, if all went well, she would be speeding south in the wake of the *Star*. For half an hour he surveyed her and then made his way back to the inn, a prey to impatience and growing excitement.

The period of waiting through the evening was the worst part. Rackham sat alone in his room in the Cinque Ports, his solitude relieved only by occasional visits from Ben, who came to report that his thirty picked men were assembling in the taverns along Fish Street. There were three here and five there; never too many together, in case someone should become suspicious, and Ben made periodic trips along the street to see that all was well and that they kept moderately sober.

At nine o'clock a knock sounded at the door, and Rackham made haste to open it, expecting Anne. Instead, it was a serving man from the tap-room with a note which he said had been handed in by a negro who had gone as soon as his message was delivered.

Frowning, Rackham turned the little packet over in his hands. It bore only the superscription 'Cap. Jn. Rackham', and was sealed with a blob of wax. Signing to the man to wait, he broke it open and carried it close to the candle to read it.

'He discovered us from Nicodemus (it read) and keeps me close here. In the morning he goes to seek the Governor. Quickly, for God's sake.' The note was signed 'A.'

For a moment Rackham stared at the words, then he wheeled round. 'A black gave you this? Where is he?' He took two quick steps and caught the drawer by the shoulder. 'How long since?'

'But a moment.' The drawer grimaced under his grip. 'He – he went. I never saw—'

With an oath Rackham sent him staggering towards the door, where he nearly collided with Penner, who loomed suddenly behind him. The Major took in the situation and jerked his thumb in a gesture of dismissal.

112

'Out, my lad,' he said, and the drawer made his escape. Penner turned to Rackham.

'What's amiss?'

Rackham held out the letter in silence. He was blazing with rage inwardly. That this should have happened, and at the most vital hour. Anne Bonney should have been in the room with him at this moment, and Penner should be preparing to take her aboard his sloop. Instead, she was locked up in her house, a mile from town, and their whole enterprise was in jeopardy.

Penner, having scanned the note, was considering that very point, but he was not the kind to waste his breath in senseless recrimination.

'It's devilish inconvenient,' he said, watching Rackham.

'Inconvenient!' Rackham swore savagely. 'That prying little bastard Bonney has poxed us nicely, rot his soul! You and she should be on the sloop, and I should be on my way to the *Kingston* by this. What the devil's to be done?'

Penner scratched his lip. 'The sloop stands ready. Ben's below, and nodded to me as I came up, so I judge he has your men to hand. It might be best to go to work as though nothing had happened.'

'And leave her behind?' Rackham put out one hand to take hold of the Major's lapels, and there was something like madness in his hot, glittering eyes. 'Look you, Penner, we made a bargain. We'll keep it. I'm no buccaneer, but by God, I'll stick to my articles and so will you. She sails with us if I have to burn that bastard's plantation about his ears. He thinks because I'm a pardoned man he has me fast; that all he has to do is roll down in his carriage to Rogers in the morning and have me set in irons for tumbling his wife.' He laughed harshly. 'He thinks I'm asleep, likely. Jesus, we'll see who's sleeping.' He strode over to his bed. From beneath the mattress he drew out his broadsword and baldric, and slung them over his shoulder. Then from the chest beside the bed he took out a pistol, and examined the priming while Penner watched him bleakly.

'What d'ye intend?' asked the Major.

'What d'ye think? I'm taking those men of mine out to his house and have her out of there. Then we'll see to the *Kingston*.' He thrust the pistol inside his shirt. 'You can get aboard your sloop. It may take us an hour longer, but I'll have the satisfaction of paying her score with Master Bonney.'

Penner moved his great bulk into Rackham's path and held out the note. 'Tell me first, how came you by this?'

'Some nigra brought it. I didn't see him; he gave it to the drawer.'

'Just so,' Penner nodded grimly. 'And ye can swear it's in her hand?'

Rackham had been about to push past, but this checked him. He took the note and looked at it again.

'I never saw her writing,' he admitted slowly. 'You think it may be forged?'

Penner shrugged. 'Were I Bonney I'd take good care my erring wife got no chance to send such a note as that. But I might easy write one myself, if I hated her lover and I knew it would bring him running.' He paused. 'You see the implication. Whoever wrote the note, it's obvious Bonney has found out she was to meet you here to-night. And it's odd, too, that he should choose to wait till morning before bearing his tale to Rogers. If he ever does intend to bear it. I think myself he'd take more satisfaction in dealing with you – and her – in his own way. And that's what you'll be giving him the chance of doing if you go blundering out to his plantation in the middle of the night.' He planted his hands on his hips and rocked gently on his booted heels. 'A pretty plot, faith. I'll go a strong wager there's blacks heating irons in his cellars now, for it's not the mercy of a bullet you'd get from Master Bonney once he had you under his foot. It's a lonely spot, and there's not so many would be asking questions about you afterwards.'

Rackham shredded the note to pieces between his fingers. 'You may be right. I believe you are. Still, it makes no difference. He can know nothing of our plans for the *Star* and the *Kingston*. He doesn't know I have thirty rogues at my call. He expects to catch me out there alone. He'll find more than he bargained for.'

'Wait.' Penner was beginning to feel really concerned. 'For God's sake, man, d'ye think ye can start a war and no one take notice? Ye'll have the militia on the back of your neck within five minutes. What chance have ye got of taking the *Kingston* once ye've roused the whole island?'

'Penner,' said Rackham, 'you talk like a soldier. Leave piracy to me. By the time the island's roused – which I doubt it will be, knowing how much your pot-bellied militia dislike activity – I'll have Anne out of there and be down to the shore where our longboats are lying. Let the Governor and his lobster-coats go sweating out to Bonney's place. It'll make the taking of the *Kingston* all the easier.'

He pulled open the door and shouted for the drawer. When that individual appeared, keeping a respectful distance, Rackham dispatched him in search of Ben. Penner sighed and shook his head.

'If we come through this alive we'll have had more than our share of luck,' he said heavily. 'D'ye love the girl, then?'

'You'd best be away to your sloop,' said Rackham

pointedly. 'There's nothing to keep you here. We've trouble enough without having you late at Salt Cay.'

'By your leave,' said Penner, 'I'd rather come with you. I've no wish to be biting my nails aboard wondering whether you're coming or not. Time enough to get aboard the sloop when you set off for the *Kingston*. And I can take Mistress Bonney with me. She'll be safer so.'

The truth was that he was concerned for the safety of the rescue party. Rackham in a raging temper might commit some rashness which would imperil the whole expedition, and Penner's thoughts were with that cargo of silver speeding south to the Windward Passage. With himself to counsel and restrain in what lay immediately ahead they might still be sailing in its wake before dawn.

Ten minutes later Rackham and Penner with their followers were assembling in a hollow by the east road a stone's throw from the edge of town. It was too dark to see more than a few yards, and Ben made his roll-call by moving from man to man as they lay or squatted among the bushes. Those who had pistols were ordered to draw their charges, for Rackham would take no chances of an accidental shot which might announce their arrival at Bonney's plantation and so rob them of the element of surprise.

Presently Ben muttered that all was ready, and a moment later Rackham was leading his little force in single file away from the roadside towards the shore. He counted a hundred paces and then turned eastwards, following the line of the road but keeping a safe distance from it. Here they were moving through light scrub which dotted the sandy ground, but only a little distance ahead the undergrowth thickened into larger bushes and small trees. To their left lay more woods, shutting out the sea, but above the incessant drone of the tropic night they could just make out the sound of the distant breakers. All about them were the shadows, and above the dark Caribbean evening sky, with the tiny star-flecks glinting.

They came on the first sign of ambush about quarter of a mile from Bonney's plantation. They were filing through a small grove when Rackham caught the sound of movement somewhere to their right, in the direction of the road. Signing to the others to be still, he beckoned Ben, and together they stole cautiously through the trees until they were on the edge of the low scrub bordering the road. There they heard the noise again – the soft scuffling of a foot on the sandy earth. It was only a few yards from them, and after a moment Rackham detected its origin.

Close by the road grew a single palm, its slender bole and feathery head outlined sharply against the night sky, and at its base, so close to it as almost to seem part of the trunk itself, was a vague shape, darker than the surrounding shadows. Gradually as he watched, it began to take form. A negro was crouching behind the tree, watching the road.

He was squatting on his heels with his back towards them, and only ten yards away. They could make out the powerful spread of his shoulders and his thick, muscular neck, which made his head seem ridiculously small by comparison. He was crooning gently to himself and swaying slightly backwards and forwards as he watched.

Ben drew his dirk, closed his teeth on the thin blade, and putting his palms flat on the ground, began to edge himself forward, an inch at a time, towards the unsuspecting sentry.

Suddenly the negro stood up. He stood by the tree like a huge black phantom, and turning directly towards Rackham and Ben, said something in a deep guttural voice.

117

Ben froze on the instant, but before they had time to decide whether they had been detected or not, an answering voice came out of the brush to their left and a second negro stepped into the open and came padding softly in their direction, apparently to join his companion.

In that dim place, with shadows all over the open ground, he might have walked within a foot of the two sailors without being aware of them. Both were lying motionless, and were no more than dark shapes on the floor of the glade. Even had the negro been picking his steps he might have missed them, but he was paying no heed to where his feet fell until one of them descended on Rackham's leg.

To the negro it seemed as though the firm earth had come to life beneath his feet. He stumbled, and a huge shape whirled up from beneath him and struck him a paralysing blow in the stomach. His breath rushed out of him with a sound between a gasp and a scream, and he sank writhing to the ground.

Rackham swung away from him to see Ben closing with the first negro. For a moment they were locked together in the shadow of the palm; then they stumbled and went crashing down, with Ben beneath his larger opponent. Steel flashed in the air as the pirate tried to drive home his dirk, but a sinewy black hand shot out and clamped on his wrist. The dirk was twisted from his hand, but even as the negro grabbed for it, Rackham's fist descended with crushing force on the nape of his neck and he slid forward without a sound.

The other negro was lying doubled up and moaning, his hands pressed to his midriff. He was obviously in no case to escape or do harm, so Rackham left him and whistled softly to bring up the rest of his force.

That he took a risk he fully realised. There might be other

sentinels on the road, but he doubted it. The two negroes were both unusually big men, and since it was only himself who was expected at Bonney's plantation that night they would have been enough to account for one unsuspecting man. He said as much to Penner when presently the others had come up, and the Major looked at the unconscious black and shuddered.

'Ye can thank God ye took them by surprise and not they you. Look at that animal! Why, he's a good foot taller than I am myself. Even you would have been a baby to him. Here, Jemmy, put a bit of line round this brute's wrists and ankles before he comes to.'

While the negroes were being trussed, Rackham and Penner held a brief council beside the road. Penner agreed it was unlikely that there were any more sentries outside the plantation; if there were they must have heard the noise of the scuffle and be on their way back now.

'Anyway, whatever way it is, it seems to me best that we should get in and out as fast as we can,' he added. 'The main gate'll be as good as any, and so up to the house. They won't be expecting a boarding party.'

Moving as quickly as he could without undue noise, Rackham led the line of men through the scrub that bordered the highway until they approached the last tree-shrouded bend on the road before the main gate itself. Much depended on whether the gate was open or not; if it was closed there would be no alternative but to storm it and risk a running fight with Bonney's negroes in the plantation grounds.

But the gate was open, and between the palisades a solitary sentry, another negro, was squatting on his heels and drowsing with his head against the barrel of a fowling-piece. He was keening softly to himself when a huge white figure seemed to materialise in front of him and he was struck a crushing blow between the eyes which flung him backwards half-senseless. Before he could recover sufficiently to bawl the alarm sinewy hands had pinioned and gagged him and he had been flung into the bushes beside the gate.

Rackham, standing in the drive, listened intently for any sign that the scuffle had been overheard, but apart from the incessant hum of insects and the mournful call of a night bird in the trees there was no sound at all. Satisfied, he turned to Penner, and pointed ahead up the drive. Less than a hundred yards in front of them it widened out into a small carriage-sweep, beyond which was the house itself. Light gleamed through the shutters of the three windows at the left-hand end of the building: Rackham knew that all three gave on to Bonney's long dining-room.

He stooped down and rubbed his fingers in the dust, drew his heavy broadsword, and flexed it between his hands. Penner sighed as he unsheathed his rapier, and laid a hand on Rackham's arm.

'I know ye've got a lot to mislike him for, boy,' he whispered, 'but be easy, for your own sake. Vengeance is mine, saith the Lord, an' that. Let's take the girl and leave the others be, eh?'

Rackham turned towards him and disengaged his arm. 'You've better things to concern you than James Bonney. When we reach the house have six men to each window. Let the others stay here. The men at the windows will burst in when I do, understand? And no killing unless I give the word, or if they have to. Right, bring them up.'

They padded up the drive in a long line, and spread out abreast when the carriage-sweep was reached. Then together they advanced in silence to the verandah, and crouched down while Rackham mounted the rail and flattened himself in the shadow between the two left-hand windows. All three were close-shuttered, but through them he could hear the sonorous rhythm of a native drum and the tinkle of a tambourine. On both sides of him the dark figures of the pirates were clambering softly on to the verandah and lying close by the shutters. When all were in position Rackham knelt beside Ben at the centre window and peered in through the lattice. At the same moment the throbbing of the drum ceased, and a man's voice was raised in high-pitched laughter.

11. THE QUARRY

The room was brightly illumined by candles set on the long
table which stretched from the right-hand window to the
centre of the apartment. To the left, crouching on a small
rug, like a carved nymph on an Italian fountain, knelt a naked
girl. She was half-caste and her golden shoulders, gleaming
pale in the light, were heaving from the exertions of the
dance she had just concluded. Even as Rackham looked in
she rose and faced the three men seated at the table.

Bonney was at the table head, leaning back in a high chair,
drowsily eyeing the girl. His yellow face was impassive, but
his little eyes were glistening as he surveyed her. He had
thrown off his wig, and a black stubble showed on his round,
bullet-shaped head.

On his left, down the table, a tall, fair man with a heavily
lined face was leaning across to speak to him. Rackham
recognised him as Baker, a plantation owner from the south
side of the island, with whom he had done some business in
the old days. He was gesturing towards the girl, and although
his voice was not audible through the shutters, Rackham

could hear in imagination the languid drawl which Baker affected.

The man who had laughed was Kane. He squatted like a great toad on a stool at the table-foot, an incongruous figure in his untidy jacket and drawers, a hand on either knee, staring at the little dancer with hungry eyes. He laughed again now, and called out something which, by the expression of distaste which Baker glanced towards him, must have been an obscene jest. Bonney addressed him, and Kane, grinning, buried his face in the large mug at his elbow.

Rackham's glance went beyond the table to the little flight of steps, oddly placed in the far right-hand corner of the room, which he knew gave on to a short passage leading to the hall. There was no door, but a curtain hung at the head of the steps to act as a partition from the corridor. On the bottom step sat a little wizened negro with a native drum between his knees, and beside him a skinny mulatto youth with the tambourine. No one in the room was armed, but on the wall behind Bonney's chair was a trophy with two small-swords crossed beneath it.

Ben stirred and spoke. 'Bonney amuses hisself. Shall we show 'im the best o' the entertainment's still to come?'

Rackham leaned forward and felt with his fingers in the crack beneath the shutter. It was only loosely fastened. He drew it gently towards him and heaved with all his strength. There was a crack of splintering wood and a cry of surprise from the room, but the shutter held, and it took a second heave to break the catch. With his sword in one hand, while the other drew and cocked his pistol, Rackham stepped over the sill and dropped lightly into the room. His pistol covered the three stupefied men at the table.

'Make a sound and it'll be your last this side of hell,' he

snapped. 'Baker, sit still and no one will harm you; I've no quarrel with you. Just these two fine birds.' And he gestured to Bonney and Kane.

Bonney sat fixed in his chair, his pallid face even whiter at the apparitions in his three windows. Bearded, swarthy faces were grinning at him from every one, and everywhere was the glitter of steel. And in front of them all was the man who by now should have been shackled and helpless while negroes dragged him to the plantation a prisoner. Bonney tried to rise, but fear gripped his limbs, and he could only cower back in his great chair. Baker sat still and staring.

The only one to act was Kane. He had bounded to his feet when the shutters were burst open, and now he vaulted over the table, oversetting a bottle with his foot as he leaped, but regaining his balance and landing like a cat on the other side. He sprang sideways once to disconcert Rackham's aim, and in a second was bounding up the steps, spurning aside the drummer as he went.

For an instant Rackham's finger tightened on the trigger, then he remembered that the crash of a shot must bring whatever force the plantation mustered about their heads.

'After him!' he snapped, and Ben was round the table and up the room almost before the words had left his leader's lips, drawing his dirk as he went. Kane was clattering down the passage, bellowing an alarm. Ben clutched at the curtain to steady himself, swung up his dirk, and flung it after the retreating overseer with all his force.

Kane's roaring broke off in a scream, and they heard the tremendous crash as he plunged headlong over some piece of furniture and brought it with him to the floor. There followed a horrid, wheezing cough, repeated again and again, and the sound of limbs threshing in agony. Then he coughed for the last time, and in the same second the bottle he had overturned in his leap rolled off the edge of the table and splintered on the floor. Just so long had it taken from the moment when Kane began his fatal flight.

Ben strode along the passage and presently returned, wiping his blade on a piece of Kane's shirt.

Rackham looked at Bonney. 'So much for your overseer. If you don't want to follow him, where's your wife?' And he raised his sword so that Bonney should see it gleam in the candlelight.

The question seemed to make something snap in Bonney's brain. Hitherto, even while Kane was choking out his life in the corridor only a few yards away, he had sat motionless, his eyes fixed fearfully on Rackham's face. Now he scrambled suddenly out of his chair and rushed to the wall, snatching down a small-sword from its bracket. Setting his back to the wall he stood panting, the sweat trickling down his face, the sword extended before him. A little ripple of laughter came from the pirates at the other end of the room.

At this point Major Penner intervened. He had no wish to see Bonney cut to pieces, which was what he imagined must happen if Rackham were not forestalled. Avoiding the half-caste girl, who crouched by the table, her hands folded over her breasts, gazing with eyes of terror on the scene, the Major confronted Bonney and gestured with his own rapier at the sword held in the plantation owner's unsteady hand.

'Best put it away,' he said. 'Resistance will not help you. Be a sensible fellow, now, and sit ye down again.'

'In God's name, do as he says,' Baker broke in. 'What can you do against so many? Put up your sword.'

Penner held out his left hand for the weapon, and Bonney hesitated, his face all wet with desperation. Then suddenly, with a cry of panic, he lunged with his point full at the Major's breast.

'Ye silly bastard!' shouted Penner, springing back. 'Must I embroider your fat carcase?' He advanced his own point. 'Put it down before I do ye a mischief.'

But Bonney, blinded by fear, only thrust again, and this time the Major could retreat no farther, for the table was at his back. He parried the stroke easily enough, and as a third wild blow was aimed at him, lost his temper.

'Take it then, you fool,' he said, and encircling Bonney's blade with practised ease, he transfixed his opponent's elbow.

Bonney screamed, dropping his weapon, and staggered back clutching his arm. Blood welled up in a great stain on his sleeve, and seeped on to his fingers, but he would still have resisted had not Penner set his own point, now sullied with blood, at his throat.

Rough hands thrust Bonney into his chair, and Rackham leaned forward and set a hand on each of his shoulders.

'Where is she?' he demanded, and placed his thumbs on Bonney's throat. 'Speak now, or I'll burn your house with you tied in this chair. Speak, you rotten slaver!'

Bonney writhed beneath his grip, and then his head lolled forward and he sank down in the chair. He had fainted.

Rackham straightened up with a grunt of disgust. 'I'll find her myself, then.' He swung round to Penner. 'Send half these lads out to the back of the house. There are other blacks on the plantation: they may have heard Kane howling for help. Three more stay here to watch our friends. The remainder can go through the house and strip it.'

With whoops of delight his followers obeyed. Some fell on the table, snatching up the silver while they stuffed the remains of the food into their mouths. Others wrenched

126

down the ornaments from the walls, while a small party burst open cupboards and ransacked drawers. One laid violent hands on Baker, and began to haul the rings from his fingers. The merchant protested to Penner, but was bidden to be thankful he was escaping with his life. He subsided in mingled wrath and fear, and was soon left to shiver in his under-clothes.

Penner himself mounted guard on the dancing girl, his sword still drawn, and bluntly told several would-be amorists to take themselves off. Growling, they obeyed, and child-like, hurried off yelling to find other amusements.

Through the hall and the west wing of the house they stormed, like terriers, ratching in every corner. None of the rooms was occupied, and as he turned towards the rear of the house, where lay the kitchens and the domestic slaves' quarters, Rackham felt a chill of fear. Perhaps Bonney had removed Anne from the plantation altogether, or confined her in some outhouse. It would take them the better part of an hour to make a thorough search, and before then they might find themselves beset by the militia, supposing any of the blacks had escaped to spread the alarm.

In growing anxiety he set the men to smashing in cupboards and partitions in a desperate attempt to reveal a hiding place. They turned the kitchen into a shambles without result, and Rackham was on the point of returning to the dining-room to force Bonney to talk when a shout from one of the searchers took him out to the hall.

Two of the more experienced rovers had remembered that a house may contain more below its floors than it does above, and had diligently sounded the boards in the principal rooms. He found them in a corner of the hall, where the matting had been thrown aside revealing the outline of a trap-door.

'Bring a light,' said Rackham, and when two of his followers were standing by with candlebranches the trap was thrown back. Stone steps led down into the darkness, and taking one of the candlebranches Rackham began to descend, feeling into the shadows with his broadsword.

He beat right and left, and the point scraped on the walls on both sides of him. The candles threw only a poor light into the gloom, but when he had gone less than a dozen steps the stone stair ended on a floor of hard-packed earth. At the same time the confining walls ceased, and he guessed he was standing in the opening to a cellar.

He looked up to the square of light above and behind him, where the heads of his four men were peering over.

'Tom, and you, Michel, come down.' The two men swung over the side of the trap and dropped beside him. One of them brought the other candlebranch, and showed that they were standing in a broad chamber, stone-walled, with three doors opening off it. All three were closed and two were secured by heavy bolts.

'Anne!' Rackham raised his voice. 'Anne! Are you about?'

In that confined place his voice had an odd, muffled quality, but it evoked no answering sound. They waited, and then from behind the centre door came the sound of a quick movement, the clatter of some object falling, and an exclamation suddenly choked off.

In one bound Rackham was at the door. It was the unbolted one, and even as his hand descended on the latch he heard the scuffle of feet beyond the door, and the quick gasps of someone breathing in exertion.

'Each side,' snapped Rackham, and as his followers leaped to either side of the doorway he raised his foot and sent the door crashing back on its hinges. He jumped back as he did so, and so saved his life, for the first thing that emerged from the dark opening was the glittering blade of a cane knife, wielded by a negro who might have been the brother to the two they had captured on the road.

He hurtled forward like a diver, the razor-edged blade held before him in both hands, so that he must have spitted anyone standing close to the door. Rackham jumped aside, and Michel, thrusting out a foot, sent the negro sprawling. Tom leaped like a great cat on his shoulders, the knife in his right hand rose and fell twice before the negro had a chance to recover, and with one shriek which rang round that confined place, the fallen man collapsed and lay still.

His sword still at the ready, Rackham faced the dark opening. 'Anne? Are you there, lass?' he called, and to his joy he heard her voice answer from the darkness. The next moment she was in his arms. For a long minute they clung together, observed approvingly by the two buccaneers. At last they parted, and he looked into her face.

'He held his hand over my mouth, to stop me crying out,' she explained. 'Pah, I can taste it yet.' And she spat in most unladylike fashion.

'He'll trouble no one any more,' observed Michel laconically, and Rackham set his arm about Anne's shoulders and began to guide her to the steps.

Under the rough blanket which appeared to be her only clothing he could feel her trembling violently, and put it down to the cold of her underground prison. But before they had reached the steps she suddenly stumbled and would have fallen but for his protecting arm.

'Oh, oh, Holy Mother!' She buried her face in his chest and clung to him, her breath coming in great hoarse sobs. There were no tears in her eyes; her body was simply giving way in reaction to the mental and physical strain she had undergone.

He aided her up the steps, slowly, for she was no light burden to support with one hand. Half-way she paused, shook her head, and pulled her blanket more closely about her. Her eyes were glistening and her face was terribly pale, but she had mastered herself, and by a great effort set off up the remaining steps.

The pirates in the hall stared at the sight of their captain emerging from the trap with a woman on his arm, her red hair tumbled over the blanket which afforded her such scanty covering.

'Jesus, don't none o' these women wear no clothes?' said one.

Rackham turned to Michel. 'Bid Ben assemble the men at the front of the house. Then tell Major Penner I'll join him presently.' The Frenchman hurried away, and Rackham conducted Anne to her room.

Once there she sat straight down in a chair, but the colour was returning to her cheeks, and her spirit with it. Her first inquiry was about Bonney, and when Rackham told her that he was wounded, she tightened her lips.

'I've a word to say to that dear husband of mine. He'll be more wounded presently.'

Bidding him turn his back, she rose and began to search out her clothing. While she dressed she explained, so far as she knew, what had happened that afternoon.

She had been in her room when Kane and a negro had entered and forcibly taken her down to the cellar. There, under Kane's supervision, the negro had torn off her clothes, and left her only the blanket. She had been locked in, and although she had screamed and hammered on the door, no one had paid any attention. Guessing that Bonney had discovered her visits to Rackham, she reached the terrifying conclusion that he intended to let her starve slowly to death underground, but that fear, at least, was calmed when food was brought to her a few hours later. Shortly afterwards Bonney himself had come down, with Kane and the negro in attendance. He knew, he said, of her visits to the Cinque Ports, and was expecting her lover later in the evening. He had then explained, in nauseating detail, what he intended to do to Rackham, and had turned her physically ill. With the promise that she should witness the performance he had left her, and the negro had been set as guard outside her door.

How many hours had passed before she fell into an uneasy doze she did not know, but she had awoken to find the negro in the cell with her. He had flung her down, gagging her with his hand, and threatening to kill her if she moved or spoke. Then she had heard Rackham's voice, had managed to break free, and the sound of the scuffle had reached Rackham in the outer cellar.

'And God knows I've heard no sweeter sound than you roaring beyond that door,' she added. 'It's a fine, strong voice you have, John.'

'How the devil did he know of your visits to the inn?' asked Rackham. He told her of the note, and how Penner had detected the trap.

'Nicodemus told him. I had that from Bonney himself. They flogged the poor little mite's grandfather to death before his eyes. That was Kane's work, rot his soul.' Anne Bonney spat out an oath. 'There's another hound whose account's to settle.'

'It's settled already,' said Rackham, turning round. She was fully dressed now, in her black shirt and breeches and long boots, and was tying up her hair in a red scarf. 'One of my lads put a knife through him in the passage yonder.'

'Too easy an end for him,' she said viciously. 'And for that greasy nigger that stripped me in the cellar. I'd have seen them roasting over a slow fire, by God! They served enough of Bonney's poor devils of slaves the same way, although the Governor never heard tell of it.' She wheeled round, her eyes hard. 'And so I'll serve the little swine himself. Where is he?' She started forward, but Rackham laid a hand on her arm. 'What is it you do?' she demanded, pulling free. 'D'you think you'll keep me from him? You try, and I'll—'

'Wait.' He placed himself between her and the door. 'Whatever you intend by him, we've little time left. The town may be afoot by now, and the militia on their way. Penner's to take you aboard his sloop, while I've to attend to the *Kingston*.' He laughed sharply. 'God, woman, d'ye know what it means to take a ship and clear her out of harbour? I came here to cut Bonney's heart out, aye; but I'll waste no time over what I have to do.'

Plainly Anne Bonney had different ideas. She faced him in genuine astonishment at first; then she laughed, an ugly, harsh sound, and put her hands on her hips.

'And you'll cut his heart out, will you? Faith, what a fine, bloodthirsty babe it is!' She stepped closer to him. Under the line of the scarf round her forehead her brows were wrinkled, and she wore an expression of cruelty he had never seen on her before.

'Look you, Calico Jack Rackham, he's my affair and I'll attend to him in my own way. You can take your *Kingston*, well enough, and leave me here with Penner. We'll be aboard his sloop in good time, never fear. But first I'll settle with that poisonous rat through yonder.'

Rackham was not a soft man, but there was something here that filled him with disgust. He was remembering how he had face La Bouche, unarmed, and that deep, husky voice had called out: 'Make an end, Pierre. It's over warm for such excitement.'

And yet in this very room he had loved her violently and passionately. She had seemed soft and languorous, then, and yet strong and vibrant, like no other woman he had ever known, and he had been intoxicated by her. What he was looking at now was either a mask, or else a mask had slipped from its place, revealing the sadistic, feral nature beneath. It was like an ugly dream, and in that moment the *Kingston*, the Spanish silver, the knowledge that the King's troops might soon be upon them, were all forgotten. He felt tired and sick, and something of his feelings must have shown in his face, for her eyes brightened.

'You'll let me past, then?' The plea, from lips that had been coldly promising to torture Bonney to death, was incongruous and revolting. Abruptly he stood aside, and she was past him in a flash.

He stood, listening to the sound of her boots striding down the passage, and then he remembered that the alarm might be sounding in the town, and that there was much to do, whether he felt sick and weary or not. He went out into the hall, and found Ben waiting to speak to him. The burly lieutenant came forward, wiping his lips with the back of his hand.

'Only a wet, cap'n,' he explained apologetically, indicating the mug he held. 'I kept the lads to about the same; enough to rinse their throats out, like. They're outside and ready now, but for them that wi' the Major and the prisoners.'

'Good.' Rackham forced himself to think what must be

done next. He passed a hand acorss his face, and Ben noticed the movement.

'Ye all right, cap'n?' There was genuine concern in his voice. 'None o' them blacks nicked ye, did they?'

Rackham shook his head. 'No, no. It's nothing. Nothing at all. Wait for me outside with the men. I'll be with you presently.'

He watched Ben go through the front door, and then walked slowly to the dining-room.

Bonney was still seated in his chair, his right arm roughly bound with a rag at the elbow, where the sleeve of his fine taffeta coat had been ripped away. But far from having recovered, the planter was in a state of terror far greater than when he had faced Penner's rapier, or even when Rackham had had his hands about his throat. He was huddled back as though trying to hide, his face grey with fear, and for once his eyes had lost their shiftiness. They were fixed in a terrified stare on Anne Bonney, who stood looking down at him.

Penner stood frowning, while the mulatto girl peeped out anxiously from the corner behind him. On either side of Bonney's chair stood the two grinning pirates who had been appointed his guards. Baker had been driven out of the house, having been stripped of his valuables.

Anne Bonney had possessed herself of a rapier and was holding it levelled at Bonney's face. She was speaking in a strained, harsh voice, as Rackham entered the room.

'"Down on your knees," you said. Have you forgotten, then?' The rapier flicked out and Bonney shrieked and flung himself vainly aside. Fearfully, he put up a hand to his cheek, and brought it down smeared with blood.

'Many a hundred times you said it, and I obeyed, while you sat there grinning like the foul beast you are.' Her voice

134

rose with passion. 'And do you remember calling for Kane – aye, and for your black scum of overseers, too – to come and gape at me and share the joke? A fine joke, eh, James?' And again she slashed at his face.

Bonney screwed his head round in an effort to shield himself from that razor edge, and pawed feebly with his left hand in an attempt to ward it away. Anne Bonney caught at his coat and jerked him round.

'Aye, you scream and cower, as I did, but when did you ever spare me, or any other poor soul?' She shook him fiercely. '"Down on your knees," you would say, and call me every filthy name you knew. Well, down on your own knees now, James Bonney! Quick, or I'll cut your tongue out!'

She stepped back, pointing to the floor at her feet, but Bonney clung to his chair until one of the pirates heaved him bodily up and forced him down on all fours. The planter shrieked with the pain of his wounded arm, but the pirate, setting a foot behind either knee to keep him kneeling, put a hand in his collar and jerked his body upright. He was held there, helpless in the grip of the grinning ruffian, while Anne Bonney looked malignantly down at him.

At last Bonney found his tongue. 'Anne', he croaked, 'Anne, lass. A jest – only a jest, girl. I meant no offence . . .'

She leaned down until her face, evil and mocking, was close to his own. 'Of course, James. Only a jest. You were always a great joker. We'll share another jest together, now, and I promise it'll set you in a roar, my love. You mind that little black mistress you were so fond of – one of many – and how you caught her with a boy of her own colour who worked in the cane-fields? You remember what happened to them? Kane would tell you, if he still had a tongue to tell with. That was a good joke, James. You told me about it, you remember, and reminded me of it no later than to-night, down in the cellar, when you promised we should play it over again, with myself and another as the butts.'

Bonney struggled wildly in the grip of the pirate who held him, and Penner came forward to Anne Bonney's side.

'There's been enough of this, mistress. Had you set in to cut his throat without these frolics, it's like enough you wouldn't have been hindered, or if your man, John Rackham, there, had called him out and planted his iron in him, I'd have stood by and thought no wrong. But I don't like this eye-scratching devilishness. It looks ill from a woman,' he added, oddly solemn, as though he were reproving a child.

She spat at him in reply. 'You! You great ninny, to tell me what looks ill!' She flung out a hand to point at Bonney. 'That swine has made life hell for me these two years past; he's polluted the very ground he has walked on. You and that clout-pole Rackham, who've been sea-rovers and done God knows how much bloody murder and more, to tell me that I mustn't have the carbonadoing of a scoundrel who's done worse to me than I could ever do to him! Go and chase your ships if you've a mind to, and leave me here. By the time the troops arrive Bonney'll be past speech, and I'll swear it was you lot that killed him.' She stopped, glaring at Penner.

The Major looked at Rackham. 'The woman's mad. For God's sake, John, let's do as she says, and leave her here. The militia may be about our ears at any minute. What does she care for the silver, anyway? Look at her, man – it's blood she's after.'

'She's coming with us,' said Rackham. However much his feelings had been revolted he knew he could not leave her behind.

'Anne,' he said gently, 'let him be, lass. It does no good

to take his life, any more than it does to tramp on a slug. Come away.' He put out a hand, but she ignored it. Her fury had subsided, but her voice was still hard and determined.

'I'll come when I've finished with him,' she said, and Bonney whimpered in terror.

'There isn't time,' snarled the Major, losing his temper. 'Rot it, you bloody-minded hussy, there's the *Kingston* to see to, and a tide to catch.'

'Then the sooner you let me at him, the better,' Anne Bonney shot back. 'I'll not take long, I promise you – although it may seem long to James.'

Bonney, still held by his guard, caught at Penner's coat. 'Major, for mercy's sake,' – he was literally crying – 'don't leave me! Don't, for Christ's sake! She has gone mad, she'll tear me!'

'It's no more than you deserve,' snapped Penner. 'Holy Mother!' He jerked round, and every head in the room turned towards the windows. From somewhere not far off, in the direction of the town road, the report of a musket shot echoed in the sudden silence.

For a few seconds they stood motionless, listening. Then Rackham broke the silence.

'The militia! We waited too long, by God!' He strode to the windows and shouted for Ben.

'Get the men into the woods! Get well into cover and keep quiet if you value your hides. Away with you; we'll follow.'

Penner cursed and shook himself free of Bonney's clutch at his coat-tails. 'Pray heaven it's the militia and not Harkness's soldiers, or we'll be trapped nicely.'

Rackham pointed to Anne Bonney. 'Get her out of this, Harry.' She was opening her mouth to interrupt, but he silenced her with a roar of fury. 'D'ye want Harkness to find you here, then, with a dead man in the passage and Bonney to tell his story?'

His anger permitted of no retort, but if she was baulked of her main purpose she was still determined to do her worst by her husband. The rapier was still in her hand, and without warning she whipped up her point and lunged at the kneeling wretch with all her strength.

The merest accident saved Bonney's life. The buccaneer who was holding him was in the act of jerking his captive roughly to his feet as Anne Bonney's lunge was launched, and the sudden movement marred her aim. The point passed within an inch of Bonney's face, and before she could regain her balance Penner's heavy hands were on her shoulders, dragging her away.

'Take her out,' said Rackham to the two pirates who stood by Bonney. 'Never mind him; he'll give no trouble,' he snapped as they hesitated. 'Hold her outside until the Major comes.'

They obeyed him with an efficiency that gave Anne Bonney no chance of protest. She was swept away neatly and speedily and bundled unceremoniously on to the verandah, her curses stifled by hairy fingers clapped over her mouth.

Rackham spoke rapidly to Penner. 'We still have time enough to make the tide if all goes well with the *Kingston*. Remember your part: a single light, and if we're not with you in three hours, a gun. As for Anne, take her aboard whatever she may say. She'll slip you if she can.'

Penner jerked his head towards Bonney, who had collapsed and was sitting on the floor, a grotesque figure with the sleeve of his coat soaked in blood and the livid cut on his cheek. 'What of him?'

'Let him be,' said Rackham. 'Now run, man, and look for us at Salt Cay.'

Penner scrambled over the sill, and barked a command at the two men who crouched on the verandah with Anne between them. Rackham saw her struggle in their grasp, there was a flurry of her red hair and an oath from one of the men.

'God damn, she's bit me!' he cried, and then she was swung up by their combined effort and hustled to the verandah steps. She was cursing stridently as they hurried off into the darkness, and then the flow was suddenly cut off, as though one of them had thrust a gag into her mouth.

He was alone in the room now, but for Bonney, and all but two of his men had gone with Ben into the woods. The couple who remained waited on the verandah. For a few seconds he stood listening, but there was no sound of the approach of troops; no noise to re-awaken the panic of a few minutes ago.

He stooped to Bonney and pulled him to his feet by his sound arm. The plump face was ghastly grey; he was near to fainting with his wound, and for a moment Rackham felt a twinge of pity. It was hard to imagine this cringing wreck, with his clothes torn and his face smeared with blood and perspiration, as the monster Anne Bonney had painted. But if our positions had been reversed, thought Rackham. What then? Perhaps she was right. With a mighty heave he threw Bonney over his shoulder, carried him to the window and whistled up his two men.

'Drop him somewhere out there,' he said. 'Then wait for me.'

While they were carrying the inert form into the darkness Rackham took from the table a flagon of rum which his looters had overlooked and proceeded to pour the contents over the cloth and on to the foot of the curtain which screened the passageway. He took one of the candlebranches and applied it to the stain that was spreading across the cloth. It exploded in a puff of flame so sudden that his arm was singed before he could draw back.

He hurled the candlebranch at the curtain and without another glance at his improvised bonfire crossed the room and vaulted out on to the verandah. His two men were just emerging from the darkness, having left Bonney among the bushes, and together the three padded noiselessly down the edge of the drive, while the fire crackled and spread in Bonney's dining-room.

A minute later they were in the trees beyond the road, and Rackham stood listening while the dim forms of his men moved in the shadows about him. Far away on the town road was a distant drumming; it grew into a thunder of hooves as a troop of cavalry swept up to the plantation gates, men and mounts starkly black against the red glare of fire from the house. All was confusion as they wheeled and re-formed on the carriage-way; then their commander was leading them forward to see what could be saved from the blaze.

The trees beyond the road were empty now, and the single file of pirates, with Rackham at their head, were moving silently down to the beach where their longboats waited.

Within the next hour, while the good folk of New Providence were too engrossed over the fire to the eastward to detect what was taking place less than a mile from their own waterfront, the capture of the *Kingston* was effected. The longboats crept out through the narrows past Hog Island and openly approached the brig where she swung at anchor. Those aboard her were far out of earshot of the town, but they could see Bonney's house ablaze, and Rackham turned this to advantage. He disarmed the suspicions of the *Kingston*'s anchor watch by explaining that a party of mutinous slaves had burned the plantation and murdered their master and were still at large in the woods. The Governor, fearing that they might try to escape by sea before the militia could hunt them down, had ordered armed guards to every ship in the harbour and adjacent anchorages. All available men had been pressed into service, hence Rackham and his somewhat disorderly-looking party.

It was well told, with Rackham standing in the stern-sheets of the first boat which lay under the *Kingston*'s counter, while the poop lanterns cast their pale yellow gleam over the surrounding water. It satisfied the commander of the *Kingston*'s anchor watch, who invited the newcomers aboard, more willingly in view of the alarming news they brought. His satisfaction was short-lived, for within two minutes of Rackham's mounting the *Kingston*'s side the anchor watch, taken completely unawares, had been deftly overpowered and disarmed. Thereafter they were persuaded to embark in the boats which the pirates had just left, which they did with blasphemous protest to the accompaniment of ironic cheers from their elated captors.

By the time the commander of the anchor watch had grounded his longboat on the northern shore of Hog Island and plunged his way through the underbrush to bellow to the harbour the alarm which should rouse the town, the *Kingston* was standing away to the north-east, her pale canvas slowly vanishing into the night. So the enterprise was begun.

12. UNDER THE BLACK

Overnight the weather changed and dawn came with a grey sky and showery squalls driving from the north-east. With sail spread the *Kingston* ploughed southward over Tongue of the Ocean, and two cables' lengths astern Penner's sloop danced in her wake like a puppy frisking behind a full-grown dog.

Rackham had been on deck since before first light. He had not slept during the night, the false refreshment of shaving and dressing in clean clothes had long since worn off, and he was red-eyed and tired.

They had made the rendezvous with Penner, and had lost no time in transferring twenty hands from the sloop to the brig so that the larger vessel should have a reasonable complement in the event of emergency. It had been a disquieting half hour for Rackham, however, partly by reason of Anne Bonney's behaviour. Remembering how it had been necessary to drag her from Bonney's house, he had expected to find her hostile; instead, to his surprise, she had been in a state of exultation when she greeted him as he boarded the sloop.

142

Her animation was so far removed from the viciousness and anger she had displayed such a short while before that he wondered, not for the first time, if there was perhaps a streak of madness in her nature.

Her high spirits were not shared by Penner, who, in the brief spell of waiting off Salt Cay, had discovered grounds for anxiety aboard his sloop. While the men were being transferred to the *Kingston* he announced his fears to Rackham.

'They're asking questions. Of course, it was to be expected. They sign for a cruise with me, and here go twenty of them to the *Kingston* before we're an hour out. They want to know why. I've told them to obey orders and be damned to them, but that won't serve for long. They smell piracy in the very sight of you, John. These lads I've given you are old filibusters, but I'm thinking my gentlemen-adventurers may cause us trouble.'

'How much trouble?' asked Rackham.

Penner blew out his cheeks. 'Who knows? There's a dozen taking their cues from a smooth, plume-bonnet rogue of a captain that I suspect of honesty. He'll not be made to play the pirate, for one.'

'What of the rest, then?'

'Och, most of the lads'll as soon sail under the black as under the red, white, and blue. Sooner, when they hear what it can put in their pockets, But they'll need to be told soon.'

'They'll be told to-morrow morning', Rackham had promised. 'You'll need to send them all aboard the *Kingston*, but for a skeleton crew of safe men to sail the sloop. If your honest captain – what's his name, anyway?'

'Kinsman, Captain Alan Kinsman, late of the First Foot and be damned to you common sailormen.'

143

'Aye, well, if he refuses to come aboard the *Kingston*, threaten to hang him for mutiny. And if the enterprise is too foul for his fancy fingers, so much the worse for him.'

For all his confident tone Rackham had been uneasy as he left the sloop to return to his brig, and to complicate matters Anne Bonney had insisted on returning with him. Silent during the crossing to the *Kingston*, she had been violently passionate once they were alone, and so for a while he must forget the enterprise and the difficulties that lay ahead – the sloop's crew, the engagement with the argosy, and the hundred other details which were now of the first urgency.

Yet when the first crisis had come, and he had been standing at the poop rail, looking down on that packed waist, with faces of every colour from jail-white to jet black staring up at him, he had carried it off none so badly, he assured himself. He had made a brave figure in his new shirt and breeches of spotless calico – he had even heard murmurs of 'Calico Jack' when the hands assembled – and his air of authority, abetted by vocal support of his own faithful thirty, had given confidence to everyone on board. As Penner had foreseen, the majority of the men from the sloop were no whit disturbed at the proposal of a piratical venture; many had openly welcomed it, for privateering paid none so well and there were irksome disciplines and restrictions attached. The mere mention of the prize involved had won over the waverers, and he had finished his speech in a roar of acclamation.

Nothing was heard from the gentlemen-adventurers. They had come aboard with the sloop's crew, a bewildered and disconsolate little group. Most of them had been sea-sick during the night and were in poor case to protest. Rackham was gratified to note that few of them really deserved the title gentlemen-adventurer, for while adventurers they might be, gentlemen they were not. Shabby, out-at-elbows ruffians, there were those who might have been poor officers from poor regiments, but far from voicing opposition to Rackham's address, one or two had brightened at the prospect of easily gotten fortune, and the remainder, after uneasy glances at their wild companions in the waist, had wisely kept silent. If they could not be relied on to help, they certainly would not hinder.

One, however, was apart from the rest, and he the only man who could be called a gentleman-adventurer indeed. Rackham had picked him out at once – he was of that type that will command attention whatever his surroundings – and had guessed that this was the 'smooth, plume-bonnet rogue Kinsman' of whom Penner entertained such deep mistrust. Smooth he might be, but the rest of the Major's description was an obvious libel. He was certainly a soldier, with his trim military coat, faded but well-kept, and the plain, broad brimmed castor shading his thin, angular face. His top boots fitted like a second pair of breeches, and his long rapier sat as easily on his hip as a quill behind a clerk's ear. There was about him none of the raffish finery of the less impoverished of his fellows, but the workmanlike severity of his appearance, his strong features, and his upright carriage accomplished more for him than airs and tailoring.

He had listened to Rackham attentively, his light blue eyes never leaving the speaker's face, and when the hands dismissed he had turned to the rail without a word to his companions. His attitude plainly said: 'You see how matters stand. I am your leader no longer', and his former followers presently left him and sought themselves berths in the forecastle. The philosophic spirit they displayed on discovering themselves too late to secure even a corner of that crowded place seemed to indicate an acquaintance with the hardships of life, possibly gained in the camp but more probably in the jail.

While Penner congratulated him on the success with which he had won the confidence of the crew, Rackham had found himself aware of a vague disquiet linked somehow with the figure of Kinsman, standing down there at the port rail apparently lost in contemplation of the cheerless waste of water stretching away to the horizon. It was a foreboding that possessed him for the next two hours, while he paced the poop, observing the ship's company, as they lounged in the waist, talking in little groups, dicing or playing cards.

In the end he turned his back on that silent figure and retired to the stern rail, where he tried to place himself in the mind of the commander of the *Star*, ploughing southwards a few hours ahead of him. He had no real fear that they would lose track of the prize, even in that waste of waters between the Great Bank to the west and the long line of cays to the east; he had sailed too often to the Windward Passage to suppose that any competent shipmaster would deviate much from a normal course. The *Kingston* was following as fast as canvas could carry her: faster, he was sure, than the *Star*, for all her clean keel, would be sailing.

Thus he reassured himself, but still that vague disquiet remained, and still it was illogically connected with the lean figure of the gentleman-adventurer, now hidden but clearly seen in Rackham's imagination. Damn the fellow, why should he matter? He was nothing, a mere cipher among a hundred others. And yet – and at that moment he heard the rich, husky sound of a woman's laughter and strode forward to the poop rail.

What he saw kindled his irritation against Kinsman tenfold. The adventurer still stood by the port rail, but he had been joined now by Mistress Bonney and Penner, the former leaning on the bulwarks beside him. Kinsman, Rackham noted, was smiling and leaning forward as though the joke they were sharing was a particularly intimate one. She was wearing her black shirt and breeches, with her glossy hair secured in a net behind her head, and it seemed to Rackham that every curve of her brazenly displayed body as she lolled against the rail, every gesture, and every look must be a wanton challenge not only to Kinsman but to every man in that crowded waist.

If anything had been wanted to crystallise Rackham's feelings towards the gentleman-adventurer it was supplied now. The misgivings which Kinsman's mere presence had evoked had been enough to make him dislike the man; that Anne Bonney should flaunt herself at him turned those feelings into a simple detestation.

He stood looking down at them a moment longer and then turned his attention to the starboard side of the waist, where Kemp was setting the hands to the gun tackles. But even his stentorian blasphemies and the thunder of the carriages on the planking could not drown the laughter that every now and then would drift up from the port rail, Anne Bonney's husky contralto blending with Penner's deep-bellied guffaw. Captain Kinsman must be the most damnably amusing poker-backed bastard in the whole American sea, Rackham thought grimly. They would find how amusing he could be boarding the *Star* to-morrow perhaps, but speculation on that head only led to the conclusion that the captain would likely be most infernally able when it came to close-quarter brawling in the scuppers of locked ships.

There was too much to occupy Rackham's attention for him to brood long, however. He was called forward by Kemp presently to assist in the instruction of the gun crews, and from that he was drawn away by Ben, who had suggestions to make for the improvement of certain running gear. Then came Penner for advice on the rehearsal of boarding parties, and so the afternoon passed, the hours almost unnoticed, such was the energy with which he applied himself to matters which he felt he really understood and in which he could engross himself.

Hard work gave him an appetite and restored his temper and when he went below to supper he was in an excellent humour. He shared the meal with Penner and Anne Bonney, the latter at her most enchanting in a gown of green and black silk which she had sent aboard the Major's sloop days before the sailing.

Her mood was as gay as her appearance, and the meal might have passed pleasantly enough, for Penner was an amusing and stimulating companion. Unfortunately he required intervals to apply himself to his food and it was during one of these that Anne Bonney reawakened Rackham's ill temper by suggesting that they should have Captain Kinsman to sit with them in the cabin.

He frowned, remembering how she had sought the gentleman-adventurer's company, and asked himself was Kinsman the reason for the obvious care she had taken with her appearance. Jealousy prompted him to a hasty refusal of her request, and she looked at him in some surprise.

'And why not?'

'Because I don't wish it.'

At this Mistress Bonney opened her eyes wide and her voice took on an icy edge. 'And if I wish it?'

Rackham filled his glass before replying. 'I still don't want him here. I'd oblige you if I could, but not in that.' Belatedly he made an excuse. 'It might make bad feeling among the crew.'

'As if you cared for bad feeling! Is that the best reason you can give?'

'I need to give no reason,' was his sharp rejoinder. 'I don't want him or any others of that mincing cattle that call themselves gentleman-adventurers, and there's an end to it.' Angrily he pushed his plate aside and thrust back his chair.

'"An end to it", you say?' Her eyes shone with anger. 'And who the devil may you be to tell me "there's an end to it" as though I was some serving-wench?'

'I'm captain of this brig,' he retorted, 'and that means captain over every man-jack – and woman – aboard. So you'll do as I bid you.'

'You dare – you dare to tell me that?' She was on her feet, her eyes blazing.

'You've ears, I think,' snapped Rackham. 'God knows you have a tongue.' He got up and kicked his chair aside.

'So.' She considered him, standing with her hands on her hips, her mouth twisted into a spiteful smile. 'I see. I noticed you seemed to like it mighty little when I spoke to him on deck. Well you're not my husband, by God, and I'll do as I please and be damned to your jealousy.'

'Jealous!' He turned on her. 'Jealous? Of that mealy, spindle-shanked pimp?'

'Aye, because he's a gentleman—'

'Gentleman! The nearest that ever came to being a gentleman was when he stole his master's breeches to go whoring after the milkmaid.'

'To be sure you'll be a fine judge,' she flung at him. 'To

the devil with you and your carping at a man that's something you'll never be. Aye, you can mouth and rant as much as you've a mind to, but your bellowings don't matter that to me.' She snapped her fingers under his nose and turned contemptuously away from the table.

Rackham started after her, brushing aside Penner's attempt to restrain him. 'Wait!' he began, and then, across his harsh command, there rang the cry of the look-out, carrying faintly down from the mainmast-head.

'Sail ho! Ho, the deck! Sail ho!'

It froze them as though in a tableau: Rackham half-way across the cabin with Penner grasping his arm; Anne Bonney with one foot on the companion. She and Penner looked to Rackham with the same thought, and the Major gave it utterance.

'The *Star*!' He released Rackham's arm and thumped the table with excitement. 'Holy Saint Patrick! Johnny, d'ye suppose it is?'

There was a rush of feet on the deck overhead as the hands ran to the rails. Anne Bonney stood with parted lips and a flush of excitement on her cheeks, echoing Penner's question.

'Wait.' Rackham frowned in concentration. He had not expected to sight the *Star* for several hours at least, but it was possible he had overestimated his quarry's capabilities. 'It's only a sail, after all. There's more than one in the Carribean.'

'But on this course?'

'Who said aught of the course? It's a ship, but we don't know where it's sailing.' He pushed past the Major. 'The sure way is to go and see for myself. By your leave, mistress.'

Anne Bonney had moved forward as though to detain him,

150

but he stepped aside. This unexpected turn had been sufficient to cool his temper, but not to quench his resentment. Nor was he impressed by her sudden change from icy rage to an attitude which, to judge from her expression, was designed to be conciliatory. He was beginning to distrust these changes.

He ran up the companion, and ignoring the noisy rabble crowded at the rail, swung himself into the mainmast shrouds. They fell silent as he began the hazardous ascent; for all his bulk he went up as nimbly as a monkey until he reached the main-top where he wriggled on to the narrow grating beside the look-out, breathless with the exertion of his climb.

Far below the *Kingston* was like a slim knife-blade, her decks white against the turquoise water around her. The wind sang in his ears, and as the vessel rolled the deck vanished from directly beneath him and he was hanging over the heaving trough of the sea fifty feet below. Slowly, like a great pendulum, the mast came up again with a thousand shrieks and groans from cord and timber as the vessel paused for a moment on even keel and rolled again.

'Where away?' he shouted. The look-out pointed almost dead ahead, and Rackham followed the line of the outstretched arm. The sun was setting, and its rays had turned the south-western sky the colour of flame. Straining his eyes he made out a tiny smudge disturbing the perfection of the curve where dark blue and amber met on the horizon; a smudge, nothing more to the naked eye, but certainly a ship if that eye were a seaman's.

Through the look-out's glass the smudge leaped into clarity – two masts almost in line, with canvas spread. A prolonged observation told him what he wanted to know – the ship was sailing with the *Kingston* and apparently on the same course. It might be the *Star* – so much he admitted to the demand of the eager crowd who surrounded him when he regained the deck, and his words were greeted with a roar of acclamation which alarmed him because it was a measure of what the reaction would be if he was wrong.

'Ye can hope and pray it is the *Star*,' he told Penner when they had regained the privacy of the cabin away from the exultant tumult of the deck. 'If it's not, God help us. Listen to them! They'll be yelling for our blood – my blood – if that sail turns out to be some bum-boat making for Caicos Bank, as it well may be.'

'Dear lad,' the Major was effusive, 'it has to be the *Star*. It must be. Aren't ye convinced yourself, now? And by my soul it's a credit to your captaincy, to your navigation. It's nothing short of a miracle, so it is.'

'Bah!' said Rackham. 'It's luck and nothing else – if it is the *Star*.'

'The crew won't call it luck,' said Penner complacently, eyeing his glass against the light. 'And if they do, what then? It's all a pirate skipper needs. Luck, my lad,' and he drained off his wine.

'Luck,' said Rackham absently. He raised his glass but set it down again untasted. 'Where is she?'

The Major hesitated. 'In her cabin. And if you take my advice you'll let her stop there. Quarrels aren't breeches – they don't have to be patched. You'll do more good by letting well alone, and by morning it'll all be forgotten. Besides,' – his face broke into a jovial smile again – 'there's the *Star* to be thought of, and half a million tinkling, lovely dollars that we'll be wading ankle-deep in this day night.' He laughed for delight and applied himself again to the bottle. 'The wealth of the Indies! Silver from the mines of Peru, gold from the deserts of Mexico, pearls from the Rio Hacha big as your fist, dollars and crowns and pieces of eight from God knows where! And what does it matter? We know where they're going!' He chuckled and shook his head. 'And to think – to think if I hadn't clapped eyes on you that morning at the Fort it might never have happened.'

'It hasn't happened yet,' Rackham reminded him. He found the Major's optimism annoying, but the other waved him aside with airy assurance.

'Have we come this far to be bilked by fortune? I tell you I feel it in my bones, and my instinct was never wrong yet.'

But in spite of this carefree confidence in his partner Rackham was too well aware of the difficulties yet remaining to be able to abandon himself to an anticipatory carouse. He sat while the Major babbled on about the treasure they were to reap on the morrow and proposed numerous toasts which he honoured himself, but as the light began to fade Rackham's nervous irritation increased and at last he rose and went on deck, leaving Penner to drink himself to sleep.

In the quickly gathering dark the *Kingston* must follow as best she could the quarry they had sighted; they must hold the course that they believed she would take during the night. Rackham issued his orders, and in renewing contact with these practical if trivial details which were no more than formalities to the experienced steersmen, shed a little of his anxiety. There was an air of excitement about the *Kingston*'s decks which could not help but communicate itself to him; they were active and eager for the chase and the capture, and it seemed that the first reckless enthusiasm had been replaced by a steady purpose which heartened him more than all Penner's flights of fancy could have done.

It was dark when he went below. Penner was snoring gently in the main cabin, and Rackham stood hesitant for a moment at the foot of the ladder. To his right was the cabin where he had spent last night with Anne; she would be asleep in it herself by now. The other was the one he had occupied in the old days; it would be empty.

He turned to it and opened the door, closing it again behind him in the darkness. He took the two steps he knew were necessary to reach the bunk, and the hairs on the nape of his neck rose as something moved in the blackness before him. He stopped, tense and ready, but before he could move or strike a hand touched his own and held it. Fingers caressed it lightly, and then drew him downwards. He felt for the arm in the darkness, and followed it to a smooth, naked shoulder. He could hear her breathing, swift and urgent, and then the other hand was touching his face and he was drawn to her without resistance.

13. THE ACTION

Captain Bankier of the *Star* watched through his glass the brig that had been following in his wake and steadily drawing closer since dawn, and asked himself for the twentieth time what the devil she could be about. That his pursuer was the *Kingston* he knew, and since she had been snug at anchor in Providence two days ago he could not doubt that her presence was legitimate, but he knew also that she had been due to careen, and that only an emergency could have brought her out after the *Star*.

He was reassuring himself that it would be best to continue on his course until signalled to do otherwise, when a thin jet of smoke shot out from the *Kingston*'s side, followed by the dull thump of an explosion. The signal to heave-to was unmistakable; the question was whether to obey or not. Common sense told Bankier that the *Kingston* had been dispatched after him on some lawful errand; no other logical explanation offered. In which case his duty was clear.

He snapped his glass shut and addressed an order to his first lieutenant, and a few minutes later Rackham, on the

155

Kingston's poop, saw the *Star* behaving precisely as he had calculated she must, swinging round to heave to.

He drew a deep breath. For the next hour a hundred pairs of eyes would be watching them from the *Star*'s decks; for an hour there must be no sign that the *Kingston* was anything but what she pretended to be. The least slip to arouse suspicion and the *Star* would be away like a bird, her well-greased keel covering four miles to the *Kingston*'s three. Surprise was their only hope.

Himself he relieved the steersman, and the *Kingston* ploughed on before the light breeze over a brilliant cobalt sea. Slowly she narrowed the distance as the long minutes passed, and the tension mounted among the silent men in the waist and those aft. Penner, his crimson coat providing the only patch of colour on the poop, paced up and down behind Rackham, pausing every now and then to gaze ahead at the *Star* before resuming his interminable walk. Once he stopped and said, 'D'ye suppose . . . ?' and left the question unfinished. His nerves were beginning to wear at the silent waiting broken only by the creak and moan of timber and cordage as they ran swiftly down towards their quarry.

Rackham called an order to Kemp, his voice sounding deep in that strange silence which was yet so full of noise. The red-haired gunner jerked upright from his seat on the ladder and padded gently to the rail, as though he were afraid the *Star* might hear his footsteps. For a moment he studied the *Star* and the swell of the sea, and then turned to summon his crews, without haste, to their guns.

Suddenly the *Star* seemed much closer; the men on her decks were recognisable as such and not as doll-figures. There was the little group on the poop; Rackham could see the coloured coats and the scarlet of the marine sentry. Soon they would be within hailing distance, and Penner would be called on to play the second act of the drama.

'In good voice, Ned?' asked Rackham softly, his eyes on the ship ahead, and the Major started.

'What's that?'

'Be ready. We'll hail them in a moment.'

The Major sighed nervously. 'Aye.' He moved over to the port rail and stood waiting, his hands clasped behind him.

Rackham put his weight on the wheel and the seaman beside him copied the action. Ben, in the waist, bawled an order that sent the hands to the braces and the *Kingston* swung over almost imperceptibly. Rackham judged the distance to the *Star*: three cables' lengths, and as they shortened sail he spoke.

'Now, Ned.'

Penner stooped and grasped the speaking trumpet at his feet, and his hail rang across the water.

'*Star* ahoy!'

A figure detached itself from the knot on the *Star*'s poop and an answering hail demanded their business. Penner roared out his answer.

'Major Penner, of the brig *Kingston*. We have dispatches from Governor Rogers for Jamaica. Urgent dispatches. A sloop brought news that Spanish ships are on their way from the Florida Channel.'

Rackham could guess the sensation this would cause aboard the *Star*. If only the fool who commanded her wasted no time with stupid questions. They were too near as it was; every minute was precious if Kemp was to be given the chance he needed – he was fidgeting among his guns, snapping his fingers with excitement, casting appealing glances towards Rackham, and inaudibly cursing the delay.

157

The reply to come aboard came from the *Star* with tantalising deliberation, and Penner turned away from the rail, his face bathed in perspiration.

'Ready, Andy!' shouted Rackham, and Kemp waved in reply.

He barked an order, and the caps were whipped off the tubs containing the slow-matches. Beside each tub crouched a man, fanning vigorously to disperse the tiny drifts of smoke which might otherwise be seen from the *Star*'s look-out.

Rackham fixed his eyes on a point on the *Star*'s poop – a lantern that gleamed brassily in the sunlight. They were off her starboard quarter now, little more than a cable's length away, and in bringing the Kingston down level with the other brig his judgement must be faultless. Two minutes and they would be broadside on, and Kemp's guns would provide the answer to the question every man on board must be asking.

The lamp was moving nearer. In one minute the *Kingston*'s bow-sprit would be level with the *Star*'s after-rail, and still there was no sign that she had been discovered for what she was. Men were lining the *Star*'s side, watching as the *Kingston* crept up on their quarter. Rackham could see their faces plainly now; there was one man standing on the rail, a great bronzed fellow with a shock of yellow hair. He held with one hand to the shrouds and waved the other in greeting. Ben, on the poop ladder, waved in reply.

The scream of blocks overhead drew Rackham's attention back to the *Kingston* as she trembled violently and the wheel kicked beneath his hands. Her head fell away a little; he brought her up, and they were gliding in level with the *Star* with a bare hundred yards of open water between them. There she lay, on a smooth sea, her side as broad as the proverbial barn door, as perfect a target as any gunner could have wished; if Kemp bungled he could not blame his quartermaster.

'Ports!' yelled Kemp, and the crash as the wooden flaps were flung back was followed immediately by the shrieking and rumbling of the guns as the crews ran them forward. The *Kingston*'s mask was off; the men of the *Star*, so indifferent a moment ago, were looking death in the face as they stared at the unwinking muzzles that had suddenly sprouted from the *Kingston*'s side.

There was a yell of alarm and a frantic order bellowed from the *Star*'s poop. Something was being shouted through a speaking trumpet, but Rackham never heard it. Kemp was kneeling by the nearest gun, his handspike going furiously while the match spluttered openly now in the hand of his mate.

'Quickly! Christ! Quickly!' Penner plucked off his hat and dashed it on the deck in an anguish of excitement. They were dead level, bow to bow and stern to stern, and Kemp leaped back from his gun. He shouted his order in a cracked voice, there was an instant of silence, and then the *Kingston* seemed to explode beneath their feet.

The ship leaped and rocked beneath the shock of the broadside and Rackham staggered at the wheel. Through the clouds of acrid smoke that swirled back from the guns, filling the waist and rolling up to the poop, he heard the ponderous thunder as the carriages were run back. Kemp was yelling like a madman as the crews ran to swab out their barrels and ram home fresh charges; above the babble of sounds Ben was roaring orders to the topmen and hands at the braces.

Rackham looked through the thinning smoke to the *Star*. That one broadside had taken terrible effect. The brig's bulwarks looked as though they had been swept by some huge flail; at one point a great yellow splinter trailed down into the water, carrying a tangle of canvas and rope with it, part of the poop rail had been carried away, and there was one gaping hole near the waterline.

Two voices, one calling orders and the other shrieking, carried across the water. He could see men ascending the rigging, like insects creeping on a web, and on the poop a hatless figure was shaking his fist at them.

'Stand by to go about!' Ben's voice cut through the hoarse cheer from the *Kingston*'s deck as she drew away from the other ship. Men were pointing and shouting; Kemp, the lower half of his face a black mask of powder, was wrestling with the second gun as it was run forward.

They went about in a great arc that left a creamy horse-shoe on the blue water and ran down on the *Star*'s port side. She had her guns out now, but Rackham guessed the upheaval there must be on her decks and was not anxious. It was one thing to take a broadside in battle and fire one in return; it was quite another to be surprised and have to drive to the guns men shocked and dazed by the impact.

'Fire as your guns bear!' yelled Kemp, and as the *Kingston* cruised past she poured shot after shot into the King's brig, raking her mercilessly at the main-deck level. The *Star* seemed to stagger in the water beneath that hammering; one of her forward guns went off and a ball screamed over the *Kingston*'s stern, while another shot ricochetted off the water and struck the pirates' side with a resounding crash.

Rackham whistled another man to the wheel and dropped down the ladder to the waist where Penner was marshalling his men. One quick survey of the havoc wrought by the second broadside was enough. There was no useful purpose to be served by punishing the *Star* further; it would only

160

mean useless slaughter and would render her a floating wreck. As they bore down for the third time the running out of Kemp's guns was a precaution only; what was still to do would be done by the three lines of boarders drawn up to the *Kingston's* rail and stretching the length of the waist.

As they bore down on the *Star's* quarter Penner waved his hand and a cheer burst from the triple ranks. It was answered by a feeble chorus from the *Star*, and then a series of little grey plumes of smoke broke out like flowers from the side of the King's ship, and musket-balls whizzed over the *Kingston*. One pirate gave a cry of pain and collapsed on the deck, and then from the shrouds above came the answering rattle of musketry as Penner's sharpshooters fired down into the *Star*.

'Stand by to board!' bawled Penner. Only a few yards separated the ships now; the crackle of firing mounted as the *Kingston* swung in, and a pin in the rail at Rackham's side was smashed to splinters by a stray ball. He grasped a line to steady himself against the coming shock as the grappling irons sailed over the water on to the *Star's* deck. Through the musketry smoke he could see the scarlet file of marines and an officer with drawn sword at their head, while about them milled the *Star's* seamen.

The vessels met with a jar and groan of timber that sent a shudder through the *Kingston's* length, fell away slightly and then ground together as the men hauled on the grapples. Penner pulled himself on to the rail and leaped for the rigging across the gulf between the ships, and the first rank of boarders followed on his heels. The volley of the marines crashed out, and then Rackham found himself in a mob of tearing, striking, cursing men on the *Star's* deck.

Directly in front of him a seaman was levelling a pistol,

but in the same moment a boarding-pike thrust by a pirate took him in the chest and he fell back into the press. Penner was plunging forward ahead of them with a seaman dragging at his legs, and just beyond him the marine officer was calmly issuing orders, sword in hand, with one eye on his file and the other on the battle raging almost at his elbow, as cool as though on a barrack square.

Rackham turned, cutting at a sailor who was rushing at him. He missed his stroke but recovered, and with one hand protecting his face and the other swinging his broadsword, drove his way through to the open space at the foot of the poop ladder. From within a yard of where he stood to the other end of the waist the deck was a madhouse of struggling, stabbing men, but even as he watched the third wave of boarders swept over from the *Kingston* and their impetus carried the fight forward, leaving the after part of the deck clear of all but half a dozen who had fallen. Above him, on the poop, he could hear the clamour of fighting, and as he set his foot on the ladder an officer in a blue coat came hurtling down and landed almost at his feet.

Before he could rise Rackham was on top of him, one hand on his throat, pinning him down. A glance at the newcomer's dress, also the fact that he had been on the poop, made Rackham suspect that here was the *Star*'s commander. He shortened his sword and brought the blade up in front of his captive's face.

'Strike!' he shouted. 'Bid them strike!'

The officer glared and tore at the fingers on his windpipe, Rackham slipped sideways, and then they were under the feet of men racing for the ladder. Rackham fetched up in the scuppers, scrambling to his feet, and as he did so he heard a voice above the din, shouting.

'Quarter!'

Another took up the cry, and as he regained his balance it became a chorus from the forward part of the ship.

He looked about him. The officer was being hauled to his feet by two pirates while a third threatened him with a dirk. Dazed and helpless, the officer turned an agonised face towards the fore part of the waist and groaned at what he saw. Ringed against the rail by the body of pirates the seamen of the *Star* were throwing down their arms, and in the bows a similar scene was being enacted.

Unbelievably almost, the capture of the *Star* had been completed in a few minutes. Even now there were as many of the *Star*'s seamen fit to fight as there were pirates, but the sudden double shock of the broadsides, followed by the fury of the boarding, had proved too much for them. One had cried 'Quarter!' and then another, and in a moment the fight had been won and lost.

Rackham, with Penner jubilant beside him, and the eyes of every man in that crowded waist upon him, turned to the captain of the *Star*. Bankier's face was working with fury, and when Rackham addressed him he replied with an outburst which culminated in an assurance that he would see every man of the *Kingston*'s crew rotting in chains before the month was out.

Rackham was amused. 'We've heard the like before, so you can save your breath. You've a long pull ahead of you.' He stepped closer. 'Now, then, where's your cargo?'

'Find it yourself and be damned' was the fierce retort.

One of the pirates holding him growled and raised his fist, but stopped at a sign from Rackham, and Bankier's mouth twisted in contempt.

'Observing the niceties,' he sneered. 'We'll see your

manners in a different light, no doubt, when you stand on the scaffold.'

Rackham considered him. There was something odd about this fellow's behaviour. He had seen captains of captured ships before – cowards, blusterers, cold, hard merchantmen, and those who were simply downright hostile. Bankier would seem to belong to the last category, but he was a shade sardonic for a man who had just suffered an ignominious defeat.

Abruptly Rackham turned away. 'Hold him close, Ben. Ned, Bull, come below with me. We'll find the dollars for ourselves.'

He led the way below decks with Penner, Bull carrying an axe at their heels. Behind them came every pirate who could struggle down the narrow companion into the ill-lit 'tween-decks. This was their moment, and they trooped below whooping and laughing like schoolboys. Lanterns were lit and they descended into the hold.

It was close and stuffy, with only a faint glimmer of light from the hatchway. Rats scampered away as the yellow glare of the lanterns illuminated the shadows, and Penner gave a yell of delight which was echoed by the men behind at the sight of the score or more heavily bound chests which lay between the sacks of ballast.

'Glory be!' said the Major. 'There they are, Johnny! There they are!' He thumped Rackham's back and started past him down the ladder. 'Our fortunes made!' he crowed. 'A king's ransom for us all! God bless His Majesty and Governor Woodes Rogers, say I!' He seized a padlock and rattled it. 'Quick, quick! Let's have them open and see the pretty, pretty dollars!'

Even Rackham was laughing as they crowded round the

164

chests, each with its locks sealed with great blobs of wax bearing the royal crest. They were like children, pushing and jostling to get near enough to touch the massive iron bands that bound the lids, shouting foolish computations of the contents and already spending in riotous imagination the fortune under their hands.

Rackham shouldered them away from the centre chest, a ponderous case with the arms of Castile worked in metal on the lid. It was secured by a stout padlock and chain, but Bull's axe would make short work of that.

'Back and give him room,' he ordered, as Bull spat on his hands. 'And when it's open keep your fingers clear of it. Look all you've a mind to, but leave the silver alone. Right, Davie.'

Bull stepped forward, swung the axe above his head, and brought it down with all his strength, the heavy blade biting deep into the hasp that held the padlock and striking sparks from the metal. A second blow shore the lock away, and there was an immediate surge forward by the men as Rackham prepared to throw back the lid.

'Here they come', gloated a voice. 'Let's be seein' them, Jacky.'

Rackham crooked his fingers under the lid and tugged it free. He heaved it back, and the gasp of expectation from the onlookers died stillborn as they stared unbelievingly at what should have been a mass of glittering coins and ornaments but was not. The chest was filled with stones.

Rackham gazed down at them in horror, and Penner actually fell back a step. For a full three seconds there was dead silence, and then Bull, with a horrible oath, expressed the bewilderment of all.

'What the hell's yon?' His eyes glared from the stones to Rackham and back again. 'They're stones; bloody stones!'

Penner thrust his hand into the chest. 'It can't be . . . underneath . . . packed down . . .' His fingers scrabbled among the little rocks, tearing them aside. 'Holy Saints! It must be here!'

'Bubbled!' roared Bull, smashing his axe down in a frenzy of rage. 'Bubbled! D'ye know what it is? It's a bloody blind! A blind!'

In a moment there was pandemonium. Men flung themselves at the chest, swearing and striking, pulling out the stones in the vain hope that the silver might be concealed beneath them. Others, less distracted, turned their attentions to the other chests, and one by one the locks were forced. But in each case the result was the same: the chests were packed with stone and shingle, with not the trace of a single coin among them.

Rackham stood like a man in a nightmare. All about him men were jostling and cursing, pouring out floods of filthy invective against Woodes Rogers, the King, and each other. As yet it had not occurred to them to turn their rage on Rackham, but he had no illusions that they would not remember him when their first anger was spent.

He forced his way to the ladder and mounted the second step. He saw Bull catch sight of him and throw out an arm to point at him, but before the denunciation could be spoken, Rackham had attracted the mob's attention.

'Wait!' he shouted, and the noise subsided a little. They pressed round the foot of the ladder, glaring up at him. 'This isn't played out yet,' he went on. 'We don't know what it means . . .'

'I know what it means!' shouted Bull, elbowing his way forward. 'It means we've sailed like blind bairns after a shipful of stones!' A roar of approval greeted this, and he went on fiercely: 'Aye, and mebbe worse. Who's to say it's not a trap, eh? Tell us that!'

'You hold your tongue!' shouted Rackham. 'If you'd as much wit as you've wind you'd know that the one man who can tell us where the silver's gone is on deck, under guard, and that nobody baits a trap unless they know there's game to walk into it. And nobody knew that.'

'Nobody but you and that red-headed bitch you've been tumbling,' began Bull, but his words were lost in the general uproar.

'Get the King's captain! Up and get him!' There was a rsuh for the ladder, but Rackham, with Penner at his heels, was first through the hatchway with the disappointed pirates swarming behind them.

Word of what had passed had flown to the deck, and Ben and his guards were with difficulty restraining those who surged about the little group of white-faced officers. When Rackham appeared they fell back, and he advanced on Bankier, drawing his dirk from his waist.

Bankier was pale, but there was no trace of fear in his eyes as Rackham gripped him by the collar and presented the point of the dirk at his chest.

'Now,' said Rackham, and his voice was strained and husky, 'I'll ask you once, and that's all, and if you don't answer I'll put this knife through your throat. Where's the silver?'

Bankier knew it was no melodramatic threat; in fact he regarded his own fate, and the fate of his men, as foregone already. But he smiled even as the dirk pricked him beneath the chin.

'The silver?' He spoke loudly, so that all should hear. 'To the best of my knowledge it should be on its way to Charles Town. Too far away for you, pirate. You'll never see it now – unless it's to Charles Town they take you for your hanging.'

'Charles Town?' echoed Rackham. He stared into the sneering face, and then shook Bankier in his rage. 'You're a liar! Rogers would never risk it in Spanish waters! He would be a fool, and that he's not.'

'Less of a fool than if he sent it to Port Royal,' snapped Bankier, and Rackham knew he was telling the truth, impossible as it seemed. Rogers could not possibly have known that an attempt would be made on the treasure, and yet his dispatching of the *Star* to Jamaica as a blind was the kind of precaution that would appeal to his calculating brain. Rackham began to see a dozen reasons why Charles Town might be a safer destination, and knew again the sickness of despair.

The realisation of how they had been tricked brought an uproar of rage from the pirates. They surged about the officers, one of whom was felled before Ben's guards could protect him. Bankier's coat was half torn from his back, and he and his subordinates would have been battered to death on the spot if Ben had not hustled them up the ladder to the safety of the poop. Rackham mounted the ladder and faced the throng in the waist, but his attempts to make himself heard were drowned in the uproar.

Bull's voice was raised above the others. He thrust his way to the front, a fearsome figure towering above his mates.

'The bastard's lying!' he shouted. 'Charles Town be damned! Give him down here and we'll find soon enough where t'silver's gone!'

There was a roar of approval and a rush for the ladder with Bull in the van. He bounded up and stopped with a startled oath just in time to save himself from impalement on Rackham's dirk.

'Wait.' The sharp command as much as the naked weapon made them pause. 'There's no time for this. We'll deal with the prisoners as I think fit. In the meantime, there's this vessel to search and strip and make seaworthy again. Malloy, have Kemp sent to me from the *Kingston*, and signal Bennett in the sloop to come alongside. You, Bull,' – he let the point of the dirk fall away – 'see that this brig's cleared of every dollar aboard.'

It was a shrewd reminder that there might still be some profit to be gained from their prize, and he was asserting his authority at the same time. Malloy, obedient by instinct, turned away, and as Bull hesitated, Rackham sheathed his dirk and ascended to the poop as though his orders were the end of the matter. For most of them the prospect of loot was enough, and there was a hurried dispersal in the waist in which Bull and his followers quickly joined.

Rackham summoned Penner, and the Major ascended the ladder slowly. The last few minutes had wrought their change in him: he was suddenly old and tired, and the high colour had faded in his cheeks.

Rackham drew him aside. 'Look you, Ned, there's little time for what's to do. If things go ill we may find ourselves on a lee shore. We've promised these scum a fortune, and they haven't got it, but I doubt if they'll go the length of wanting our blood for a bit yet. They don't know where to go or what to do, and whoever can tell them is their master – for a time.'

Penner nodded. 'And then?'

'I don't know. I must have time – time to think, to see us safe out of this business somehow – you and me and Anne. Now, this is what's to do. Bankier and his men must go. If the like of Bull had his way they'd go over the side with shot tied to their feet – after he'd had his fun with them. That I'll not have. I'm going to give them your sloop.'

'The sloop!' ejaculated Penner. 'Dear God, they'll never let you! Turn them free to set the Jamaica Squadron after us? Why—'

'There's no other way. We haven't enough crew to sail three vessels. Don't fret yourself. I've sent for Bennett, and before Bankier's folk are put aboard I'll have the running rigging torn to shreds. They'll take long enough to set her right, and we'll be far away by then. Hell's gates! It's either that or murder them all!'

'Aye,' said Penner doubtfully. 'You may be right. Maybe they'll let them go at that. But what then?'

'We'll split our crew between the brigs. The *Star* I'll give to Bennett. You and Anne – and Bull and any like him – will be with me in the *Kingston*. I want the worst of them under our hands. Then we can be away out of this damned stretch of sea, because before long it'll be too hot to hold us.'

Penner passed a hand over the grey stubble on his shaven head and looked about him, blinking against the heat as he surveyed the tangle of gear in the waist and the scars of the recent encounter. A dead marine was lying in the scuppers, his carefully powdered wig clotted with blood; two of the pirates were helping an injured comrade to hobble towards the forecastle, and from below came the shouts and crashing of Bull's searchers as they hurried through the ship.

'And afterwards, then? When we've sailed – away? Where do we go?'

Rackham shrugged. 'D'ye think I know? Perhaps I can find a way. If not –.' He took the Major's arm. 'Get you to Anne. Keep her below.' A thought struck him and he laughed

170

bitterly. 'D'you mind something. It was her plan, in the beginning – all this! I wonder, would she not rather be back with Bonney after all?'

He may have been near the truth: at least he was presently left in no doubt that with the disappointment of their enterprise Mistress Bonney's volatile temperament had again changed suddenly, and it appeared permanently, as far as he was concerned. She came to embarrass him at a critical moment when, Bennett having done his work of crippling the sloop, Bankier and his men were being forced to embark. Unfortunately Bull and his companions had finished their ransacking of the brig, and returned grumbling on deck, for they had found meagre spoils. At once Bull raised a tremendous outcry against Bankier's release, demanding that he should be kept and tortured to obtain possible information about the treasure, and but for the fact that Bennett, who commanded considerable respect, supported Rackham, the big Yorkshireman might have won his way. As it was the majority realised that there was little purpose in keeping the prisoners, and they were being herded down into the sloop with kicks and abuse while Bull damned Rackham for a bungler and a coward. It was at this moment that Rackham's eye caught a familiar figure in black stepping through the tangle of timber and cordage that still cluttered the gangway. Anne Bonney, broad-brimmed hat on head and rapier on hip, was skirting round the press of the pirates, and behind her, concern on his face, came Penner.

She ascended the ladder, graceful as a cat, and stood before Rackham. She was unsmiling, and there was the nasty twist to her mouth that he had seen when she had confronted her husband two nights before.

171

'So the cupboard was bare, John,' she began, but he cut her short, addressing Penner.

'I thought I told you to keep her aboard the *Kingston*.'

The Major shrugged helplessly and Anne Bonney's eyes narrowed.

'Ye've yet to learn that I do as I please,' she reminded him. 'And don't tell me you're the captain and must be obeyed, for from what I see ye'll be lucky if you're captain much longer.'

It took his breath away, and she swept on: 'And now that there's no silver, what d'ye intend to do? Or d'you intend to do anything at all?'

He was aware that the noise in the waist had died, and that the hands were watching them. He kept his voice low.

'I'm going to do what I can to get myself and you and Harry out of this,' he said. 'And I'll do it best if you'll not interfere. If ye'd known what was good for you you'd have stayed off this deck and out of sight.'

To his surprise she laughed softly and cast a glance over her shoulder at the men in the waist.

'So?' Her grey eyes were hard. 'Ye know, Jack, I don't agree at all. I think I know how to preserve my own skin: so I'll make it my own concern, and do you look to yours.'

Bull came to interrupt them, demanding again that Bankier should be turned over to the crew, and meeting Rackham's refusal with a flood of vile abuse. Doubtless he conceived that he was making a profound impression on his companions on the lower deck, but they were unappreciative enough to show less interest in his tirade than in the rum casks and wine-kegs which the astute Penner ordered to be broached as soon as the sloop with its castaways had been warped away from the *Star*'s side. Whereupon Bull, Achilles-like, strode

172

off in dudgeon, and presently, Anne Bonney having returned to the *Kingston* with Penner, Rackham was again alone on the *Star*'s quarter-deck.

The thieves, having tasted the bitterness of failure, were beginning to fall out.

14. MOSQUITO BANK

The *Kingston* lay at anchor in a green-fringed cove of the tiny islet of Mosquito Bank, her bare yards almost touching the tangle of tropical foliage that grew in dense walls to the water's edge. Above the oily surface hummed the clouds of insects which had given their name to this pest-ridden haven off the Cuban coast: a spot shunned by honest sea-traffic, and so a refuge for pirate vessels and their crews. Even these were reluctant to anchor in the bank's foul atmosphere unless forced to do so; it was a token of the *Kingston*'s necessity that she had been there four days.

The storm that had come sweeping out of the north on the evening of the day they took the *Star* had driven them southwards under bare yards. They had lost sight of the *Star* at nightfall, and when morning came the *Kingston* was alone on the sea. Rackham had taken the precaution, however, of fixing a rendezvous at Mosquito Bank, and thither the *Kingston* had hastened to wait for Bennett and lie secure from the hue and cry which would be raised from New Providence to the Windward Passage.

Four days had gone, and Bennett did not come. Rackham had won a temporary respite, for there could be no inquiry into the whys and wherefores of the enterprise's failure until the whole crew were present, and half of them were still aboard the absent *Star*. When and if they came there would be a council and Rackham would be required to account for the past and provide for the future. If he failed – and he knew he must – there was an end to his captaincy.

For he found himself now with only a single influential ally: Penner. If he had hoped for such support as Anne Bonney might have lent him he had been disappointed. That she could have been of considerable assistance he now knew; for strangely enough as Rackham's stock had fallen hers appeared to have risen with the crew. Now she was their 'lucky lass' and hail fellow with the worst on board. Not for her the companionship of Captain Rackham – she made it as plain to the crew as she had done to Rackham himself, and thereby caused much obscene merriment. Whatever befell she at least was safe, for while she moved among the pirates with a boisterous familiarity, she made it plain that she discouraged liberties. She might crack jokes with such a ruffian as Bull, laughing her husky laugh while he grinned and his eyes wandered over the firm breasts beneath the black shirt and the long straight legs booted to the thighs. But Bull knew better to do anything more than laugh and look, for constantly at her elbow, impassive as ever, was Kinsman, cool, watchful and deliberate. The others never knew what to make of him. His ignorance of the sea would have made any other man a butt, but Kinsman was in no such danger, and they kept clear of him.

Rackham found he could watch them with only a little bitterness: quite plainly Anne saw in Kinsman a protector, and so was content to use him. Rackham had been used the same way, in the hope of profit, and when her use for him had passed he had been discarded. It amused him to think that the same might happen with Kinsman, but he had a feeling that Anne Bonney might find the discarding more perilous than she supposed.

He was musing on these lines on the afternoon of the fourth day when Penner joined him on the poop, and the pair of them watched developments in the waist, where Bull, surrounded by a large group of pirates, was haranguing them noisily. Apart from them, lounging by the rail, Anne Bonney sat beneath a rough awning that had been erected for her by the worshipping Malloy. She watched with a lazy smile, one booted leg crossed over the other, nibbling at a tropical fruit and spitting the stones at one of the men – he was hardly more than a boy – who plainly regarded himself as singularly favoured by this attention.

Beside her stood Kinsman, upright and immaculate even in that broiling heat, and missing no word of the noisy debate.

It resolved itself into a deputation at last, headed by Bull. They trooped aft to demand that Bennett and his crew be considered lost and that a council be convened forthwith. The unpleasant grin with which Bull delivered himself left no doubt that he was assured what the outcome of that council must be.

Had Rackham been alone they must have had their way. A denial from him would have exploded the discontent that was brewing; but Penner was a different matter. He could talk, and he was respected up to a point. To hear him, he might have been answering a friendly argument, so easy was his manner, and the result was that he won from them an agreement to wait a day longer. Thereafter – and here Rackham was forced to agree – they would hold a council.

It was a decision that suited Bull not at all; however, he had no choice but to bow to the will of the majority with a bad grace and retire with his comrades to the waist. There, a moment later, he was deep in conversation with Kinsman and Anne Bonney.

Pacing slowly up and down at the poop rail, Rackham kept them under observation. They were too far away for him to hear what was passing, but he saw Bull gesticulate twice towards the poop, and heard Anne Bonney's rich contralto laugh. Kinsman remained silent save for what appeared to be an occasional question put to Bull.

Penner, who had gone below to the cabin, reappeared and joined Rackham at the rail. He carried a bulky canvas bag which contained such surgical equipment as the *Kingston* boasted, for since the engagement Penner had been self-appointed surgeon by virtue of a smattering of medical knowledge picked up on his military campaigns and elsewhere. He had been in the habit of visiting the sick in the forecastle twice daily, and it was time for his afternoon round. His eyes fastened on the little group at the rail.

'So dear Davie hasn't run out of wind yet. God, was there ever such a man for trouble? I wonder now, if I might be better applyin' me medical talents to him? A small blood-letting, say – about a quart and a half. T'would do him a world of good. What d'ye say?'

'Keep your instruments for the wounded,' said Rackham. 'You'll maybe get a chance at Davie yet.'

'It's a happy thought,' said Penner, and stumped down the ladder. As he drew near the group at the rail, they fell silent, but their eyes followed him as he vanished in the forecastle hatchway.

He was below for half an hour, and the *Kingston* drowsed

177

in the boiling afternoon. In the waist men slept wherever there was shade, or diced in little groups. There was no breath of air and the green walls of jungle were silent but for the sudden scream of a bird and the continuous drone of insects in the steaming swamps.

Penner emerged from the forecastle at last, and life seemed to return to the groups in the waist. Rackham was conscious of it, and glanced down to see the Major crossing the deck.

As he passed the awning beneath which Anne Bonney sat, she called to him, and Penner stopped in mid-stride.

'Where away so fast, Major? Faith, in this weather it makes me sweat to look at you.'

She had removed her hat and was lying back toying idly with a strand of the red hair that hung to her shoulders, and smiling in lazy amusement at Penner, who stood hesitant. Since the episode of the *Star* he had avoided her: her abandonment of Rackham had seemed to the Major to savour almost of betrayal. Still, he could hardly ignore her greeting without offence, and offence, he knew, might be impolitic just now.

'We see very little of you these days,' she went on. 'You're grown less gallant than you were, Major. You disappoint me, for I've held you as a model to Captain Kinsman here. He's wanting in the graces himself and I had looked to you to instruct him.'

Penner perceived himself mocked, and shot a look at Kinsman to see if the saturnine captain was sharing her amusement, but there was no hint of laughter in the adventurer's cold eyes.

'Aye, changed days,' murmured Anne Bonney. 'It was not so in Providence. He used to dance attendance on me like a schoolboy,' she went on to Kinsman. 'Handing me to my coach and scowling like a sword-bully at any that as much as bade me good morning.'

Penner muttered impatiently, and was preparing to turn away when she brought him up short.

'Mind you,' she went on, and her smile was unpleasant, 'it's hard to blame the poor soul when ye think on the bonny vixen he was married to. How came ye into her clutches, Penner? Were you drunk?'

For a moment Penner stared, shocked by that brutal speech. His anger surged up under the goad of her mocking smile and the guffaw of laughter from her audience. It had been notorious in Providence that the Major's lady was a shrew and that he had left her after a series of violent exchanges, but to hear her miscalled by this wicked slut was more than he was prepared to bear. He struggled to master his temper, and partly succeeded.

'Good day,' he snapped, and unwisely added: 'You'd do better not to miscall a lady who's your better in everything that makes a woman. I'll say no more.'

He was turning on his heel when a hand descended on his shoulder and he spun round to find himself looking into the face of Captain Kinsman.

'Indeed,' said Kinsman, 'I think you've said too much already.'

For a moment Penner was too astonished to reply. Then: 'Go to the devil,' he said brusquely, and shook off the restraining hand.

'I think not,' said Kinsman sharply. He moved to bar Penner's way. 'I find you offensive,' he added coldly, 'to this lady.' He gestured in Anne Bonney's direction, and Penner turned to look at her. She was sitting back, a bright flush on her cheeks, and her eyes were glittering.

'Lady?' Penner exclaimed. He checked a contemptuous laugh, and the look of surprise faded from his face, to be replaced by a questioning shrewdness.

'And just what the devil are ye after, then?' he demanded, the thickening of his brogue a sure sign that he was losing his temper. 'Faith, if it's a quarrel ye want ye might have chosen better cause. Lady, b'God! I wonder what society ye've moved in?'

'Now you add offensiveness to me to your other rudeness,' said Kinsman very softly. 'I think you must retract that.'

'Do ye though? Hell's bells, here's news! Well, ye can think till doomsday and be damned to you! Retract, is it? Go to the devil!'

Before the words were out of his mouth Kinsman's left hand cracked like a pistol shot on Penner's cheek. The Major staggered as much from amazement as from the blow. For an instant he stared open-mouthed, then he snatched at his sword-hilt.

'Ye mincing pimp!' he roared. 'By God I'll cut ye in two!' and his blade flashed in the sunlight.

Rackham had watched the beginnings of the quarrel from the poop ladder; now he bounded across the deck and threw himself between the two.

'For God's sake, Ned!' He seized the Major's sword-arm. 'What the devil are you doing?'

'Leave me loose, by God, and ye'll see!' shouted Penner. He wrenched free from Rackham's grip, but by now there were others between him and Kinsman. 'Stand away, damn you!' he shouted. 'Let me be at him!'

'Don't be a fool,' snapped Rackham. 'Are ye too blind to see he trapped you into it? Him and that bitch there? Look at her, man, if ye don't believe me.'

If Penner had obeyed he would have been reminded, perhaps, of the scene in her husband's house only a few nights ago, when the tigerish streak of cruelty in her nature was uppermost. She sat smiling with wicked pleasure, but Penner was too enraged to think of anything but his smarting face and Kinsman.

'Will ye fight then, ye lousy coward?' he shouted. 'Ye wear a sword and call yourself a soldier! Will ye prove it?'

'Have done,' said Rackham. 'He'll prove nothing, nor will you. There'll be no blood-letting over this.'

This was greeted with a roar of protest from the hands and a string of oaths from Penner. In vain Rackham tried to reason with him; it was like talking to a stone wall. He managed to make the Major understand that he was being made the victim of a carefully engineered plot, but Penner's answer was only: 'Plot, is it? He'll plot no more when I'm done with him.'

Thereafter there was nothing Rackham could do. The pirates, bored with inactivity, insisted that the matter be settled according to sea law, and that the two fight at once. Penner asked nothing more, and Kinsman nodded agreement, so Rackham was forced to submit to the general demand.

'It's your own life,' he told Penner bitterly. 'If ye're fool enough to fling it away because some poxy dancing-master clouts your ear that's your affair. But ye're daft, man, they're making sport of you.'

'Likely I'll make sport of them,' was the grim reply. Penner's fury was beginning to subside, but his eyes still shone with anger. 'Perhaps it won't be my life that's flung away, neither.'

At the mouth of the creek in which the *Kingston* lay a long sand-spit ran out towards the open sea. It was perhaps seventy yards long by ten wide, and since Mosquito Bank offered no other suitable place for a trial at arms Rackham ordered out the boats to carry the contestants and spectators across to it.

Gleefully the pirates hurried to work, eager for the spectacle, while Rackham looked on gloomily. Obviously Anne Bonney or Kinsman or Bull – perhaps all three of them – wanted Penner out of the way. Bull he could understand, for with Penner gone Rackham would be unable to exert any control over the crew, and Bull might be elected to fill his shoes, but what Kinsman's interest could be was beyond him. Of Anne Bonney he was prepared to believe anything; presumably she was simply using Kinsman as a tool.

And a remarkably useful one he looked, Rackham admitted, when a few minutes later he stood in the fine loose sand of the spit watching the two men prepare for the combat. Around the spit itself, some of them standing knee-deep in the shallows, the crew were laughing and shouting as they wagered on the outcome or called advice. The *Kingston* had been left deserted save for the wounded; there was no need for a watch, and no one was ready to forgo the unexpected entertainment.

Rackham's heart sank as he watched Kinsman remove his coat and roll up his shirt sleeves. He had divested himself of his boots and stockings and rolled up his breeches to give his feet freedom on the loose footing the sand-spit afforded, and now he bound back his long hair with a strip of linen. Lean and vigorous, he looked a formidable opponent even for the best: compared with Penner he was the very picture of a swordsman.

The chatter and laughter died away as the two men faced each other in the middle of the sand-spit. Kinsman came on

182

guard in a low crouch much favoured by those who delight in spectacular sword-play, and the sight sent Rackham's spirits soaring, for by adopting that stance Kinsman was sacrificing precious inches of his greater reach. Penner, for all his corpulence, fell easily into the academic guard, presenting his right shoulder to his antagonist. For a moment they stood, the long slim blades glittering between them, the lean, rangy captain and the solid major, eyeing each other and waiting.

Steel slithered on steel as Kinsman led the attack, sending up little sprays of sand about his feet. His blade leaped in and out, feeling and probing, but everywhere it was met by a guard which turned it with the minimum movement of the Major's wrist.

For a full two minutes Kinsman's onslaught continued, and he succeeded in gaining a yard or so of ground, but Penner continued strictly on the defensive, husbanding his strength until his opponent should tire. The Major could feel the steel-spring toughness of the wrist behind the other's rapier, and he had every respect for a speed of footwork which showed no signs of flagging.

Suddenly Kinsman fell back, his point in the high lines, and his body for a second unguarded. It was an open invitation to Penner to lunge, but the Major was too old to be led into the trap, neatly timed though it was. He made as though to launch his point into the opening provided, but the thrust was no more than a feint. He was still perfectly balanced and ready for Kinsman's swift side-step and attack from the flank which should have found him extended. As it was he caught the other's point on the foible of his blade, turned it with ease, and lunged full at Kinsman's unguarded breast.

Speed and luck alone saved the captain. He pivoted like lightning, but even so he must have been killed if he had not lost his footing and slipped beneath the Major's blade. As it was, the point caught him on the left ribs, gashing him to the shoulder, but he recovered with one hand on the ground and leaped back before the Major could press home his advantage.

They faced each other across the bank, Kinsman pale from the shock of the wound which was staining his torn shirt, his left arm covered to the elbow with sand clinging to his sweating skin. Penner, his teeth showing, moved to attack with all his speed, crowding Kinsman back to the water's edge, calling on every hard-won trick of sword-play to end the fight while he had his man shaken.

Kinsman's shirt was red and wet from neck to waist down the left side, sweat flew from his face with every movement as the Major drove in for the kill. Kinsman parried a low thrust by the merest fraction, his guard was open, and Penner struck again. The two figures were caught for a moment as though in a tableau – Penner at full stretch, his whole body behind the thrust: Kinsman erect and poised almost as though offering himself as a target. And then somehow the Major's point was driving through empty air inches past his opponent's hip, and Kinsman, without haste, ran him through the body.

A sudden shout from the pirates died into a hush as Penner staggered away, his hands clasped to his stomach. He swayed, then the strength left his limbs, and he collapsed face down in the sand. He tried to pull himself to his knees, rolled over on to his back, and lay still.

One of the men behind Rackham spoke, his voice loud in the silence. 'He's paid his shot. Ten you owe me, Carty.'

Rackham ran to the fallen man, but as he knelt at Penner's side he could see the Major was past help. His face was dead white and drawn, and his teeth chattered as though he were in a fit.

Rackham slipped his hand beneath the Major's head and raised it. The dying man opened his eyes: for a few seconds his stare was that of a blind man, then it cleared. His mouth worked as he tried to speak, and a trickle of blood ran out on to his chin.

'Damn you,' he said huskily, 'Damn you and rot you, Calico. You – you brought . . .'

A spasm shook his body, his eyes closed again, and his cropped head fell back on to the sand. The breaths hissed softly between his lips, growing weaker and weaker.

'An' I thought the old bastard would spit him like a beetle,' grumbled a voice. 'D'ye see it? He had him trussed an' open; an' then – whist!'

'That long 'un's smart,' said another, in the complacent tone of a winner. 'Told ye he would last longer. He's paid my drink for a day or two, anyways.'

'Rot 'im,' said the grumbling voice again. ''Ere, Penner, everyone else has had summat out o' me, you can too.'

Someone laughed, and a coin was flipped across in front of Rackham. It tinkled on the sword that had fallen from the Major's hand, but he did not hear it.

Rackham stood up. A few yards away Kinsman was sitting in the sand, stripped to the waist, sponging his wound with linen torn from his shirt and dipped in water. Anne Bonney was kneeling at his side chattering her congratulations, while around them stood a little group of interested observers, the more sycophantic loud in their praise of the captain's sword-play.

One of them noticed Rackham watching them, and fell silent. The others followed suit, and Anne Bonney looked round. She threw back her head at the sight of Rackham, and there was no attempt to conceal the triumph in her face. Kinsman glanced round, stared briefly at Rackham, and returned to his wound again.

The sudden silence of the group was infectious. It spread to the others on the bank, and Rackham knew that they were watching him, wondering, knowing that with the death of the man who now lay staring up at the sky a sudden change had been wrought.

He looked about him at the silent faces, and picked out one in the group beside Kinsman.

'You, Malloy,' he said. 'Get spades and see him buried.'

But Malloy, dullard though he was, sensed the change, and he hesitated. He looked at Bull, and Bull spoke pat as though on cue.

'There's no call to bury him. The sea's handy, eh? An' he'll know no different whether he goes in sand or water.' He grinned defiantly at Rackham.

So it's come already, thought Rackham. He had no doubt what the issue would be, but he owed it to Penner to stick to his guns.

'I said "Bury him!" I don't give orders twice, Davie.'

Bull spat in the sand and laughed. 'An' who the hell are you to be givin' orders at all, eh? Happen we've had enough of your orders, like.' He looked about him, inviting support. 'Happen the company want a change. Them as doesn't can bury your pal if they feel like it. For me, he can lay there an' rot.'

It came to Rackham suddenly that the one way out was to kill Bull where he stood, and instinctively his hand dropped to his waist. Bull saw the movement and whipped out his own knife, but at that moment Kinsman, who had never looked up during these exchanges, raised his head.

'Wait.'

Bull stopped in mid-stride.

'Put up your knife.'

Reluctantly, Bull obeyed, and Kinsman climbed slowly to his feet, his hand holding the pad of linen against his chest. He looked at Rackham, glanced at Penner's body, and beckoned two of the pirates who stood nearest.

'Bury him.' His voice was hoarse and his face tired, but his authority allowed of no dispute. 'The rest of you go back aboard.'

He turned away, and with Anne Bonney at his side walked slowly to where the boats were beached. Watching them, Rackham knew that whether they held a council or not; whether Bennett came in the next hour or never came at all, the command had already changed hands.

15. ON THE ACCOUNT

Yet next morning, when a new commander was elected, it was not Kinsman, who would certainly have received an enthusiastic vote had he not refused to allow his name to go forward.

'I'm no sailor, thank God,' he replied to the remonstrances of Anne Bonney, who had seen in his election her best hope for the immediate future. 'There are more ways than one to command. Let them choose our lusty Yorkshireman; I've no doubt they can persuade him.'

This was in reference to Bull, the only other contestant for the command, and since he possessed at least the characteristics of bravery and a vigorous personality, the Yorkshireman was presently ascending to the command of a ship for the first time in his deplorable life while Rackham, now an ordinary member of the crew, stood in the waist and listened to the new captain submitting his plans.

Bull took the poop in an old blue broadcloth coat which, while it was far too small for him, had the virtue of covering his soiled shirt and breeches to the extent of his elbows and thighs, and served to emphasise his bulk, which was the most commanding thing about him. The addition of a broad-brimmed castor and two incongruously dainty ribbons in his beard, in imitation of the late Captain Teach, completed a striking and distasteful costume.

There was nothing frivolous about his address, however. They were finished, he told them, with harebrained chases after imaginary argosies; henceforth the *Kingston* would engage only on sound, practical enterprises which should show handsome profits with the minimum risk. To this end he proposed a cruise along the Cuban coast to the eastward in which they would despoil the coastal villages and such small shipping as plied those waters. He urged the ease with which they should come by loot, food, equipment, and women. He dwelt on this last at some length, knowing that it was a sure card – surer in this case by reason of the unattainable woman on board, whose presence had been making Bull himself increasingly restive. Finally, when they had stripped the coast towards the Windward Passage, they would take to the open sea on the account proper.

On this he concluded, standing puffed out on the poop deck, awaiting their agreement.

Rackham, who had listened with growing contempt, was roused from his apathy to the extent of protest. He pointed out that the Windward Passage was the one place in the Caribbean where it would be most inadvisable for the *Kingston* to venture, since it would certainly be under patrol by King's ships, particularly now when there would be a hue and cry for the despoilers of the *Star*. There was a muttered agreement from some of the older hands, and Bull glared down from the poop.

But for the fact that he needed Rackham as quartermaster,

Bull would have felt inclined to deal with him briefly and bloodily on the spot. He scented here an attempt to undermine his new-found authority. Curtly he answered that they need not necessarily sail as far as the passage, but merely in that direction.

'Why sail east at all?' was Rackham's reply. 'Any other course should be less dangerous. And will the returns justify it?'

Here was a direct challenge on the most important point of all, and Bull knew it. In fact he was none too confident that the coast villages would prove fruitful; the fact that they would be easy of conquest was what had recommended them to him. But he dared not admit it, or there would have been an end to his command before it had begun.

He spat out an oath. 'If I though there was no profit d'ye think I'd make the venture? I say there's dollars an' women in those villages a-plenty, for them as knows how to look. Them as doesn't can watch me.' And he gave an ugly laugh. 'Anyway, there'll be better pickin's than we've seen up to now, an' ye can lay to that. As to the risk, I've sailed these waters as long as you, an' I think the risk's none so great. So you, or any other that's too lily-livered, can take yourselves out on the bank yonder an' stay there to rot.'

He emphasised his words with a slap of his horny hand on the rail and glared round, inviting contradiction.

There was none, and Rackham turned away. What, after all, did it matter? He could not doubt that Bull would pay the price of folly sooner or later, and the Cuban coast would do as well as any other.

Bull, satisfied at having answered opposition with what he supposed was overpowering logic, saw no reason for further delay. Forthwith he gave orders that the *Kingston* should sail, and shortly after noon the brig was warped slowly from the inlet. By this time, however, the captain had had time for reflection, and he found lurking in his mind a suspicion that perhaps Rackham's warnings were not entirely unjustified. This served to kindle his fury again, and he stood scowling on the poop as the rhythmic heave of the oarsmen in the ship's boats drew the *Kingston* out of her green, tunnel-like haven into the limpid waters of the lagoon.

Danger he was prepared to face, for there was no room for cowardice among Captain Bull's varied vices, but the thought of King's ships was an uncomfortable one; thus it was that as the *Kingston* slid away from the bank before a light afternoon breeze, he alone aboard felt no uplift in spirits; rather he regretted having lost the comparative safety of their hiding place. His imagination was stimulated by contemplation of what might lie ahead, even when reason told him that there were long miles of empty sea between him and the waters patrolled by the guardians of His Britannic Majesty's colonies of the west.

As he stood brooding, Bull's eye fell on Rackham, who sat precariously perched on the port rail immersed in calculation of the brig's speed by timing against his own pulse beat the progress of a billet of wood dropped by an assistant in the bows. The sight of the author of his forebodings engaged on a task beyond his own understanding was a double irritation to Bull. He strode across the deck and abruptly demanded the other's attention.

Absorbed, Rackham completed his counting before sliding off the rail. Bull eyed him balefully.

'Have ye done, then? Never mind me, like. Ah's only the bloody captain.'

Rackham looked at him without emotion. 'What's your will?'

'At my service, eh? Much obliged.' Bull thrust his thumbs into his belt and straddled his feet, pondering the man in front of him.

'Ah's been thinkin' of what ye said afore about King's ships,' he said at length. 'Haply there's summat ye forgot – summat makes hash o' your argument.'

'And that is?'

'Ye talked of King's ships as though they was God Almighty's Own. If thee's scared of 'em, like, I don't wonder. Some'll scare at their own shadows. Not me, though. Mebbe Ah's got a longer memory than thee.'

'And what is it you remember?'

Bull laughed. 'Just a week since we took a King's ship board and board. We took her for the loss o' three men – less the wounded, o' course. Well, what's happened once can happen again, can't it? Mebbe ye hadn't thought o' that. Or mebbe—' his face twisted into an unpleasant grin – 'mebbe ye was ready to cry down my plans because Ah's in your room as captain. Eh? Mebbe your tale o' King's ships is all bloody wind to scare hands?'

Rackham looked at him with contempt. 'If ye choose to think that you're as big a simpleton as I've always thought you.'

'Simpleton, eh? By God, Ah'll—'

'You prove it when you talk of taking the *Star*. Is there no difference, then, between taking a ship by trickery, catching her unawares, and engaging with the kind of vessel we'll find down the Windward Passage waters?' He laughed. 'Ye'll not surprise them. Because they'll be looking for you. What's more they'll be Jamaica Squadron vessels of seventy,

192

eighty guns, carrying crews of ten-year service and more. Where d'ye think you'll go against them with your thirty lousy guns and Kemp at sea with Bennett, God knows where?'

Bull was stunned into silence, but not for long.

'That's what thoo says,' he shouted. 'An' who says thoo knows an' no one else? Eh? Happen Ah can fight a ship as well as Kemp, or thee, or any poxy navy skipper! D'ye doubt it?'

Rackham checked a blistering retort. 'If ye don't doubt it yourself, what matter? You can fight the ship, you say. Fight her, then; fight the whole West Indies fleet. You're the captain. But unless ye want to drive your head into a noose you'll be warned in time. Raid the coast, since ye can fly no higher, but put about while we're still far short of the passage. That way we might still be safe.'

Bull consigned his warning to hell and beyond. 'You stick to your lousy charts an' canvas!' he bawled. 'You're quarter-master, understand? You sail where you're bid. An' it's the captain as does the bidding.'

On which authoritative note he stamped away, more determined than ever to carry out his plans in despite of the dangers, real or imaginary, which lay somewhere to the east beyond the cobalt waters which slipped rapidly away beneath the *Kingston*'s keel.

193

16. THE KING'S COLOURS

It was partly a perverse determination to ignore Rackham's warnings that drove Bull to venture farther eastward along the Cuban coast than he would otherwise have dared to go: that and the fact that the two settlements which the *Kingston* raided in the first week of her voyage were poor fishing villages hardly worth the looting. It was not an auspicious beginning, and Bull found himself faced with the choice of holding to his course in the hope that something better would turn up, or of yielding to Rackham's cautions and turning back.

Supposing that the latter would involve loss of face, Bull insisted on continuing eastward, and this in spite of an additional hazard which Rackham had pointed out as early as the second day of their cruise. This was that the *Kingston*'s sailing was perceptibly laboured, and that she stood in need of careening. Bull was appalled at the suggestion.

'Careen, d'ye say? On this coast? I'd as soon careen in Lake Maracaibo.'

Rackham had suggested that the coast thus far was not too

dangerous, and that it would be well to have the *Kingston* beached and scraped before venturing in more perilous waters. But Bull, conceiving that Rackham was intent only on undermining his authority, had flatly refused. The *Kingston* had been nimble enough to catch the *Star*, therefore she was well enough for the present, and Bull had no intention of wasting time in careening because of a white-livered quartermaster.

He said so loudly, and received the unexpected support of Kinsman, who privately expressed his confidence in the captain's judgement. This flattered Bull, and served also to subdue the resentment he had felt at Kinsman's natural gravitation to the poop during the voyage. Bull had sensed the mastery of the man and grudged it: there were many ways in which he found Kinsman inconvenient, not least in the matter of Anne Bonney. In fact, Bull had come to the conclusion that sooner or later Kinsman must go, and if afterwards Mistress Bonney should stand in need of consolation she would receive it, whether she wanted it or not.

In the meantime he welcomed Kinsman's support in the matter of careening, and when Rackham made his final appeal on the seventh day of the voyage, Bull, with Kinsman and Anne Bonney behind him on the poop, rejected it with derision. And this although Rackham's urgings were seconded by one of the most experienced seamen on board, a weather-beaten filibuster named Carty, now acting gunner in place of the absent Kemp. It was Carty who, pointing ahead along the sunlit, rock-bound coast to the distant outline of Cape Lucrecia, made the last plea for reason.

'That point's no more'n thirty leagues from the passage. God help us if we have to try to weather it again wi' our bottom foul as it is an' a King's ship behind us. Put about, cap'n, while there's still time, like Johnny says.'

'Johnny says!' Bull exploded. 'An' is all that Johnny says gospel?' He proceeded to demonstrate that it was not, citing for instance Rackham's warning of the probable danger of King's vessels. There had been no word at the raided villages of British ships; that was enough for Bull. With threatening emphasis he announced that they would round Cape Lucrecia immediately and seek what plunder they could in Nipe Bay. Against this Rackham was powerless, and he left the poop with Bull's guffaw in his ears.

They rounded Cape Lucrecia that day and put into a little bay barely a hundred miles from the Windward Passage. Here Bull proposed to lie overnight while a hunting party went ashore to procure fresh meat. To Rackham this was the ultimate folly, since they could take supplies from the next village raided, but he knew that argument with Bull was useless. He said nothing, and a hunting party of some thirty – about a third of the ship's company – went ashore. They were to remain there throughout the night and the next morning, returning at noon with their game.

All that evening Rackham was in a fret of impatience. He walked the deck, turning every few minutes to scan the eastern horizon, while the short twilight came and went and the velvet Caribbean night fell over the lagoon and the brig riding at anchor. But even the dark, which brought a great peace over the rest of the ship, the sixty men and one woman who drowsed or talked in the starlight, could not allay the fear that was growing in him as the hours limped past. Without consulting Bull he had sent a man to the mast-head – a precaution which Bull had deemed unnecessary – and when it became too dark to see beyond a few yards from the ship's side Rackham kept glancing aloft through the spider's web of rigging as though to will his sentinel to vigilance.

A little after midnight he settled down with his back to the rail and fell into a doze from which he was awakened by a hand on his shoulder which brought him to his feet with his tongue tingling. It was his sentry reporting that he had seen a light along the coast to the eastward, but whether at sea or on shore he could not be sure. It had only been a twinkling far off, coming and going so swiftly that it was only by chance he had seen it at all.

Rackham heard him out and sent him back to the mast-head. He had no doubt that what the look-out had seen had been the light of a ship – he had no real justification for thinking this other than his own intuition – and any ship, Spanish or British, was a potential enemy. And the *Kingston*, quite apart from being badly barnacled, was under-manned and anchored close to shore in as poor a position for defence as possible.

From the stern cabin came the sound of a hoarse voice singing to the accompaniment of pannikins beaten on the table, and as it reached the end of the verse other voices joined it in discordant chorus. Late as it was the captain of the Kingston, finding the night warm and sleep difficult, had assembled his cronies for a carouse. So much the better, thought Rackham; at least he would not be to waken.

He mounted the poop and descended the ladder into the tiny well leading to the cabin. The door was ajar and within Bull was seated with half a dozen of his companions about the table. The great lamp was reeking above them, and bottles and pannikins littered the board, while the cabin itself was filled with wraiths of tobacco smoke.

The laughter died on Bull's lips as Rackham appeared in the doorway.

'An' what the hell d'you want?' His speech was only partly

slurred as yet. 'Damn me, if tha's come to bid me careen again Ah'll keel-haul thee an' let thee scrape the bloody barnacles off as ye go.'

When the sycophantic laughter which greeted this biting wit had subsided Rackham told him of the light that had been seen to the eastward, and it was noticeable that only Carty gave the least sign of alarm. Bull scowled.

'An' what then? He's seen a light, or thinks he has. D'ye want me to go aloft an' make sure for him?'

'You might do worse,' said Rackham bluntly. 'If I was you I'd have a boat away now to bring back the hunting party and then stand out of this bay until we see whether or not it's a ship that's coming up the coast.'

Bull stared in incredulous anger. 'Bring 'em back for a bloody light? An' what o' the fresh meat they was sent for? Are we to go hungry because thoo's seen a poxy firefly?'

'Or a ship.'

'Ship be damned. Who says it's a ship?'

'I say it might be. And while there's the chance . . .'

'Thoo says a hell of a lot more than Ah like to hear,' shouted Bull. He reared up in sudden rage. 'This week back ye've been whinin' after me wi' your coward's talk o' King's ships and barnacled keels an' the rest of it. Since we left Mosquito Bank, by God! An' now it's a light ye've seen – or say ye've seen. Well, what of it, then? Are we to turn tail for that?'

'I don't ask ye to turn tail. I'm telling you that if it is a ship, as I think, we'll be in no case here to fight, fly, or do aught but swim for it, thanks to you.'

Bull's jaw dropped in sheer amazement. 'To me? Thanks to me, d'ye say? Why, ye lousy, cuckoldy maggot, ye . . .' He loosed a flood of foul abuse, lunging over the table in his rage.

'Ye've ignored every warning I've given you', Rackham swept on. 'Ye would cruise this coast, ye wouldn't careen, and now ye won't heed danger that a child could see.'

With a roar of fury Bull snatched at the knife in his belt, and Carty sprang to his feet and grabbed the captain's wrist. For a moment they strove, Bull bawling to be released, and then a precise metallic voice cut through the din and stilled it.

'And what is this danger, if you please, that a child could see?'

The two men wrestling at the table stopped abruptly. Rackham swung round. Captain Kinsman stood in the doorway, his cold eyes surveying them. Behind him the door of the tiny side berth which Anne Bonney occupied was ajar: he had stepped from it unheard in the confusion.

He repeated his question, looking from Rackham to Bull, who stood knife in hand, glaring like a schoolboy caught in mischief.

It was Rackham who answered. It occurred to him that Kinsman at least was no fool, and if he could be convinced of the danger threatening the *Kingston* Bull might be forced to look to their safety

Kinsman's face remained expressionless as he listened. 'So. A ship, you think?' His voice rose slightly. 'A King's ship, perhaps?'

'Perhaps.' Rackham looked at him curiously. 'Whatever she may be she's an enemy of ours.'

Kinsman nodded and looked across the table. 'And what does Captain Bull propose?'

Before that quiet authority Bull found himself answering without conscious intent.

'Bah, what is it, when all's said? A light, maybe.' He

shrugged impatiently. 'Whatever it is can wait till morning.' He tossed his knife on to the table and feigned a yawn. 'Them as likes can stay up an' watch for it,' he added, with a black look at Rackham.

Kinsman turned back to Rackham. 'That ends the matter, then.' He met the quartermaster's eyes for a second before stepping aside as though to let him pass first through the door. Plainly he intended that there should be no further argument, and Rackham was on the point of protesting, but a moment's thought convinced him that it was useless. Kinsman was intelligent, and if what he had heard did not convince him nothing else would. Yet there was something odd about his manner, as though he wished to have Rackham out of the cabin and harm's way. With another curious look Rackham walked past him and went on deck, wondering.

Dawn came in glorious sunlight which revealed the blue expanse of empty sea beyond the headlands of the little bay. In the brightness of the morning, with the rollers gently lapping the narrow stretch of silver beach at the foot of the cliffs, and the seabirds wheeling and crying above the *Kingston*'s masts, the fears of the night seemed far away, and Rackham was prepared to believe that his alarm had been unfounded. But he still viewed their position with uneasiness, for at the least it would be several hours before the hunting party was back aboard.

A careful commander would have found employment for the *Kingston*'s crew, but Bull, when approached by several of the pirates who found the glitter of the beach inviting, granted a request that the remaining two boats be taken ashore so that their crews could stretch their legs and search for fruit in the thickets. This accounted for another thirty of the company, leaving thirty aboard the brig, but Rackham reflected bitterly that it would make little odds how many manned the ship if an emergency arose. He watched the boats pull towards shore, the oarsmen singing as they bent to their task, and then, when the boats were beached, playing like children in the shallows.

An hour passed and the sun climbed slowly above the headland. Aboard the *Kingston* it was easier to sit in the shade than stand at the rail, and easier to drowse in silence than talk to one's neighbour. Anne Bonney lay in the shadow of her awning, blinking sleepily in the heat like a lizard, watching Kinsman polish the blade of the great rapier which lay across his knees.

In the shade of the forecastle Carty sat with his back to the bulkhead, idly tossing up and catching his clasp-knife, now with his left hand, now with his right. Beside him Malloy chewed placidly on a piece of tobacco leaf, his shirt hanging open exposing his skinny brown chest. He began to whistle softly through his teeth, a reedy, piping sound, and Carty stopped his juggling.

'Whistlin' for a wind? I know a better way than that.' He spat on his knife blade, and with a quick thrust of his forearm sent it spinning away. It glittered through the air and thudded into the mast.

Malloy shook his head. 'Knowed that trick afore you was born. Never brought a wind yet. I seen it tried a hundred times.' He got to his feet with an effort and shuffled across the deck. 'I mind it aboard the old *Duke*, when I sailed with Avery. Precious luck it brought him.' He grasped the knife and jerked it out of the wood, and as he did so he happened to glance towards the entrance to the bay. His jaw dropped open in amazement, and for a second he stood speechless, pointing with the knife out to sea.

'Holy Mary!' he yelled. 'A ship! A King's ship!'

Round the eastern headland, her red hull gleaming beneath a mountain of snowy canvas, a great ship came gliding into view, and before the astonished and horrified eyes of those on the *Kingston*, veered steadily in towards the bay. The shrill of a bosun's pipe came across the water as her huge foresail snapped and filled, and the tiny figures of men scrambled into her rigging to shorten sail. The vessel seemed to hesitate for a brief moment, then she came round and was standing in towards them over the blue water of the lagoon.

A great cry of panic and dismay rose from the *Kingston*'s decks. One moment the brig had been drowsing peacefully in the calm, the next she was a madhouse of blindly scattering men, thrusting and tumbling over each other as though by flying below decks they could escape the nemesis advancing across the bay.

Within seconds the cry was being taken up ashore where many of the pirates were already taking to the woods. Some, bolder or more intelligent than their companions, tried to run out one of the boats to reach the *Kingston*, but they were careless in their haste and the boat foundered in the surf only a few yards from the beach.

From the poop of the *Kingston* Bull stared incredulously at the man-of-war with the red, white and blue fluttering at her main-truck. It seemed to him impossible that such a thing could be, and it was several seconds before complete realisation came home to him. He glared wildly round as Rackham came bounding up the poop ladder to his side.

'It's the King's colours!' he roared. 'We's took – trapped!' He loosed a volley of curses and shook his fist at the oncoming ship. Rackham cut him abruptly short. 'Ye can save your breath for the gibbet where you'll need it shortly,' he snapped, and then he delivered the stinging reproach that was boiling up in him.

'No King's ships, eh? A safe coast and a jolly cruise and a bellyful of rum and dollars? No danger at all. "Them that like can stay and watch for it," you said. Well, by God, you're watching now!'

Bull was too distracted for resentment. There was something very near to terror in his eyes as he turned in desperation to Rackham. 'What's to be done?' he croaked, and Rackham answered him with a savage laugh.

'You ask me what's to be done? You dare? Am I the captain? No, no, Davie, not I. Ye've peacocked it on this ship long enough, my lad, and thrust your fool head in a noose in spite of all my warnings. Pull it out as best ye can.'

'Blast you!' shouted Bull. 'It's your neck as well as mine! God's teeth, we'll be under her guns while you stand mocking!' He cast another frenzied look towards the man-of-war and his tone changed abruptly. It became almost pleading.

'Calico, man, you're a sailing-master; could we not slip by, mebbe? Look, man, she's none so nimble herself, wi' all that weight! We might be away before she's gone about!' He seized the quartermaster's arm, but Rackham shook him off and pointed to the advancing ship.

'There's two decks of guns there to say why you can't slip past her,' he said. 'Even if you could she'd overhaul us inside a couple of miles with our keel foul as it is.'

'Hell! We can't wait here doin' nowt!' shouted Bull. 'Carty! Cut yon bloody cable afore she runs us down. Malloy!' He lurched to the rail and stilled the panic of the crew by sheer lung-power. 'Get 'em into the shrouds! Tacks an' braces! Bustle damn you, or we're done!'

His face was terrible to see as he turned on Rackham. 'We'll clear this bay or feel its bottom before this hour's out!'

Rackham judged the distance between the *Kingston* and the great red vessel creeping over the water under shortened sail. There might just be time to get the *Kingston* under way before they found themselves at the mercy of the warship's guns, but even so those guns must surely blow them out of the water before they could hope to slip past towards the open sea. Still, there was a chance – a tiny, ridiculously slender chance – that the *Kingston* would escape without injury from the other's broadside and at the same time deal her a crippling blow. A lucky shot to a magazine or the rudder chains – little ships had beaten big ones before now.

Bull strode up and down, roaring like a madman, while the crew of the *Kingston* worked with the energy of despair. With the gentle land breeze in her favour she was turned in a matter of minutes from a floating, near inanimate hulk into a living ship; a laboured, unhandy ship, but able to give battle even so.

As she came round a faint wail came over the water from the pirates abandoned ashore. To them, with the cliffs at their backs, and beyond that a hostile land, the deck of the *Kingston* was preferable, even though it must soon be swept with shot and running with blood.

Smoke sprouted from a bow gun aboard the King's ship, followed almost instantly by the thud of the report, and a round-shot sent a spout of water flying up a hundred yards beyond the *Kingston*'s bows – the signal to heave to. Bull yelled a curse and shook his fist.

'Burn your powder, you bastards!' he shouted. 'We'll drown afore we swing!' Brave at the best of times, he was exhibiting now the courage of the trapped animal, and some of it spread to his crew. There was a ragged cheer as the *Kingston* glided slowly forward, her sails filling, Rackham holding her head for the centre of the entrance to the bay.

The distance between the two ships began to close rapidly. Down in the waist Carty was frantically mustering his gun crews: if he was lucky he might be able to get in three shots, Rackham calculated. Three shots to balance the ponderous weight of metal that would sweep the *Kingston*'s decks, tearing her hull and shattering her upper works, turning her from a ship into a riddled, drifting mass of timber with the dead strewn on her deck.

'Stand by!' It was Bull bawling beside him, and Rackham and the pirate who was with him at the wheel braced themselves. There was an explosion from the bows of the King's ship and a shot rushed overhead and ripped through the mainsail. Another followed, and there was a jarring crash of splintering timbers and a scream from the waist.

'Now!' snapped Rackham, and the two men flung their combined weight on the wheel. The *Kingston* shuddered and came round, and as she did so there was the triple crash of gunfire and three sickening thuds against her hull, one after another like knocks on a door. Smoke welled up from the waist as Carty's guns gave answer – 'Too soon! Too soon!' a voice was shouting, and Rackham recognised it for that of Bull, stamping beside him.

He saw the red ship looming up on their larboard bow, and groaned aloud as the *Kingston* answered sluggishly to the wheel. There was nothing he could do as their opponent veered slowly round, presenting her huge flank with its double tier of black shining muzzles; he watched them with a kind of dull fascination, heedless of the yells and howls from the waist, Bull's storming beside him, or the acrid bite of the powder smoke in his eyes. This was the end.

The side of the King's ship seemd to burst into flame, and the *Kingston* staggered and lurched as the broadside smashed into her. Rackham was hurled from his feet and thrown against the rail, where he lay, half-stunned. Someone fell on him, and a second later he felt the hot stickiness of blood on his face. He struggled up, throwing the body aside, and saw it was the man who had held the wheel with him, but now he was dead, with his head battered to pulp. Rackham clung to the rail as another salvo boomed out with deafening violence and the *Kingston* heeled over again. She half-righted herself, drifting with her deck canting beneath his feet as he staggered blindly towards the ladder and looked down into the shambles of the waist.

It was as though a gigantic scythe had been swept over the *Kingston*'s deck. The foremast, struck by a round-shot, had come crashing down and hung outwards over the starboard side, caught in the mesh of its own gear. There were two great gaps in the port-side rail and the deck planking was ploughed and scarred with shot. One of the port guns had broken loose from its tackles and careered across the deck, smashing half-way through the opposite bulwark where it hung precariously over the water. There were men on the deck, too, some of them stirring or crawling, and others who lay grotesquely still. Several lay huddled round one of the guns, and he saw a stream of blood begin to trickle down across the tilting deck.

Bull was roaring behind him on the poop, and as though awakened by that stentorian voice the *Kingston* began to come to life again. Carty was on his feet in the waist, and perhaps half a dozen others. As Bull bellowed his commands they

206

started forward obediently, and then the *Kingston* lurched again. She was beginning to go down by the head, and the chorus of shrieks grew louder.

'Aft!' roared Bull. He was bleeding freely from a gash in his cheek, and there was more blood on the leg of his breeches, but he moved with the assurance of a whole man. He stood at the opposite ladder to Rackham, his broadsword naked in his hand, his face purple with the effort of making himself heard above the din.

The King's ship was going about only a cable's length away on their port quarter. Rackham, ironically enough, had accomplished his object: the *Kingston* now had an unhindered passage to the entrance of the bay, but she lay yawing and helpless, her hull a riddled hulk that must founder in half an hour or less.

Men were scrambling up the ladder, tearing at each other to reach the temporary security of the poop, heedless of the screams of the wounded abandoned in the waist. Rackham saw a red head on the deck below where Anne Bonney was picking her way carefully through the tangle of gear and timber, stepping gracefully as ever even in the carnage that surrounded her. Beyond her a man was hobbling across the deck on one foot, catching at any handhold he could reach, and Rackham recognised Ben, the leg of his breeches sodden with blood and his foot trailing behind him. He stumbled and fell, and Rackham started down the ladder to his assistance. As he reached the deck he came face to face with Anne Bonney.

Her face was deathly white and there was a look of terror in her eyes. He put out a hand to steady her, but she brushed him aside.

'Alan,' she asked, her voice trembling. 'Have you seen Alan?'

It took him a moment to realise that she meant Kinsman. He shook his head and she put up her hand to her mouth to check a sudden uncontrollable sob.

'Oh God,' she muttered. 'Where is he? He was with me by the gun, and then . . . then they fired on us and there was blood everywhere . . . and . . . and he was gone! He was gone!' Her voice rose in a shriek, and she covered her face with her hands and half-collapsed on Rackham's shoulder. He steadied her and guided her feet to the ladder.

'Up with you while there's still time,' he said. 'If he's alive he's up yonder with the others.' He released her and started out over the tilted deck to where Ben was trying to free his wounded leg from a tangle of cordage. Slipping and stumbling Rackham reached his side and knelt down, pulling out his knife to slash through the lines that were tangling his comrade's foot.

Ben looked up at him, his pain-drawn face breaking into a grin.

'Good for you, cap'n,' he said huskily. 'I reckoned I was gone wi' this game pin o' mine.'

Rackham cut away the cords and was slipping his arm round Ben's shoulders to help him rise when the uproar from the poop was redoubled. The King's ship was drawing along-side again.

Rackham looked aft to see the pirates who only a moment since had been fighting their way up the ladders coming down them again in headlong flight. Others had thrown themselves down behind the shelter of the bulwarks or any other cover they could find.

'Jesus, they ain't goin' to hammer us again, surely?' muttered Ben, his eyes wide as he watched the approach of the King's ship.

There was a crash of musketry from the poop, and Rackham saw Bull with a smoking piece in his hand. Before the sound of the shot had died away it was answered by the deep blast of a gun. A storm of langrel swept across the poop, knocking splinters from the rail and cutting almost in two a pirate at the ladder head, but by some miracle Bull was untouched. He hurled away his musket and snatched up his sword, yelling defiance at the oncoming ship.

There were armed men at her rail, and perched above them in the shrouds were musketmen who fired down into the *Kingston* as the distance narrowed between the two ships. A grappling iron soared over the water, lodging behind the *Kingston*'s rail; then came a second and a third. Bull leaped down the ladder and slashed one of them free, but two more followed, and the half-sinking *Kingston* was hauled towards the side of her great red opponent.

The *Kingston* was in no case to repel the boarders who dropped to her deck. Apart from Bull there was hardly a man aboard with any thought of resistance; they were a disordered rabble with no thought but to escape the murderous fire poured on them from the musketeers aloft, and the steel in the hands of the boarding party.

As the first navy men came over the rail Bull leaped to the attack, burying his broadsword in the body of a seaman even as the man's feet touched the deck. Before he could deliver another out he was borne back by the weight of numbers and stretched weaponless on the deck.

A voice aboard the King's ship shouted an order, and another volley of fire was poured over the heads of the boarding party at those survivors of the *Kingston* who were scurrying for safety. Another man went down, and before the volley could be repeated a voice screamed out above the noise.

209

'Quarter!'

The command to hold fire was shouted from the rail of the King's ship, and a young officer with the boarding party stepped forward ahead of his men, his drawn rapier in one hand and a pistol in the other. He looked round him about the ravaged deck and shouted, 'Do you surrender?'

Rackham nodded wearily and somewhere behind him a hysterical voice answered the officer. 'Aye, aye. Christ, aye! No more, no more!' It trailed off into a sob. It might have been the voice of the *Kingston*, beaten and broken. The young officer sheathed his sword and ordered his men forward into the doomed ship.

Rackham and Ben were dragged to their feet and held each between two burly sailors, and Rackham looked about him to see who else had survived. There was Bull, senseless on the deck, but still alive, and Carty with a broken arm that hung limply in its blood-sodden sleeve. Dobbins, the ship's boy, was weeping as he was kicked to his feet, and herded together at the stump of the foremast were Earl and Bourne, two of the jail-birds, with Malloy, crumpled up between them, his grey hair streaked with blood.

Somehow he was surprised to see Anne Bonney still alive, and near her Kinsman. So she had found him after all. Her face was so grimed that he would have been hard put to it to recognise her as a woman at all, in spite of her hair, which hung wildly disordered about her shoulders. The sailors evidently took her for a man, or else they were indiscriminate with evil-doers, for one of them pushed her roughly forward, sending her sprawling in the scuppers. Kinsman made as though to help her, but another sailor jostled him aside.

Bull, Dobbins, Earl, Bourne, Malloy, Carty, Anne Bonney, Kinsman, Ben, and himself. No, there was Fenwick, another dock-rat, being hauled out from under a mass of rigging where the foremast had gone overside. That made eleven – eleven out of thirty. Eleven of two hundred who had sailed from Providence.

'Mr Williams!' A voice rang out from the quarter-deck of the King's ship. 'Come away, Mr Williams, why d'you wait?'

The young officer looked up. 'If you please, Sir John, there are wounded men caught in the wreckage.' He spoke in an apologetic tone, as though he had put them there. 'It may take some time to free them.'

'How many of the villains have you?'

The side of the red ship towering above them was lined with men, and aft, at the gilded rail of the quarter-deck, stood a group of officers, foremost among them a slight gentleman in a magnificent suit of apricot taffeta. His face, pale among the bronzed skins about him, was refined and almost like a woman's. He held a snuff-box in one hand and tapped the lid impatiently.

'Eleven, Sir John,' said Williams.

'You don't say so? Then I think you have done well enough. You'll be swimming back to the ship if you wait much longer. Bring them aboard.'

Williams hesitated, and the *Kingston* lurched again with a clatter of broken timber sliding across her deck. The men aboard her had to cling for support.

'Come, come, now.' Sir John's voice was almost conversational. 'She'll sink, you know.'

Williams struggled to keep his balance. 'But the wounded men—' he began.

'Come aboard, Mr Williams,' came the order, and Williams hesitated no longer. The pirates were driven to the rail and forced to scramble up the red hull to the deck of the King's ship. The sailors followed them, Williams last of all, and even as he swung himself off the rail the *Kingston* shuddered and sank lower in the water.

On the broad open deck of the King's ship the pirates were pushed into an uneven line under guard of the seamen's muskets. Williams, who went in evident apprehension of his soft-spoken commander, supervised their marshalling with a great show of energy and one eye on the quarter-deck. When he saw a trickle of blood dripping from Carty's wounded arm to the spotless planking he rapped out an oath.

'Have that man's arm bound up,' he cried, adding in a lower tone, 'And clean that mess away. If Sir John sees it he'll go mad.' He strode along the rank, pushing the prisoners into line so that no irregularity of dressing should annoy the great man, exclaiming impatiently when Malloy, too weak from his wound to stand, tottered and sank to the deck.

'Blast him, pick him up,' he commanded. 'Here you,' he pointed to Bull, who had recovered his senses but was still dazed and was staring about him vacantly, 'help him up and hold him, d'you hear?'

A sailor prodded Bull with his musket butt, but at that moment Williams' attention was distracted by a scuffle at the end of the line. He wheeled round furiously, to see Anne Bonney attempting to wrench free from a sailor who was gripping her wrist. As she did so, swinging a fist against the side of his head, another seaman sprang forward to his mate's assistance.

'Fight would ye, ye bloody pirate,' he snarled and grabbed at her shoulder. He missed his hold and caught her shirt, and as she wriggled free there was a tearing sound and the garment came away in his hand. The sailor who had her wrist gave a yell of surprise and released her, his jaw dropping.

212

'Hell!' he shouted. 'A mort!'

Williams started towards them. 'What the devil—' he began, and stopped as he saw Anne Bonney stripped to the waist. 'My God!' he exclaimd, colouring with embarrassment.

One of the sailors, grinning broadly, reached out towards her, and Williams leaped as though he had been stung.

'Drop that!' he snapped. 'And you, woman, whoever the devil you are, cover yourself. You, you there, give her a coat or a shirt. A cloth or anything. Rot me!' A thought struck him. 'Who – what – are you one of these villains, woman? Or were you their prisoner, or what?'

Anne Bonney snatched the torn remnant of her shirt from the sailor and calmly arranged it over her shoulders and breasts. She nodded to the pop-eyed officer.

'You can look away now,' she said.

'Eh?' Williams was bewildered. 'But who—'

Ben, who was standing only with the support of Rackham's arm round his waist, raised his head.

'She's one of us, an' twice the man you'll ever be,' he growled, and had his face slapped by the petty officer.

'Have you done with them, Mr Williams, or shall I wait your convenience?' The elegant captain was descending the ladder, followed by his officers, and Williams jerked round, his face scarlet.

'I'm at your service, you know, Mr Williams,' the captain continued. He crossed the deck, glancing from one end of the line to the other and back again.

'Which of you is John Rackham, or is he with those ashore?' he asked.

Surprised, Rackham looked up. 'I am.'

Bright eyes considered him from the pale, effeminate face,

213

and then they passed on to Anne Bonney. 'And the woman, of course. Perhaps I should have warned you, Williams, that we might have a lady with us.' He turned his head as Kinsman stepped out at the end of the line, and Williams started forward, outraged. But before he could intervene Kinsman had caught the captain's attention.

'By your leave, sir. My name is Kinsman. I'm an officer of the King and an agent of Governor Rogers of New Providence.' He put out a hand to restrain Williams. 'I can prove what I say, Sir John, if you please.'

Williams stopped, staring in disbelief.

'You're a what?' he exclaimed. He stared at Kinsman's grimed face and torn clothing. 'You? Why –.'

'Mr Williams,' Sir John spoke as though to a small child. 'Would you be so obliging as to step aside? I thank you. You must learn to govern yourself, Mr Williams. You are too impetuous by far, a fault of which I am continually reminded every time I have the misfortune to partner you at play. What is claimed can easily be tested.' Williams fell back abashed, and the captain advanced across the deck towards Kinsman. 'Now, sir, this proof you spoke of.'

Kinsman stooped and took hold of the top of his boot with both hands. He tugged with all his force and the lining parted with a sharp tearing sound. From the tear he drew out a small flat packet of oilskin which he ripped open, revealing a folded paper which he handed to Sir John. The captain unfolded it, raised his eyebrows, and began to read.

It was a brief enough warrant: two lines to say that the bearer was the trusted servant of Government. It made no mention of the organisation which Woodes Rogers, patient and thorough, had built up for the security of privateers and merchantmen, so that no vessel sailed from Providence without a secret agent aboard. In ninety-nine cases out of a hundred they sailed unnecessarily, but here was the hundredth case, and the Governor's system had paid its dividend. Kinsman had not been able to prevent crime, but he had done his next duty, which was to help bring about the ruin of the criminals.

With a sudden animal growl Bull flung himself out of the line and flung himself at Kinsman, but a seaman thrust out his foot and Bull tripped sprawling on the deck. Before he could rise he was pinioned and dragged away by the bosun's mates, yelling threats until one of them cracked him hard across the head with a hand-spike, and he was silent. His fellow pirates stood silent, watching Kinsman and hating him, but making no move, while their guards hovered about them ready to quell any show of resistance.

Rackham was remembering and beginning to understand. He should have known that there was something wrong about Kinsman. Now everything became clear – why Kinsman had been so willing to encourage Bull in his folly. Rackham had been ready to put it down to ignorance of the sea, or to a desire on Kinsman's part to stand well with his commander. He knew better now.

He wondered, had Anne Bonney known, and glanced along the line towards her. He was shocked by what he saw. She stood motionless, her face pale, biting her lip and staring straight ahead at nothing, bewildered and miserable. If she had behaved as Bull had done, and flown at their betrayer like a wild-cat, he could have understood. That would have been like Anne Bonney. But the drawn, hopeless look in her face was something he felt he should not have seen, and he looked away.

Sir John had finished his reading, and Kinsman was

speaking. 'As you see, sir, the document bears my signature. You'll observe it is part covered by the Governor's seal, a precaution he took lest it be thought I had forged it.'

The captain nodded. 'Ingenious,' he murmured.

'I'll write my name again, and you can compare them,' offered Kinsman, but the captain waved the suggestion aside.

'I think that will not be necessary.' He looked sharply at Kinsman. 'You took a great risk, captain. It seems Governor Rogers has hard men in Providence. You shall tell me later how far we are indebted to you for the capture of these villains.' He turned to one of his officers. 'Conduct Captain Kinsman to a berth, James. See that he has all he needs.'

As Kinsman was led aft Sir John turned his attention again to the pirates. 'Mr Williams, these gentlemen shall be in your charge. Have them in irons – all except these three,' he indicated Malloy, Carty, and Ben. 'Their wounds must be dressed. Thereafter you will confine them unchained, apart from their fellows. As for the woman, have her confined alone with a trusty man to guard her. If,' he added resignedly, 'there is such a thing as a trusty man aboard. Perhaps you had better have two trusty men, and each can watch the other.'

'Aye, aye, sir,' said Williams.

'Very good, then.' He turned away. 'Mr Hamilton, I'm obliged to you and we shall make ready for sea.'

'The men ashore, Sir John,' ventured one of his officers, and the captain frowned.

'Ah, yes.' He walked to the rail and looked across the cobalt waters towards the cliffs. 'According to Bankier's information there must be close on sixty of the brutes. Do you know, Mr Hamilton, I think they are very well where they are? They'll go a-pirating no more, or I'm much mistaken.

216

The Spaniards will see to it. Besides, at the first sign of boats being lowered they will take to the woods like rabbits. I think we have done very well as it is.'

Williams watched him mount the ladder. 'Now then, sharp about it,' he snapped to the master-at-arms. 'These three to the surgeon's mates, the others below. Keep the woman apart; we'll deal with her in a moment.'

Anne Bonney was taken out of the line, and as the guards pushed him towards the hatchway Rackham saw that she was sobbing. The seaman who guarded her eyed her doubtfully, then muttered, 'Never fear, honey, they won't let you swing. Not a fine-looking lass like you.'

A voice behind Rackham spoke. 'She's goin'.' Rackham looked up and in the brief moment before he was jostled down into the ship he saw the *Kingston* for the last time. She was barely afloat less than a cable's length from the King's ship, the water gushing in over her rail, swirling among the wreckage of the deck. For a few seconds she was awash, with a tangle of broken spars, rigging and canvas forced up by the water, her broken foremast pointing up like a jagged finger. Then the water boiled above her, bubbling through the wreckage, and the *Kingston* was gone beneath the placid surface of the bay.

17. THE KING'S JUSTICE

The court-room at St Jago de la Vega, capital of the British island of Jamaica, was a mixture of the old world and the new; or rather of the old adapted to new conditions. At one end of the long, white-washed room was the bench, with its pulpits of oak and high-backed canopied chairs, and beneath it the massive table with its bewigged and black-gowned clerks and officials. There was the long box for the jury on one hand, and the stand for witnesses on the other, and in the well of the court the dock, a large pen fringed with the inevitable steel pikes.

All this was of the old world, and the huge fans which hung from the ceiling beams, swishing softly to and fro as they were twitched into motion by black slaves who squatted at the side of the room, the little black boys who stood at either side of the empty judge's chair with fly-switch and fronds, the latticed screens, the walls with their glaring white-wash – all these things were strangely at odds with the impedimenta of a court of law.

But the most vivid contrast was in the occupants of the public

218

benches assembled to witness the trial of the *Kingston* pirates. Down one side of the court behind the witness box ran a spacious gallery packed with spectators, and Rackham could guess before he even looked at them that they would be the exact counterparts of the audience who had watched in the Fort at New Providence when he and his fellows had received the Royal pardon – planters, merchants, officers of the garrison and navy, and their womenfolk. Jamaican society, in fact.

There they were, in their finery of plumes and silks and taffetas, with their affectations and their mannerisms, their wealth and – in some cases – their beauties ostentatiously displayed, their chatter and their laughter, a carefree, uninhibited multitude eager to enjoy the spectacle. They stared at the dirty little group of chained men and one woman in curiosity and amusement, discussing them freely and loudly, although every word was audible in the dock.

The talk of three in the front row of the gallery directly opposite Rackham caught his attention. There were two men and a woman – one of the men a magnificently dressed elderly rake, yellow of face and somewhat shrivelled, but with a wicked eye which he fastened from time to time on the blonde young woman who sat beside him. She might have been his grand-daughter except that she looked a little more worldly than a grand-daughter has any right to be. The other man was a typical planter, substantial and middle-aged.

'And they will hang them all?' the blonde girl was asking.

'Every last one, m'dear,' said the old rake. 'Higher than Haman, dammit, and they hanged him high enough, didn't they, Jerry?'

The planter frowned. 'No punishment can be too severe,' he said ponderously. 'There's every crime in the calendar in that dock. Hanging's too kind for 'em.'

'Quite so,' remarked the other. 'Robbery, murder, rape – begging those pretty little ears their pardon – and attack on a King's vessel, rot it, into the bargain. What more could a jury ask?'

'But it seems—,' the girl hesitated, '—it seems . . . so many at once . . . well, rather a—'

'A waste of good manhood, ye'd say?' The old rake guffawed. 'D'ye hear that, Jerry? Praise God there are no women on juries.' He dabbed his eyes with a handkerchief and leered at her. 'And what would you have done wi' them, eh? If we mustn't hang 'em, what then?'

She tossed her head. 'They could be sold as slaves, to work in the plantations, or some such tasks.'

'Some such tasks, d'ye say?' He winked at the planter. 'Ladies' maids, or footmen, perhaps. I don't doubt they'd leap at the opportunity, if ye follow me.' He chuckled and shook his head. 'But I think I'd sleep safer o' nights if I knew they were swinging in irons – and so would others I could mention.'

The planter scowled savagely. 'I'd have 'em flogged to death by inches.'

'Gallows-bait, gallows-bait,' nodded the old rake happily. 'Jerry is so right, my love. Bloody, desperate fellows. Why, this same Rackham, I'm told, once rifled the great Spanish silver fleet off Florida. 'Codso, he did. Took a fortune from the cursed Dons, rat me, from under their very noses. Oho, I warm at the very thought of it. But ye must see that such dangerous rogues are safer – far safer – hanged and out of harm's way.'

The girl was studying the prisoners with interest. 'Which one is Rackham.'

'Eh? Rackham?' The old rake peered at the dock. 'Stab

220

me, how should I know? One looks as bad as t'others. That big one, perhaps, with the fair beard.' He pointed towards Bull. 'What matter, anyway? Ye'll know soon enough. Plague on 'em.' He drew closer to her. 'Let me tell ye the story of Bill Noodle and the milkmaid. What, ye ha'nt heard it? Well, then—.'

Rackham felt hot rage mounting inside him as he listened. He who had never truly hated in his life was learning at last the hate that is fiercest of all – hate inspired by fear. He was a brave man, but he was mortally afraid of what they were going to do to him – the rope, the fire and the disembowelling knife had been in his mind all through that voyage when he had lain chained in the depths of the King's ship, and in the cell at Port Royal's Fort Charles where he had been confined alone because as the supposed leader of the *Kingston* pirates he was held to be doubly dangerous. He had been afraid, he was afraid now; but it was the kind of fear which when it reaches its peak is translated not into panic but into a dreadful anger. He hated these fine ladies and gentlemen, not because they might be guessing his fear and gloating over it, but because they were sitting at ease, watching idly, and he was chained and in rags and waiting to die.

He looked up at the gallery again and his gaze fell on a woman on one of the middle benches; a fleshy, over-painted female of middle age, still well-preserved enough to be accounted handsome, with dull eyes that were fixed steadily on a point beyond him. She was watching Bull, and Bull was eyeing her in return, swelling out his mighty chest, conscious of the imposing figure he cut with his great blond beard and magnificent physique.

Rackham could read the thoughts that were passing between them: Bull was lusting, even now, and the woman

221

up there, for all her expressionless eyes and mask-like features, was considering Bull as a lover. It was ghoulish and unnatural, and it sickened him on the woman's account rather than on Bull's, for Bull, after all, was little better than an animal and would remain so to the end.

Four knocks sounded, and the babble of conversation stopped in the court-room. A door was flung open behind the judge's bench and a small procession emerged headed by an official, wigged and gowned, who glanced about sharply to see that all was as it should be. He noted the prisoners and the scarlet-clad sentries on either side of the dock, nodded to an acquaintance in the gallery, and stood aside to admit the judge and his chaplain. As his lordship entered, the court rose with a swishing and rustling of gowns and dresses, standing until he had seated himself and his chaplain had ensconced himself on a stool at one side.

Chief Justice Peter Bernard, in his red robe and flowing wig, was an impressive figure. He was also slightly drunk, and everyone in the court knew it, except the prisoners. They watched him in fearful fascination, unconscious of the winks and nods being exchanged in the gallery, seeing only the personification of the King's justice which was shortly to provide for their sentence and execution.

They saw a florid, handsome man on the threshold of middle age and already inclining to portliness. The face framed by the full-bottomed wig was youthful despite the flush that denoted the drinker, with a mobile sensitive mouth and rather prominent grey eyes which were concealed by heavy lids as his lordship settled himself comfortably in his padded seat. He had breakfasted heavily on Malaga, to which he was addicted, and was not inclined to exert himself.

He seemed to be dozing in his chair, hardly stirring when

the jury filed in and were sworn, and rousing himself only briefly to nod agreement to a question from his clerk, a nervous little man who sat in front of his lordship's pulpit and had to stand on tip-toe to make himself visible to the judge. Then his lordship settled back again while the charge was read – a charge of piracy only, since the Crown was confident of convicting on that count and did not wish to waste the time of the court by pressing other charges of murder, robbery, arson, assault, and putting into fear. This was explained to the jury, who were given to understand that the accused would hang just as surely for piracy whether the other crimes were taken into account or not, and the jurors, wearing the expressions of gravity and bewilderment common to juries of every age and clime, nodded and were silent.

The clerk began to recite the names of the accused.

'John Rackham, hold up your right hand.'

There was a buzz of interest on the public benches. Rackham started involuntarily at the mention of his name, and slowly rasied his hand, the shortness of his manacles forcing him to lift his left hand breast-high at the same time.

'Are you guilty or not guilty?'

It would be easy to say guilty and get the whole hellish business over. He knew he was doomed, whatever he said, and there seemed no point in prolonging the farce. But there was another side to it, too. Even if he could not make a fight for his life, there might be others among the pirates who had hopes of winning acquittal – a ridiculous hope, in his view, but that would not stop some of the simpletons from entertaining it. A plea of guilty on his part would certainly damage their chances, and besides, why should he save the law the trouble of proving him a pirate? The bastards were paid for it, let them work.

'Not guilty.'

His plea was echoed by the others as their names were read, and the judge drowsed on, even through the titter that greeted Bull's growl of 'Not guilty, o' course,' accompanied by a broad smirk for the benefit of the spectators. Bull was determined to give them their money's worth.

The clerk came to the last name. 'Anne Bonney, hold up your right hand,' he intoned, and the judge opened his eyes.

'Are you guilty or not guilty?'

Chief Justice Bernard leaned forward and addressed the clerk. 'Have the prisoner stand forward, Mr Prentice.' It was a voice completely at variance with his appearance; a sharp, incisive voice that made the little clerk leap as though he had been stung.

'Come forward, Anne Bonney,' he cried. 'Let her past, you two. There, now, answer the court: are you guilty or not guilty?'

She hesitated, and the clerk supposed that she was dismayed at having been singled out and thrust to the front of the dock with the eyes of the court upon her. In this he was quite wrong. Anne Bonney had never known cause to be dismayed by public regard, and she knew that his lordship's attention was excited by more than mere curiosity. She had seen that look on men's faces before, and it occurred to her that here might be an opportunity. She gave him time to look at her, from the red hair tumbling about her shoulders to the patched and outrageously revealing black shirt, and said in her soft, husky voice, 'Not guilty.' And she added, almost as an after-thought, 'my lord.'

His lordship looked at her, and somewhere at the back of the gallery a woman tittered and was hushed by her neighbour. The judge took no notice but sat back, motioning to the clerk to continue.

The clerk, however, had come to the end of his catechism, and it was for Mr Mitchum, who was to conduct the case for the Crown, to begin his preliminary address. He had watched the foregoing passage with a cynical eye, for he knew his lordship and he had an excellent view of Mistress Bonney. However, that had nothing to do with him, and he addressed himself to his case, which, he assured the jury, was a simple one, but none the less damning for that. He gave a brief recital of the facts, and drew attention to the unusual abundance of evidence which the prosecution had at its disposal, including that of Captain Alan Kinsman who had sailed unknown to the pirates as an agent of the Crown.

This announcement caused something of a sensation in the court, and Mr Mitchum paid tribute to public curiosity with a few comments of the gallantry and shrewdness of the intrepid officer whose evidence, in his opinion, was by far the most conclusive that could be advanced against the prisoners. Then, sensing that the spectators would rather see the hero himself than hear eulogies of him, Mr Mitchum concluded his address and called Kinsman as his first witness.

As the Captain, trim and soldierlike in a new suit of buff and with his own hair tied neatly back from his lean, sunburned face, took the stand, Mr Mitchum permitted himself a smile of approval. Such authority and bearing could not fail to convince the jury as they were even now having their effect on the spectators.

Kinsman proved an ideal witness. In a dead silence the court listened while he described the voyage of the *Kingston*, the attack upon the *Star*, the subsequent change of command at Mosquito Bank, the voyage along the Cuban coast, and the final capture. Of his duel with Penner he said nothing, but on every other point he was painstakingly explicit. He named the prisoners in turn, showing how each was undoubtedly a conscious participant in the piratical activities of the ship, and concluded with a reminder to the jury that if they thought him suspiciously exact they must remember that he had been acting throughout with a view to collecting evidence for just such an occasion as the present trial. With that he laid down his notes and looked inquiringly to Mr Mitchum.

There were echoes of approval from the public gallery which went unchecked by the court as Mr Mitchum rose to remark that His Majesty's subjects in the West Indies no less than the Government itself owed to Captain Kinsman a debt which they trusted would be amply repaid. All this Kinsman accepted with an impassive face and only the least bow of acknowledgement, which heightened the already favourable impression he had created.

'The one matter in which I would have the gentlemen of the jury informed beyond all possible doubt is this, sir,' continued Mr Mitchum. 'You can say, can you not, that each one of the accused did knowingly and willingly act in the seizure of His Majesty's ship *Star*, and that none sought to hinder or impede that crime?'

'That is so, sir.'

'In effect, you know every one of them to be pirates?'

'I do.'

Mr Mitchum looked significantly at the jury. 'And can you think – I ask you as one who, I am sure, will wish above all to see justice done – can you think that there exists in the case of any of these accused, extenuating circumstances which might be held to excuse their offences in any way whatsoever?'

Kinsman appeared to hesitate. He looked at the dock and for a moment his eye met Rackham's. In that moment

226

Rackham realised that it lay in Kinsman's power possibly to save Anne Bonney from the gallows. If he gave a full recital of the details surrounding the Penner affair and told of the assistance, unwitting though it had been, which she had given him, it was just possible that the jury might recommend her to mercy. Surely Kinsman would be bound to do that much at least; he who had been her lover.

Kinsman looked back to Mr Mitchum. 'I know of none, sir.'

So Anne Bonney was doomed with the rest of them. She could hang for all Kinsman cared. And yet perhaps there was something that could be done even now.

As the prosecutor sat down and the judge invited the prisoners to question the witness, Rackham held up his hand.

'Did you not,' he asked Kinsman, 'receive some help from one of the prisoners at any time?'

Kinsman's eyes narrowed slightly. 'None that I recall.'

'Did no one assist you in the murder of Major Penner, then?' asked Rackham.

There was a sudden gasp of astonishment from the public benches, and Mr Mitchum swung round angrily to stare indignantly at this presumptuous questioner. He was preparing to leap to the defence of his witness, but his witness was already defending himself in the same cool, precise voice with which he had given his evidence.

He turned to the jury. 'I did not think it needful to burden the court with details,' he said quietly. 'It is true that I fought with Major Penner, who has already been mentioned to you as commanding the sloop, and that I killed him. True also that I provoked the quarrel on purpose to kill him. But that I murdered him I most emphatically deny. I regarded him as outlawed, and executed him because he was a clever,

227

capable rogue who would certainly have undone my plans had he been allowed to live. And that I was given assistance by anyone knowing me to be in the King's service I also deny.'

'D'ye say she didn't abet you to put the quarrel on Penner?' demanded Rackham, pointing to Anne Bonney. He realised he might be making her case worse instead of better, but it was too late to stop now.

Kinsman considered the question. 'That she helped me I do not deny. But that she knew me for what I was – an agent of His Majesty – is not true. She aided me for her own ends.'

'Because she was your lover?'

'Exactly,' said Kinsman, his face as emotionless as ever.

Here was more sensation than the spectators had ever dared to hope for. It took repeated commands by the sergeant-at-arms to still the chatter and when they were quiet at last the judge put a question to Kinsman.

'You slew the pirate Penner because you feared his ability to sway the other rascals? You believe they might have avoided ultimate capture had he remained to command them?'

'Yes, my lord. Although he did not command in fact he had influence enough with them.'

His lordship nodded and up bounced Mr Mitchum to assure the jury that no blame could be attached to Captain Kinsman for the death of Major Penner, since he had merely forestalled the hangman, as the prosecution would show. Furthermore, it was evident from the witness's testimony that the fact that the woman Bonney had been instrumental in bringing about Major Penner's death could not be argued in her defence, since she had acted without intent to assist the Crown. Rather,

Mr Mitchum submitted, it showed the type of woman she was – one who would not scruple to send a man to his death at her lover's prompting.

Approval showed on the faces of the jury as Mr Mitchum, with little regard for the rules of procedure, drew a brief and unsavoury picture of the female accused's morals and behaviour. Thereafter he summoned his next witness, Captain Bankier, and Rackham saw again the dull, heavy features which he had seen first on the deck of the *Star* – God, it seemed an eternity ago.

If the spectators hoped for sensational details from this witness, they were disappointed. Bankier gave his evidence without conviction, returning the briefest possible replies to the prosecution's questions and occasionally quoting in a monotonous drone from a sheaf of notes. His testimony served the prosecution's turn of damning Penner as the leader of the boarders, and of blackening the case against Rackham and Bull, but he was not an enthusiastic witness and to the onlookers he was merely tiresome.

The last prosecution witness was an officer from the King's ship which had sunk the *Kingston*. His evidence was short, consisting of an affirmation that the pirates had shown resistance and had attempted to escape. Mr Mitchum dismissed him without comment, and the accused were then invited to speak or to call what witnesses there might be to their defence. Since they had been given no opportunity to summon such witnesses it was an empty invitation, but at least they had the opportunity to speak for themselves and several were ready to avail themselves of it.

Rackham was not among them. He knew there was nothing he could say that would make his position any better; his plea of not guilty had been a formality and he was not going into the witness box to be baited by Mr Mitchum for the sport of the gallery.

With contempt he watched his companions one after another take the oath and submit themselves to the prosecutor's practised inquisition. Skilfully and mercilessly he brushed aside their various defences and exposed their guilt. For the entertainment of the public he played with the prisoners, weaving them round with a web of words or leading them on with series of apparently harmless questions until they were entrapped by their own answers. For Mr Mitchum it was easy sport; not a soul in the court-room but knew that these men were condemned already, and could not help but reveal themselves guilty wherever the prosecutor's cross-examination touched. It was all so simple that a child could have deputised for Mr Mitchum without jeopardising the Crown case, and indeed his own conduct verged occasionally on the juvenile.

There was his examination of the simpleton Malloy, which provoked much amusement. Malloy had conceived the amazing plea that he had been forced to the business by Rackham and Bull, who, he alleged, had threatened him in New Providence with instant death if he did not fall in with their schemes.

Asked if he had first been threatened before the attack on Bonney's house Malloy, after some thought, supposed that it was earlier that evening.

'How did they threaten you?' was Mr Mitchum's solemn inquiry.

Malloy frowned. 'Well, Johnny said 'e would pistol me if I didn't do as I was bid, an' Davie swore to knife me. I knew they was ready for anythin', 'cos they're desperate lads both.'

'Did they threaten you with a pistol, then?'

'Oh yes, yer honour.'

'They held it to your head, perhaps?' Mr Mitchum was almost genial.

''Deed they did, sir. Calico claps it to me 'ead an' "Do as I tell ye, ye lousy little rat, or I'll burn yer brains," says 'e. Powerful fierce, 'e was', Malloy added eagerly.

Mr Mitchum shook his head in mock dismay. 'And doubtless he held it to your head all evening, while you were breaking into Master Bonney's house and looting and burning it and taking the brig *Kingston* as well. Was he not fatigued by it?'

The ripple of laughter in the gallery rather than the question told Malloy he was being mocked. He saw the grins on the faces of the jury and the ponderous scorn of his questioner and looked about him helplessly. He was a pathetic figure, with his wispy white hair and bony manacled hands twisting together as he turned his head this way and that like a bewildered animal, and it was difficult to imagine him as the bloody pirate Mr Mitchum had painted him.

'I dunno, sir,' he said at last, thereby causing a fresh outburst of merriment.

Rackham found it a revolting spectacle. He bore no resentment to Malloy for the defence he had advanced – after all there was some truth in it, for Malloy was the kind of hopeless idiot who could never make a decision for himself. His hatred was all for the paunchy inquisitor, the expectant scoffers in the gallery, and the bored, impassive judge, who sat unmoved with lowered lids, never stirring a finger to stop the torment of the poor lunatic in the witness box.

At last it was over. All but Rackham, Carty, Ben, and Anne Bonney had spoken on their own behalf and had been torn to shreds by Mr Mitchum, who now prepared to address the

231

jury. He was checked at the outset, however, by his lordship, who indicated that he wished to question the accused further.

'It is not for me to counsel or instruct you,' he told them, 'but I feel myself bound to urge those of you who have not spoken to your defence to do so now while there is yet time, for unless you can make some answer the jury will have little choice but to convict you. That is more than I have a right to say, but my conscience forces me to deal with you frankly.'

He seemed almost friendly, with his youthful face and those clear eyes to which their very prominence lent a suggestion of ingenuousness. Seeing them still silent he went on:

'I shall call you in turn, and you shall answer or no as you wish. John Rackham?' He paused and the court waited breathlessly. 'Patrick Carty? Benjamin Thorne?' His lordship looked up after each name and waited, but none of the men made any reply.

'Anne Bonney?' His lordship's voice cut sharply across the hush. For a few seconds he paused, and then added: 'Come, mistress, have you nothing to say?' There was a trace of irritation in his voice that made Mr Mitchum look up in wonder. 'Have you thought of the position in which you stand?' the judge demanded.

He was looking directly at her, and his expression seemed to command an answer. She obliged him.

'The position I stand in now concerns me less than the position I'll be standing in a few hours hence.'

From a man her reply would have won a murmur of approving laughter, from a woman it shocked them, and his lordship no less than the rest.

'This is not the time for lightness,' he admonished her. 'Remember the fate which will be yours if you are found

232

guilty, as you must surely be unless you defend yourself. Again I urge you to think carefully before it is too late.'

She looked at him curiously, a little puzzled at his insistence. Her perplexity was not shared by the rest of the court, except perhaps the clerk, Mr Prentice, who was a bachelor and a misogynist.

Mr Mitchum, who was neither, understood his lordship very well. He noted with satisfaction that the men and women in the public gallery also appreciated the situation, and were watching with ill-concealed amusement.

'Come now,' his lordship encouraged, 'will you not testify?' His big grey eyes were almost pleading, and Anne Bonney felt again a surge of hope. His lordship was obviously human, and with humanity Mistress Bonney knew how to deal. She had already one card prepared to play at the last; with the judge's sympathy she could be sure that it would take the vital trick.

'What is there to say?' She made a little pout. 'Your lordship has heard.'

And your lordship has seen and the clever bitch knows it and there's an end, thought Mr Mitchum.

'Yes, but what have we heard?' His lordship was grave. 'Are we to understand that you have no answer to all this.'

She shook her head. 'I know little of courts, my lord. If it was as they say, then—' she shrugged '—I can only cast myself on your lordship's mercy.'

Mr Mitchum coughed drily, but his lordship seemed not to hear. He said nothing, but sat back and motioned to Mr Mitchum to commence his address to the jury. But he no longer appeared to doze in his high-backed chair; his eyes remained wide and thoughtful, straying round the court and returning always to the dock and Anne Bonney.

The human side of Mr Mitchum could be amused at him, the professional side was a little angry. Everyone knew Bernard was susceptible, but he seemed to be pushing matters too far when he paraded his weakness in court over a red-haired slut with a moist mouth and wanton eyes. However, that was not Mr Mitchum's concern; if his lordship wanted to play the fool let him do so by all means. Briskly then Mr Mitchum concluded the case for the Crown and sat down to watch with interest how his lordship would proceed to his summing-up.

He confessed later that he half-expected his lordship to plead with the jury on Mistress Bonney's behalf. It would not have surprised him, for he knew his lordship too well for a spoiled darling of fortune to suppose that he would permit any scruples of justice to stand between himself and anything he coveted. However, no such appeal was made. His lordship's address was as wholehearted a condemnation of the accused as the most fervid prosecutor could have wished; and presently the twelve good men, filled with honest zeal and the desire to show it, returned a verdict of guilty on all the accused without leaving the box.

Then, with the chaplain standing like a spectre at his side, the judge delivered the savage sentence demanded by law for those convicted of piracy on the high seas, his voice ringing hard and level above the whimpering of the boy Dobbins, who was crouching with his head on the edge of the dock between the pikes. The others, motionless, with their eyes on the judge, heard him order that they should be taken back to prison and thereafter half-hanged, disembowelled and dismembered, and their entrails burned before their faces.

Malloy put up his hand to his mouth to conceal its shaking; Carty's lean face remained unmoved but for the working of his jaw muscles; Bull gripped the edge of the dock while his smouldering eyes stared at the judge; Ben listened with quiet attention. Rackham was conscious of no emotional change; to him the sentence was nothing but a formality; he had been expecting it since the moment when Malloy's shout had brought him leaping from his resting-place on the deck and he had seen the King's colours at the truck of the great ship standing in towards them.

'And may the Lord have mercy on your souls,' concluded his lordship, to which the chaplain pronounced amen.

The stillness which had accompanied the reading of the sentence was broken by a gentle sigh from the gallery. It was a significant sound, charged with horror as the men and women sitting there in their security mentally pictured the fate of the prisoners. But there was satisfaction blended with the horror, too; grim pleasure on the swarthy face of the merchant who sat in the front of the gallery and happy interest in the expression of the elderly rake beside him. The rake's young blonde companion was pale but there was a sparkle in her eyes as she watched eagerly the reactions of the men in the dock.

Rackham was surprised that he could watch them now without rancour; his hatred had all vanished. It was a petty, tiny thing compared with the monstrous, overpowering horror of death. There was no room in his mind for anything beyond that, and these glittering butterflies in the gallery were unimportant specks of light in a dream-world which was already slipping away behind him. Now all that mattered was the rope, the knife, and the body of John Rackham, and he knew fear as he had never known it before.

From a long way off he was aware of Anne Bonney's voice speaking, and the quiet that immediately descended as the court gave its attention. She was pleading her belly, as the saying was; it was the usual appeal of women sentenced to death to claim pregnancy since they could not be hanged until their child was born.

The judge sat forward with as much eagerness as his exalted position permitted, and Mr Mitchum rose to provide an abrupt check to his excitement.

'This can be verified by examination by a physician and midwife,' he said, and Chief Justice Bernard looked glum. He appeared to brighten, however, as the prosecutor went on to suggest that his lordship should give instructions to the effect that such an examination be made. Mr Mitchum did not doubt that the report would confirm the prisoner's claim, but he was wise enough not to say so.

After all, they had had a most satisfactory trial and would presently have an equally satisfactory execution. Idly, Mr Mitchum looked round from his seat at the men in the dock. He could view them almost benevolently now, as having provided him with an ideal case: interesting, but not arduous. As the court rose for his lordship's exit – still a trifle unsteady – Mr Mitchum continued to study the prisoners, noting each man's expression as he was led from the dock. They certainly looked suitably condemned and hang-dog, all except the Bonney woman, of course. He saw her exchange a glance with Rackham; and Rackham's head nodded, as though in approval, and she smiled a curious, crooked smile in return. Then she was led away under separate guard, and the pirates were filing out between their sentries.

Mr Mitchum sighed and began to assemble his papers.

18. KATE SAMPSON

While the prisoners were being taken back to Port Royal a ship was rounding Portland Point and standing into the harbour. It bore, among others, the Governor of the Bahamas, his betrothed, and his personal secretary, Master Tobias Dickey.

It was an irony that Woodes Rogers should have been pointing out to Mistress Kate Sampson the ponderous splendour of Fort Charles as they cruised past, at the very moment that Rackham, a condemned man, was being led back to his cell. For his presence there had nothing to do with them who were on their way to England to be married, and were touching at Jamaica only so that they might inspect the plantation which old Master Sampson, whose possessions extended beyond New Providence, had promised as a wedding gift.

They were not to know of the capture of the *Kingston* pirates, and Woodes Rogers would hardly have troubled about it if he had. At that moment he had no thought for anything except the marvel that this wonderful woman at his side, twenty-odd years his junior and incredibly lovely, was soon to be his wife and was apparently well content with the prospect. This was a source of wonder to a man whose one permanent miscalculation was his underestimation of his own attraction.

Their courtship had been entirely formal. Rogers, after his early months in New Providence, had realised that for the first time in his life he was leading a fairly settled existence: it had occurred to him that in his new-found security and affluence he required a wife, and he had looked about to see what New Providence had to offer. It was not a promising field, but it had contained Kate Sampson. The Governor had been interested, then attracted, and finally enslaved. He knew, of course, that she had once been betrothed to Rackham, but had dismissed the matter as of small importance. New Providence had been an unruly place before his arrival: its people had perforce mingled with the pirates who used it as a stronghold, and Kate had been a mere seventeen at the time – an age at which she would naturally be susceptible to the glamour attaching to the young swashbuckler who had become famous among the islands as Calico Jack.

So the Governor's wooing had progressed and in course of time had been rewarded with Kate's acceptance and her father's approval. Rogers had no illusion that his own passion for her was returned in equal measure, but he had not expected it to be and was prepared to settle for simple duty and wifely devotion. It did not occur to him that he might fascinate a girl of nineteen.

And he was satisfied until the night that Rackham, like a ghost from Mistress Sampson's past, had come again to Providence. That had been a bad time for the Governor's peace of mind, but fortunately Kate had been the reverse of enthusiastic at her former lover's reappearance, and fate and the Bonney woman had combined eventually to send Master Rackham a-pirating again and so out of Mistress Sampson's life for the second and – Rogers fervently hoped – last time.

Still, the Governor had been left with the conviction that the sooner he and Kate were wed the better, and to assure her agreement without delay he had suggested the trip to England. She had received the proposal eagerly, and they had left New Providence only a few hours before the arrival there of a sloop bearing the news of the attack on the *Star*. Thus when they sighted Jamaica they were in complete ignorance of what had befallen Rackham since his flight from Providence.

Rogers at least was not in ignorance for long. Within minutes of their reception at King's House in St Jago, the residence of the Governor, Sir Nicholas Lawes, he heard the full tale of the *Kingston*'s capture and the subsequent trial from Sir Nicholas himself. His immediate reaction was one of satisfaction: here was the pestilent Rackham about to be dealt with once and for all, and Rogers could further congratulate himself on his shrewdness in having sent his cargo of silver to Charles Town instead of to Port Royal. He had called himself an over-cautious old woman at the time, changing his plans at the last minute and sending the *Star* off as a blind to any evil-doers who might have got word of the treasure shipment: well, he had been wrong to reproach himself. His precaution had been justified.

To sober his satisfaction came the thought that while Rackham was to swing for his crimes, the less Mistress Kate knew of it the better. She might, Rogers brooded, feel pity for the damned rascal. He reassured himself that the topic was not one likely to be introduced in Sir Nicholas's drawing room during their stay, and in this he was right, but there were other rooms in King's House besides the drawing room.

On that first evening Mistress Sampson took the notion for a walk in the gardens for which King's House was famous. She would have preferred to go alone, but one of Sir Nicholas's aides offered to escort her and she could hardly refuse him. Once in the garden, however, and having no wish to be burdened by his conversation, she dispatched the young gallant for her shawl, and continued her stroll alone, drinking in the heady fragrance of the bougainvillea which cast its heavy scent over the pleasant enclosure.

Her path ran beside the verandah which surrounded the house, so that anyone following it was within a few feet of the windows of the rooms on that wing. She had stopped to admire a bloom and was about to walk on when she heard a voice speaking from almost directly above her head. Looking up, she saw that she was opposite one of the windows, that the shutters stood slightly ajar, and that the voice was coming from the lighted room beyond.

It was a young voice, loose and loud with liquor, and she recognised it as that of one of the Governor's aides, a swarthy youth named Phipps who had been in attendance that afternoon when they arrived. She would have moved on out of earshot, and had actually taken the first step when that thick voice froze her to a standstill and the blood drained from her face as she listened.

'So they may hang Captain Calico and his rogues as high as they please, but you can lay to it they won't stretch Mistress Bonney's lovely neck. And a damned shame if they did, too; there are a thousand better uses for so fine a piece of she-flesh. Am I right, Miles?'

She heard a snigger of agreement and the clink of a bottle

240

and glass, and only then did the full import of what Phipps had said come home to her. She could not fail to recognise the allusion to Captain Calico; there was only one man in the world he could have meant, and that was the man she had once promised to marry two long years ago and whom she had seen only once since for a brief and painful moment on the Fort roof at New Providence. Horrified and trembling she found herself holding with both hands to the edge of the verandah and straining her ears to listen.

A younger voice was speaking now, a sober voice. 'I don't understand. Is this the woman that was condemned with the pirates this morning?'

'Condemned, and pleaded her belly to 'scape the gallows,' supplied Phipps.

'But then, surely she must hang . . . when the child is born?' The words were said with distaste. 'And again, I've heard it said that many condemned women will . . . er, plead their bellies whether they are with child or not. Perhaps this may be the case here.'

'Perhaps indeed,' said Phipps with mock solemnity. 'But I doubt if there's a physician in Jamaica bold enough to thwart Bernard by publishing it abroad that she's not pregnant. Eh, Miles?'

'Bad business for him if he did,' agreed a third voice. 'Find himself out of practice in no time. That at least. Most likely something worse.'

Phipps let out a hiccoughing laugh. 'I'll give five to two that Mistress Bonney don't sleep alone to-night. Nor she won't be in a cell at Fort Charles, neither.'

'But . . . but . . .' It was the young voice again. 'I don't believe it. You make game of me.'

'Nonsense, my lad,' cried Miles. 'If you don't believe us,

241

ask the others, but don't ask too loud. It's as Phipps said: Bernard'll make her his mistress for as long as it suits him – if she's half the Venus they say.'

'But . . . a woman that is to hang?'

'Bah! She'll not hang,' scoffed Phipps. 'Bernard's not so ungenerous as that. These nine others will swing to-day week and Mistress Bonney will be reprieved pro tempore and then time'll pass and she'll be forgotten.' He sighed gustily. 'And why not? It would be a mean-hearted brute that would waste a body like that by hanging it.'

'But the law? The Governor?'

Phipps roared with laughter. 'Why, man, Bernard is the law! And as for Sir Nick, why, he won't know and if he did it's odds he wouldn't care. Ye see how it is – Jamaica is very much like England, and he stands best who stands highest, for he may do what the devil he pleases. Why, Bernard would hardly have to send word to the fort commandant to-night; old Coates would have the wench on her way to Bernard's house faster than you can say knife.'

'It would be worth his while,' mused Miles. 'Daresay Bernard will toss a few crowns to him for services rendered. Wonder if it's true that Coates stands to attention at the sound of two guineas chinking together?'

'God help him if he ever has to exist on his pay,' said Phipps. 'I've heard – why, what in God's name was that?'

It took that exclamation to make Kate realise that a voice farther up the garden was calling her name. The aide had found her shawl and was now seeking its owner. She had stood motionless in the shadow by the verandah listening, but now, with the footsteps of her escort crunching towards her over the gravel, she had no choice but to move into the open.

She hurried back along the path and almost ran headlong

into the arms of the aide who came bearing her shawl in triumph. He would have explained at length the details of his search, but she cut his apology short as politely as she could and expressed the wish to go indoors as the night had become too cold. As he took her arm, murmuring his concern, she heard the shutters creak and Phipps' voice grumbling vaguely into the darkness.

The details of what took place in the interval between her return to the house and the moment when her maid blew out the candle and closed her bedroom door were never clear to her afterwards. She recalled Sir Nicholas's concern when she made her excuses, pleading a headache or some such triviality, but that was all. She wanted to be alone, to think, and from what she had seen of King's House she realised that the only way to ensure privacy was to retire for the night.

She lay in bed, gazing up at the dim ceiling, recollecting what she had heard and trying to determine what it meant to her. Rackham was to die; he was to be hanged within a week, and the very thought passing through her head seemed to strip her of self-possession and leave her weak and helpless. It was impossible, she told herself; people did not just die – not people like him, who was so young, and full of strength and the very power of living. She knew she should be sorry, because he had been closer to her than any man she had ever known, and yet sorrow was not the emotion she felt. She no longer loved him, of that she was certain, for she could look back now with dispassion and even self-disdain at those kisses stolen in her father's garden years ago. But to think of him dying was fantastic and unreal and horrible.

'They may hang Captain Calico as high as they please' – she could hear the tipsy voice, and at the mere memory she felt sick and miserable. There was a tiny, nagging thought at the back of her mind that perhaps she could not disclaim responsibility for his downfall, but she drove it away with the answer that all that had happened between them had been long ago, that he had left her and not she him, and that no one had the right to reassert a claim voluntarily forgone for two whole years. And yet the thought returned: was she to blame? How far it was the cause of the sick agony possessing her she did not know, but it stayed to torment her. She told herself that there was nothing now that she could do, and that she was suffering from a shock that had left her distraught. Common sense insisted that fate had run its course and there was nothing to be done but strive to put the matter away and hope that in time she might forget it all. Of course, that was impossible, and it seemed to imply cowardice, and Kate Sampson's soul revolted at the thought.

Back and forth, one way or another, she lay brooding while she heard the hours told away by the chiming of a clock in the house below, and always her thoughts approached, and rejected, and came closer and closer to a resolution, and on that she fell asleep.

It said much for her strength and spirit that in spite of the shock she had received and the problem with which it left her, Kate's bearing and manner were as serene as ever throughout the following day. And in the evening, at the grand reception given in her honour and Woodes Rogers', she endured with perfect graciousness the ponderous attentions and trivial small-talk of an endless succession of notables and their wives. It seemed to her an eternity before all was done and the last guest had departed, and she could have cried with relief at the prospect of being private again, but even now she was not to escape unchallenged. She was mounting the staircase, having paid a hurried good-night to

Sir Nicholas and Rogers, when she heard her name called. She turned with an impatience which melted a little when she saw that the caller approaching across the hall was Master Tobias Dickey. He was accompanied by a tall, portly officer in the uniform of the local garrison.

'We're barely in time, after all,' said Tobias, as he bent over her hand. 'Ye see us, child, slaves tae duty while the rest of the world plays itself. Ma'am, may I present Colonel Coates, who commands Fort Charles? Mistress Sampson.'

Kate inclined her head to the officer, who was bending his large body almost double in his bow. Coates, she was wondering, and then she remembered where she had heard the name before. It had been only last night, outside the aides-de-camp's quarters. Coates had been named as the corrupt official who would sink his duty to oblige Chief Justice Bernard in the matter of Anne Bonney; he would have the power, of course, to permit her being taken out of prison and back again.

It was not a pleasant recollection, and as she looked at him she was forced to mask her distaste. He was a moon-faced creature with a pendulous nose and a large mouth open in a fruity smile; there was the hint of a leer in his eyes which made her automatically raise her fan to shield the deep neck-line of her gown. He spoke in a sonorous voice that matched his heavy features.

'I count myself fortunate that I am in time to pay my devotion at Beauty's shrine,' he smirked. 'Everywhere the talk is of the fair visitor Governor Rogers has brought to us from the Bahamas. They speak as of a goddess, which is no less than justice. Ma'am, your most humble obedient.'

It was the sort of laboured compliment she had heard a thousand times, but this man contrived to make it

245

embarrassing. His large, moist hand retained her own for just a moment more than was necessary and she felt as though she were touching an unpleasantly plump reptile. Tobias, who saw most of what went on around him, sensed her unease and hastened to the rescue.

'The Colonel here has been at me this whole day seeking an introduction,' he explained. 'Ye'll mind I'm lodging in Fort Charles, and since he's commandant he has me completely in his power.' He wagged his head in mock solemnity. 'My work must wait while we come gallivanting out here. And work, did I say? Child, that man that is to be your husband has not an element of humanity about him. Here am I poring over papers down at the fort yonder – all in the interests of government, mark me – when I should be taking my ease in this island paradise.' He spread his hands. 'Is there any justice in it?'

'You shall have your reward in heaven,' she smiled.

'In heaven? That's as may be. Could I not have a wee bit in Port Royal?'

She turned to Colonel Coates. 'And your attendance is most gratifying, sir. How unfortunate that your duties did not permit you to attend earlier. We have been very gay here.'

'Ma'am, it shall be my lifelong regret,' he assured her. 'But perhaps we may be honoured with your presence at the fort during your time here. As Master Dickey says, we have little time for leisure, but you may be certain of the most cordial welcome we are able to offer. Depend upon it, ma'am.'

'Aye, aye,' said Dickey. He gave her a shrewd look. 'Ye look a wee thing weary, child. I doubt ye'll have had a yawn or two behind your fan the night. Too much excitement and entertainment and whatnot, when ye should have been snug in your bed.' He chuckled. 'Hech! I would have made the bonny minister, rebuking youthful folly. Ye cannae kill the Covenanter once he's in you. But come, Colonel.' He took Coates by the arm. 'You and me'll just leave Mistress Sampson to her rest. Good-night, m'dear, and sleep sound.'

She watched them go across the hall and waited until they were out of sight before she continued to her room. Perhaps it was the knowledge that Dickey would be at the fort, within reach if need be, that crystallised her decision for her, or it may have been that Coates' invitation provided some excuse, but she knew that the problem that had stayed with her all that day had really been solved as soon as it had confronted her. For within herself she had known since the moment that she had heard Phipps' voice outside the aides' quarters that she would go to Fort Charles and see Rackham if it were humanly possible. There was no logical reason that could compel her to go to a man who was a few short footsteps from eternity, simply because she had cared for him long ago: she only knew that she could not sit by and wait and then pass on into her new life without having done what the voice inside Kate Sampson told her must be done.

She did not lie awake that night, but fell asleep as soon as her head touched the pillow, and did not stir until dawn.

19. THE PRICE OF PIRACY

They had removed Rackham's chains on his return to the cell under Fort Charles, which meant that he could turn over in his sleep without being awakened by the fetters tugging at his wrists. For the rest his liberty was no wider than it had been before: he could walk round the long, narrow cell and look out through the barred window, and he could listen to his comrades in the big common cell along the passage. Most of the time he listened; it was the only thing that provided a distraction from his thoughts, and he did not care to think too much.

The removal of his fetters had been accompanied by another even more important improvement. During his captivity before the trial the only human being he had seen had been the stone-faced soldier who brought his food and never volunteered a remark or vouchsafed more than a grunt to Rackham's questions. Now the soldier had been replaced by an impish little warder who prattled incessantly while he was in the cell and never lost an opportunity of reminding Rackham that if he wished he could now buy extra food and liquor and even female company. When Rackham pointed out that he had no money the warder grinned slyly.

'What yer got in yer mouth, matey, eh?' He chuckled at Rackham's surprised expression. 'Regular trapful o' money, if I'm a judge. Yer teeth, matey, yer teeth. Fine sound choppers like them'll fetch a guinea or two if ye can find the right buyer. I could do that for yer, pal – for a consideration, o' course. Just say the word an' I'll find the customers. Any amount o' gennlemen – aye, an' ladies, too – what'd give a sight o' money for teeth like them.'

'You mean when I'm dead?'

'Well, no, 'cos yer out o' my 'ands then, d'ye see? 'Sides, the best people ain't so partial to usin' corpse teeth. Upsets their appetites, I s'pose. But if you was to give me your word to let the armourer nip 'em out, say the day afore you do the 'angman's 'ornpipe, I'd be 'appy to give yer credit in the meantime. Say two guineas? It's stark profit, matey. What the 'ell use they goin' to be to you where you're goin'?' he added frankly. 'An' think wot the guineas'll buy you – fruit, an' a bottle o' the best, an' I knows of a lovely little yellow girl as you can 'ave cheap as dirt. Wot say, pal?'

Rackham had refused, not because he particularly wanted his teeth but because he did not want the fruit or the wine or the highly admired yellow girl. The warder had borne his refusal without disappointment; from the noise that could be heard down the passageway Rackham judged that he had found a more fruitful field for his commercial activities there. Several times he heard drunken singing and the shrill laughter of women mingling with the husky roaring of the prisoners, and occasionally there would arise a tumult of angry voices and fighting, which would bring the sergeant of the guard to restore order.

The little jailer was persistent, however; he was not the one to spoil a profitable transaction for want of salesmanship, and he had even more ambitious plans in view, as Rackham learned next day.

'I've brought yer somethin', matey,' the jailer confided. 'See 'ere.' And he held out a razor on his grubby palm.

Rackham looked at it without interest. 'What's that for? D'ye want me to cut my own throat?'

The jailer laughed uneasily. 'Ye wouldn't do that, pal, now would yer? They'd string me up in yer place, like as not. 'Ere, take it. Ye can tidy yerself up a bit, like, if yer so minded. Seems to me ye must be heart sick o' wearin' them lousy whiskers.'

For a moment Rackham was touched. He was on the point of thanking the jailer when a suspicion crossed his mind.

'What's it to you whether I'm shaved or not? I'll hang no quicker without a beard, damn you.'

'Why, matey.' The jailer tried to look hurt. 'I was on'y thinkin' – I mean, I thought ye'd be glad—'

'You thought nothing. What do you want?'

The jailer glanced round at the door and dropped his voice to a confidential murmur.

'Well, ye see, pal, it's like this. Yer big mate along the way – 'im wi' the yellow beard, wot's 'is name? – Bull, that's it – well this mornin' there's a woman comes inquirin' for 'im. Quality she were, too – leastways, rich quality – an' she give the sergeant five guineas to let 'er in, an' me another five.' He sniggered. 'Well, there y'are. They was snug as ye like in an empty cell, an' me five guineas better off. Where's the harm, eh? No one's to know, seein' there's women comin' an' goin' all the time round the sojers' part o' the fort.'

A vivid image rose in Rackham's mind of the fleshy-faced

250

woman who had watched Bull so intently at the trial, and he suddenly felt sick. There was something unutterably horrible in the thought of Bull, who would be a mangled lump of flesh in a few days' time, and that woman. He let out an exclamation of disgust, but the hoarse voice of the little ghoul at his elbow went on:

'So, I thinks to meself, why just Bull, when there's the famous Calico Jack wi' nothin' to put by 'is time all day? See? So if you was to trim yerself up, pal, an' I'll pass the word along, why, there's good in it for the both of us—'

His snickering little laugh ended in a startled yelp as Rackham swung a hand at his head. He leaped back, stumbled, and almost pitched headlong.

'Wot the 'ell! Well, you're a touchy 'un, so 'elp me! Why—'

'Get out,' growled Rackham. 'Get out before I break your neck.'

Quite unabashed the jailer slipped through the doorway. 'All right, pal,' he said amiably. 'No offence. Just lemme know if you change yer mind.' He slammed the door, shot the bolt, and went off whistling.

Rackham heard no more from him that day, and the hours wore on until sunset, when the din in the common cell down the passage broke out afresh and continued until well past midnight. He slept in spite of it, waking only when the measured tramp on the ramparts far overhead and the shouted commands of the under-officers announced the beginning of another day in Fort Charles. There would be five more mornings like this, and no more mornings thereafter.

He fell to pacing up and down, up and down the narrow limits of his cell – for how long he had no means of knowing. The jailer came and went, leaving his bread and gruel and flask of water, but they lay untasted. Then gradually that energy which he expended in his restless march up and down gave way, and he was overcome by an odd reverie of confused thoughts and memories that held him motionless as he stared with unseeing eyes at the narrow patch of sky limited by his window.

He might have been standing there only a few minutes, or it might have been an hour, when he heard the bolt snap back. Still he did not move, and when he felt the jailer tugging at his sleeve he was conscious only of irritation at an unwanted interruption.

'Go away,' he muttered. 'Go to the devil.'

'Matey! Come on, pal!' The tugging was persistent. ''Ere, matey, you got a visitor. Wake up!'

Rackham half turned his head. 'If it's any of your . . .' he was beginning, and then he stopped, for what he saw sent an actual physical shock through his body and left him speechless. Kate Sampson was standing in the heavy grey arch of the doorway.

At first he did not recognise her in this beautiful, stately young lady, and he stared uncomprehendingly while the jailer slipped past her apologetically and closed the door upon them. And then recognition dawned.

'Kate.' His voice was hoarse. 'You . . . Kate . . . you . . . here?'

The shock of the meeting was even greater for her. It seemed impossible that such a short time could have wrought so great a change in him. Unkempt, with that scrubby beard on his cheeks, his tan faded, the dark pouches of fatigue under his eyes, and his ragged clothes, he was more like a scarecrow than the immaculate Calico Jack of old.

Pity prompted her first words. 'Oh, John, what have they done?'

252

He seemed not to hear. 'Where in God's name have you come from?' he asked.

As briefly as she could she told him. She related how she had heard no word of him from the night of his theft of the *Kingston* at New Providence until that chance conversation at King's House had reached her ears. She could not tell him what had passed in her mind during that night and the following day, because she did not truly know herself, and possibly because of that omission he was to draw a false conclusion to explain her presence. As she stood there, telling her story in hesitant, broken sentences he knew a warmth that at least he was not entirely alone, and was thankful for it.

'And so . . . and so, I came,' she finished lamely.

'God bless you,' he said, and then the strain imposed by the foregoing hours and by the sight of him and his surroundings was too much for her and she broke down, covering her face with her hands and sobbing uncontrollably.

It was a natural enough reaction for a girl of nineteen finding herself plucked from her placid everyday existence and brought face to face with brutal reality, and his reaction was no less natural. He put his arm about her shoulders and she was too distressed to resist.

'There, now, lass. For God's sake, it's none so terrible. Here, rest easy.' Gently he brought her head on to his chest. 'There, that's it, now. My shirt's not as dainty as it was two years gone, but I've no better to offer.'

Perhaps she was astonished to find comfort where she could hardly have expected it, or she may have been too overcome, but she did not draw away. He touched a tendril of blonde hair that had escaped from beneath her hood.

'It seems a long time, Kate. A long time. And ye've changed. Grown lovelier than ye were, which I wouldn't have thought

253

possible. And that's something that can't be said for me,' he added wryly. 'I think the greatest kindness they've done me is not giving me a mirror. I don't wonder you're crying.'

She heard him with mounting amazement. In coming to see him she had not known what to expect, but it had certainly not been this. Anger or bitterness she could have understood, but this gentleness, as though there had never been two years between this moment and the evenings in the garden at New Providence, was something beyond her. It served as a spur to the half-awakened conscience which had been at work in her.

'I am to blame – oh, I know I am to blame! And now you—' She shuddered against him. 'Oh, God, if only I had known!'

'What's this? You to blame? For what?' He took his arm from about her and put his hands on her shoulders to force her gently away. 'In what are you to blame, child?'

'I . . . I might have waited, perhaps,' she faltered, and then it came pouring out in a disjointed stream of words. 'When you went away, on the night when the King's ships came to Providence, I thought my heart would break. Oh, I loved you, and I believed you loved me, and I told myself that you must have been carried away by chance. I waited and waited, sure that there must be word from you, but it never came. And then it was so long – months without knowing what had become of you, and I still prayed and hoped that you might come back, but you never did. Sometimes I thought you must be dead and I wished myself dead, too. I was foolish, I suppose – my father told me so, and in time I came to believe him. And then Woodes – Governor Rogers – came to the house, and – and I was beginning to forget, you see . . . and then he asked me to become his wife . . . and so I agreed.'

254

She paused, but he said nothing, and she went on. 'I never thought, then, that you would come back at all. And when you did, I didn't imagine for a moment that it was for me. You remember that morning, at the Fort, when you came up to me, and he struck you . . . only then I realised that it was for me you had come back.' She looked up at him. 'And I did not love you then. Do you see? I can't tell why; perhaps because it was so long since I had seen you, and I was no longer a girl, and besides there was Woodes. And when you went away, I was sorry for you, I think, but that was all. But . . . but now . . .' Her lips trembled. 'To think of you . . . you see, if I had waited, this would never have happened . . . and you would have been . . .'

He considered her for a long moment. 'And you count yourself to blame? Kate, if ever there was a woman in this world without blame, it is you. Why, lass,—' he reached out to take her hand – 'what fault there is is mine, and no other's. Oh, believe me, I know. Were you to wait two years for a man gone roving, breaking his word to you as it seemed?' He shook his head. 'The wonder is that you should wait at all.'

'But you came back,' she insisted.

'Aye – after two years.' He sighed. 'But you were right in one thing, Kate; it was by no will of mine that I went out to sea with the *Kingston* that dawn when the King's ships came to Providence. You would hear how it was with us, how a frightened fool touched off a gun and the King's men thought we were firing on them and sailed in to board us. There was no way but escape then, and I knew that there was an end to you and me.'

He turned away from her and walked slowly towards the window, looking out at that blue patch of sky.

'That was why I never sent you word. Could I believe you were waiting for a pirate who was beyond pardon? But I never forgot you, even though I knew I should never see you again. Then there was talk of this new pardon – oh, eighteen months after or perhaps more, and within a day of hearing of it from a ship we spoke, we put into Tortuga and I met Hedley Archer, who was lately from New Providence. He told me you were not wed. And I thought, perhaps . . .' He stopped and shrugged. 'Ye may ask how vain a man can be. But to say you were at fault – no.' He shook his head. 'You had waited overlong for a man who was lost two years. It was no fault of yours if that man came back to claim you too late. I'll own I was sick and sorry for myself, but it passed, and if I resented you it was for a moment only.'

'The resentment was not all on your side,' she told him. 'When I heard how you had fought over that woman I was . . .'

'Fought over whom? I fought over no one. Ye mean with La Bouche? That was no more than a tavern quarrel, God knows over what, for I was not sober at the time. As for Anne Bonney, she dressed my wounds, poor soul. Better for her if she'd left me be – aye, better for all of us. Penner would be alive, and she would still be riding in her carriage about Providence. Instead she'll go with the rest. And I'm sorry for that.'

Seeking to cheer him, she recounted a detail of what she had overheard at King's House.

'I think you may set your mind at rest over her. She is not likely to hang, if what they say is true. This Bernard, the justice, has looked kindly on her. The talk is that she has become his mistress, and that he will contrive to postpone her execution. It may be gossip, but I think not.'

'Well, then God be thanked for that,' he said.

'I suppose you loved her,' she said quietly.

'Loved her?' He smiled wryly. 'No. Men don't love the Anne Bonneys of this world. They only think they do, for a little while. She knew that, and so she must use every man for what she can get. Who shall blame her? Not I, God knows. I can pity her, now, although but for her it's odds I'd be an honest privateersman this day. It seems women are unlucky for me, and I for them. I've brought little good to you, my dear; we should be thankful it's no worse.'

'Could it be any worse?' she demanded. 'Can anything be worse than death?'

He smiled. 'No – although there are some will tell you it is preferable to dishonour. Myself, I think they cannot know what death is like. They should go roving a while; it might teach them things.'

Her lip trembled and she bit it in an endeavour to keep back her tears. He put his hand beneath her chin and raised her face.

'Nay, now, what's the matter?' His voice was gentle. 'What would you have me say? Cry and whimper because I must pay my shot, or curse and rant against the King and the law and aught I can lay tongue to? That would mend nothing.' It was remarkable how easy it was to sound brave when he spoke to her; it seemed almost virtuous to lie if it would comfort her.

'I know.' She drew in a little quick breath and tried to keep her voice steady. 'But it is . . . different for a woman. If only . . . oh, if only it had gone otherwise . . . any one of a thousand things could have happened rather than this. Perhaps if you were angry or hated me it would seem better – I don't know how. But you talk as though it was no more

257

than . . . than, oh, nothing at all!' Her voice choked and she turned her face away. 'I am sorry. I only make things worse for you. But I cannot forget that but for me . . . oh, but for me it would not be like this.'

He shook his head. 'That's not so, as I've told you. And if it was that belief that brought you here, why then, you were wrong.' He paused. 'Was that why you came – to blame yourself to me?'

'I . . . I don't know . . . perhaps.'

'Was it because you still loved me, Kate?'

She turned and looked at him, her face very pale. She could lie, and say 'Yes,' or she could try to explain what she did not truly understand herself – that she could not stay away while there was that tiny voice forcing her on. It was impossible to tell him what had brought her. It was a question she had not been able to answer in the past thirty-six hours: she wondered could she ever answer it.

While she stood irresolute there was the soft pad of feet in the passage followed by a rapping at the door.

'Commandant's rounds in a few minutes, m'lady,' said the jailer's voice, and after a pause he sidled in, looking apologetically at Kate. 'Beggin' your pardon, but I thought as you'd wish to be gone afore he come, m'lady. Not that 'e minds womenfolk in the cells, but seein' you ain't one o' *them*, I thought . . .'

She nodded. 'I shall come at once,' and the jailer slipped out.

She forced herself to meet Rackham's eyes again. There was that question still unanswered, and her own doubts still unsettled in spite of his protestations. And time was running out.

'Oh, if only there was something I could do!' It was a cry of frustration born of her own helplessness. 'Some way . . .'

His voice was not quite steady. 'God bless you for that.' He seemed to be about to add something more but changed his mind. Then he motioned towards the door. 'Best be gone.'

To stay longer would only be to protract her own misery, to say nothing of the risk of detection.

'Good-bye, then,' she said. It was almost a whisper, and she realised with horror that the phrase held a terrible finality.

'Good-bye, Kate. It was . . . it was like you. To come, I mean.'

Then she was in the passage, and the little jailer was snapping home the bolts.

'Pardon me, m'lady, but we'd best make haste. If ye'll follow me as quick's ye can.'

She had the presence of mind to pull her hood forward to shield her face as they passed through the vaulted guard-room at the end of the passage. There were a few soldiers lounging there, but their ribald invitations went unheard, and presently she was at the main gate, having parted with another ten guineas to the grateful jailer.

She passed the sentries and was in the street once more, in a thoroughfare coloured and alive, a place of noise and bustle where the sun shone and the strong salt breeze from the sea held its own even with Port Royal's varied odours. It seemed impossible that two such worlds could be so close together – this one and that other of stone and iron that she had left.

She heard behind her the rattle of a side-drum from the fort and turned to look back through the gate. On the other side of the parade was the solid pile of the main fort building from which she had lately emerged, and down the stone steps from the battlements a party of officers was descending.

There was something familiar about the leading figure, something unpleasantly familiar, and she recognised him as Colonel Coates. She stepped quickly back into the shelter of the wall, but he and his party turned aside at the foot of the steps and vanished presently round the angle of the keep.

The sooner she was away the better; if Coates had noticed her and made enquiries it could have been embarrassing both for her and Woodes Rogers, and Coates, she was certain from her brief acquaintance with him, was the kind who would enjoy stirring up mischief. She could not picture him turning a blind eye unless it was in his interest to do so. Since he was reputed corruptible he would possible even sink to blackmail, and . . . She stopped dead in the act of stepping into the street, overwhelmed by the thought that drove everything else from her mind.

The sentry outside the gate watched with mild interest the behaviour of the young lady who stopped so abruptly as she was passing his post. He saw her go pale, and stare back at the empty gateway with a tense expression for which he could see no good reason, and then set off down the street at a pace which he considered undignified in one who, if he was any judge, was of the quality.

Kate found her carriage where she had left it in a narrow by-street. She took her seat and ordered the coachman to drive to the address of her father's agent in Port Royal – she had intended to visit him over that gift of land which was to be her wedding-present, but that had nothing to do with her present urgent business. As the carriage jerked and rolled slowly along to the accompaniment of a flow of imprecations from the driver at the lumbering vehicles which impeded them, she sat in an agony of impatience, fearful that the resolve taken so quickly outside the fort would cool if she were delayed in committing herself. She knew the folly of the course she intended; it was frightening to think of it, but even more frightening to think that her courage might fail her if she was not quick to put it into execution.

At the premises of Matthew and Wayman, her father's agents, she was received with all the deference due to the daughter of so important a client. Here she drew on her father's account, as she had his permission to do, but to a much greater extent than he would have readily approved. In fact the size of her withdrawal made even Mr Wayman, who waited on her personally, catch his breath, but if he had doubts he kept them to himself. He guessed that it would be impolitic to question the action of this self-assured young woman who was, after all, heiress to an immense fortune and therefore not to be crossed lightly.

Having been bowed out and handed to her coach she hesitated for a second before giving instructions to her driver. There was still time to draw back from what she knew was a wildly dangerous business, but she had her father's gift for calculating chances and it appeared to her that she ran an even risk. With courage in the balance she could succeed, and she had never known reason to doubt her courage.

She leaned back in her carriage, bestowed a gracious smile on Mr Wayman, and addressed the driver.

'Back to Fort Charles.'

20. THE PASSAGE

Rackham sat listening, straining his ears against the silence that mantled the fort, but beyond the heavy cell door all was as quiet as the grave.

This was the last day. In a few minutes he would hear feet along the passage, and the rasping of the bolt, and his door would be flung back, and he would look up and see the red coats of his escort in the passage and the armourer with his bilboes and handcuffs. They would chain him and drag him out into the sunlight, and then the hangman would choke him almost – but not quite – unconscious and they would rip him open from crutch to chest and drag out his entrails and burn them in front of him. With any luck he would be dead before they had finished.

Oddly enough, it seemed less frightening now than it had done a few days ago. It would be a few seconds of sickening, frightful agony, but then it would be suddenly dark and the pain at an end.

He was glad he had seen Kate: that at least was something worth remembering. He had had bad luck there, but then he had never been particularly lucky in anything. At least it was something to have known her, a time of peace and sunshine in a short, turbulent life that had known little of either.

It was still as silent as ever. He wondered why they did not come for him. At least ten minutes must have passed since he had heard the sound of his companions being led out of their cell along the passage. He had listened to the irregular clank of the armourer's hammer as he fettered them, and had stood waiting with a cold sweat on his face, expecting them to come for him as well. But they had not come. Perhaps they were saving him for the benefit of the spectators who would be assembling at Gallows Point. The final act of the play. The great tragedy of Captain Calico Jack Rackham.

Hearing the others go had been horrible. He had not slept, and through the hours he had listened to the hellish din they had made in their last desperate carouse. There had been no women, of course – men were liable to lose their reason on the last night before execution; there were those who would kill a woman out of sheer blood-lust and cruelty, knowing that they were to die anyway and that nothing more could be done to punish them than the hangman would do in the morning. But even without the trollops they had been howling drunk, roaring their choruses and yelling abuse, fighting with each other and smashing bottles, and hammering at their cell door until it seemed they must be in the last stages of exhaustion.

Some time shortly before dawn Rackham had fallen asleep, and had been summoned back to consciousness by the ring of the armourer's hammer. Then Bull's voice had broken out in a bellow of song – evidently he was still drunk – and added to that there had been a high quavery voice – Malloy, singing

263

a psalm. They had sung together, the animal bellowing of a filthy ballad mingling with the flat cracked notes of the sacred song.

Then the boy Dobbins had begun to cry, begging the jailers to leave him behind, and suddenly breaking out into hysterical shrieks. Rackham had heard Earl's voice, swearing, and Bull bellowing louder than ever, and then there had been the sound of a body falling and the screaming was replaced by a soft whimpering while the hammer clanked on relentlessly. Bull had still been ranting when he left the cell, his huge voice drowning even the shouted orders of the sergeant of the guard.

> 'List an' I'll sing thee of Howell Davis
> Hob-a-derry-dando!
>
> Caught a shark i' the Bay of Nevis
> Hob-a-derry-dando!'

And then suddenly: 'Where's Calico? Where's that long white bastard, hey? I want to see his guts come out. Where the hell are ye, Rackham? I want to see thee swing, tha Bristol pimp!'

And then Malloy's voice had piped up again.

'Good cheer, friends, be of good cheer.' It was a flat, strange tone that Rackham had never heard him use before, and he realised that Malloy, never very sane, must have gone mad at last. 'Remember the thief that died with Our Lord and was made whole by the blood of the Lamb. There is no stain so dark but it may be washed out, so ye all repent your sins. It is but a short road now to the Throne of Glory and none shall be turned away that truly repent. Take heart, take

264

heart, and lift up your eyes to see the light of the Lord his Grace that shines through the darkness of death, and by which ye are made whole.' Then he stopped and after a moment spoke again in his usual voice: 'Billy! Brother Billy Tyrrell, Mary's here. Aye, so she is, and young Pen, as ever was. Run and tell them, quick. Run, I say.' His voice rose suddenly into a blood-chilling screech. 'Run, damn you, run!'

His shout trailed away into a hysterical laugh, while the boy Dobbins began to weep and curse afresh. Rackham had listened, horrified and yet fascinated, until the crying and the rattle of the guard's accoutrements died away and there was nothing but silence in the fort.

Now fifteen minutes had gone, and he had had time to think of death and Kate and a thousand other things, and still they did not come. He wondered where Anne Bonney was – a ridiculous, illogical thought. Was she yearning for Kinsman, he wondered? And from that his thoughts flew to Penner, dead and buried in the sand on Mosquito Bank.

At least he had been granted the mercy of a quick thrust and a speedy release. No horror of mutilation under the disembowelling knife for Penner. Yet he must have suffered too, and Rackham remembered the glaring sunlight and the sickly smell of his own blood and the wicked glittering sliver of steel in the hand of La Bouche moving in to kill him. That had been a bad moment; he had felt then as Penner must have felt when Kinsman pinned him. And both times, she had been there, languid and yet eager, smiling, and filled with hot excitement, and even as the image crossed Rackham's mind he heard the soft slither of a footstep in the passage.

He caught his breath and swung round. Then the bolt snapped back and the door creaked inward on its ponderous hinges.

A man stood on the threshold – a man Rackham had never seen before. He could be certain of that, for the face beneath the brim of the broad black hat was a sight not readily forgotten. It was the kind of face he had seen on corpses, grey and lifeless, with the skin taut over the cheek-bones, its death-like quality belied by the liveliness of its bright sunken eyes.

With a jerk of his head the creature motioned Rackham out of the cell, standing aside to let him pass, and then carefully closing the door and rebolting it. Mystified, Rackham looked about him for other guards, but the passage was empty. There was no one but this weird figure in his rusty black hat and tatty coat, and not a sound to indicate the presence of a living soul.

But if the situation was beyond Rackham's understanding he could at least see the opportunity it offered. The chance of escape might be infinitesimal but it was better than no chance at all. The thought formed in the second which passed as the thin man shot home the bolt, and as he straightened up Rackham was turning in a movement that would have ended in a plunge at the other's throat. The thin man saw the sudden turn and made a leisurely movement of his right hand, and Rackham was staring into the cold twin barrels of a heavy pistol. He checked himself abruptly and the thin man's bloodless lips parted in a grin. With a thrill of horror Rackham saw that he had no tongue.

But tongue or not, there was no doubt of the professional ability behind the pistol. The mute gestured with it, and Rackham obediently moved down the passage, his strange escort stalking a few paces behind. The passage turned sharply and terminated in a winding flight of stone steps, but a grunt from the mute urged him on, and they mounted to a second passage which Rackham judged must run directly above the first. Here, however, there was matting on the flags, and instead of iron wall brackets there were were small brass lamps. There were doors on the left side with little rush mats before them, and an air of warmth and habitation about the place. Curiosity contended with Rackham's fear as he went on, until opposite the third door another grunt from the mute brought him to a halt. Still there was no sound in the fort and he began to wonder if the place was deserted after all.

The mute rapped on the panels. A voice answered and the mute raised the latch and pushed the door open. Grinning, he jerked his thumb, and as Rackham went past him, put out a hand and patted him on the shoulder. It felt like a handful of dry sticks rattling together.

Rackham went into the room and heard the door close at his back. He knew without looking that the mute was no longer there and that the only other occupant of the room was the man who sat writing at a table before the window. It was a broad, panelled apartment with matting underfoot, a fire spluttering merrily in the grate, and a brass clock ticking on the mantel. The man at the desk looked up.

'Aye, there ye are,' said Master Tobias Dickey.

For a moment Rackham did not recognise him. The chubby face and neat wig were familiar, so was the brisk voice; but they seemed to belong to a time far back in memory. Then recollection came, and he realised that it was only weeks, not years, since he had seen this man before.

He stared, wondering what this might mean, while the lawyer regarded him gravely.

'I'll break the news as best I may,' said Master Dickey. He leaned forward in his chair and looked intently at the other's face. 'You are not to hang,' he said carefully. 'Not to hang. Ye understand?'

If he had expected an immediate display of emotion he was disappointed. Rackham did not react because at first the meaning of what he had heard did not penetrate his understanding – could not because it was so much at variance with sense and logic and what he had been conditioning his mind to for weeks.

The lawyer spoke again. 'Don't ye understand? Ye're not to be executed at all. At least, if ye are, ye'll be in grand company, wi' myself alongside you.'

Rackham found his tongue at last. 'What do you mean?' His voice was hoarse. 'How . . . how . . . not to . . . to . . . die?'

'Not unless ye're careless, or aught miscarries.'

Rackham looked round helplessly, bewildered. Master Dickey watched with interest for a moment. 'There now,' he said. 'Come over here, in front of the table, and pay heed to what I say to ye.'

Rackham came forward, hesitantly. He was trembling, but a great excitement was constricting his chest and his breathing.

'I don't understand,' he said, and Dickey caught the mounting edge of panic in his voice.

'Of course ye don't. But ye shall in a moment, when ye're your own man again. In the meantime let me tell ye that you're not out o' the wood yet, not by a good step. Ye'll need all your faculties if ye're to 'scape the gallows – and there's more than your own life in it. There's mine and another's – aye, and a third, too, perhaps, and that more precious than the rest o' us together. So take a grip on yourself, Master Calico, for one blunder and we're done.'

Rackham nodded and took the chair which Dickey

268

indicated while the lawyer crossed to a sideboard and returned with a glass and decanter.

'Medicine for a shaking hand,' observed Dickey. 'Sup that, but go slowly. And listen.'

Rackham lifted the glass – it was rum – and the burn of the spirit made him realise that he was cold, but he took only a mouthful before setting it down again.

'First,' began Dickey, 'ye're to escape. Ye've been bought off – for a sum which to my mind is a great deal more than ye're worth, although I don't expect ye to share my view. Aye, ye can stare, but bought is what ye've been.'

'But . . .' Rackham was beginning, but Master Dickey waved him to silence.

'Aye, how does one buy the life of a condemned felon, ye would ask? I'll confess it was new to me, but Jamaica's a grand place to go to school.' He resumed his seat and clasped his hands in front of him on the table.

'Ye're dead. Officially dead. Ye died by hanging, secundem artem, at six of the clock this morning on a spot known as Gallows Key. There ye were buried. Your execution took place before the others because it came to the ears of the authorities – in this case the commandant of this fort, one Colonel Coates – that there was popular sympathy for you on the waterfront. A demonstration was feared.' Master Dickey smiled wryly. 'That's the tale and who's to doubt it? If any did, I'll wager a guinea to a groat there's a body in the sand of Gallows Key this minute. Corpses are not hard to come by, and if there's lime in the grave no one will ever ken the difference.'

'But the commandant, this Coates?' Words burst out of Rackham in a sudden flood. 'You mean he managed this?'

Master Dickey nodded. 'That he did. For five thousand

pounds. A substantial fee, as I said. And when ye consider, was the risk so great? He issues the dead warrant, the folk grumble that they didn't see ye turned off, but does anyone suspect for a moment that ye're not dead at all? The point is that the military have charge of executions, and soldiers not only do what they're told, they think what they're told. They'll ask no questions.'

Rackham tried to digest this, but there were a hundred things he did not understand – principally who should pay five thousand pounds on his behalf.

'The next step is by far the more dangerous,' went on Dickey. 'You'll be taking it yourself very shortly. Ye see, Coates is bribed wi' five thousand pounds, for which he hangs you in absentia and none the wiser. But there his part ends. Oh, he was adamant on that. So other agents go to work – myself, for one. With the . . .'

'But why?' interrupted Rackham. 'Why you?'

'Wheesht a minute. As I say, with the result that when the *Willem Damman*, a Dutch brig, puts out of Port Royal to-day for Dominica, you'll be aboard her. That,' added Master Dickey, 'cost another three hundred. Take another sup o' the rum, man. Ye look as though ye need it.'

Rackham obeyed and repeated his question. 'What have you to do with all this?'

'Ye may well ask. Coates near died o' fright when he learned I had been let intae the business, but the fool had brought it on himsel' by refusing to act beyond arranging your execution and having your cell door unlocked. Someone was needed, someone who could be trusted, tae make arrangements for a ship and tae guide you to it.'

'But you? Rogers' closest friend – who in God's name would come to you, and why would you—' He broke off.

'Who the devil paid this money for me, and why?' he demanded.

Master Dickey considered him solemnly. 'Does that matter, after all?'

Rackham nodded. 'It matters.'

Dickey picked up a quill, brushed it thoughtfully against his chin, and laid it down again. 'Mistress Sampson,' he said.

Rackham stared at him. 'Kate?' he said unbelievingly. 'Kate Sampson? But . . . oh, you're mad! Or lying, one or the other.'

'Name me one other soul in the world that would – or could – give five thousand pounds for your neck,' said Master Dickey calmly.

There was no answer to that. However fantastic Dickey's story, it was borne out by present circumstances. He was sitting here, drinking rum while the clock ticked precisely on the mantel over the crackling fire. And there was a ship waiting to take him away, to Dominica. It was like a dream, but with none of a dream's vagueness. Here the details were clear. And he had no choice but to accept what Dickey said.

Kate had saved him, then. He could not doubt why she had done it – obviously she loved him, in spite of Rogers and everything else. And for him she had been prepared to risk so much – perhaps her life.

Quietly the lawyer said: 'Well?'

Rackham met his eyes. 'I don't know . . . what am I to think? It's . . . it's hard to believe. That she should do so much.'

'She didnae do it for the reasons you're thinking,' said Dickey gently. He got up and went to the window, looking out at the rain pattering the sill. 'Ye'll be thinking she loves you – a romantic notion, and like most romantic notions,

271

wide of the truth.' He turned impatiently. But why talk of it? The thing's done, for which ye may be thankful, why or wherefore is beside the point.'

Rackham got up and went round the table until he stood beside the lawyer. 'How can you say? What did she tell you?'

Master Dickey smiled a little sadly. 'I'm an old lawyer, lad. Folk dinnae need to tell me things. Ye'll ask me why, if she doesnae love you, she risks her very life and gives a pickle money to free you. And my only answer is that there are folk like that – like Mistress Sampson. Good folk and brave. Here there was a wee spark of conscience to prick her on. It was misplaced, but then she's only a lassie yet. But it wasnae love. A woman who had gone so far as this for you wouldnae jib at going the whole hog if she really cared for you. Aye, she would let money and marriage and all go hang, this one, so she could be where her heart was set.' He paused deliberately. 'And she hasnae, ye see.'

It was not in Master Dickey's nature to be cruel, but he had weighed up his man and he wanted no complications, no foolish notions that might some day bring this fellow back in pursuit of a dream. Kate Sampson must be free of him for ever henceforth; if Rackham conceived that she still loved him there was no telling what tragic foolery he might perpetrate. So Master Dickey drove his point home.

'I'll make myself abundantly clear, Master Rackham. And while I'm about it, I may say that your calm acceptance of my part in this dirty business is far from flattering. Here am I, with as nice a conscience as any Presbyterian that ever sang psalms, colloguin' wi' knaves and a misguided lassie to take a buccaneer's head frae the rope. Doubtless ye think I'm being well feed: well, I'm not. Not one penny piece, God be thanked. If I betray my master I'll do it wi'out that stain, at least.'

'I'll tell ye this,' he went on, 'if Mistress Sampson had come to me when first she conceived this . . . this damned folly, I would have moved heaven and earth to turn her from it. I would have seen ye hang and thanked God to be rid of a knave, and hauled on the rope mysel'. But she had been tae Coates first and she was not to be turned. What, then, was I to do? Go to Woodes Rogers and say: "Look here, your lady wife-to-be is aiding the escape of the ruffian Rackham that used to be her jo'?" Eh? Could I do that?' His face was flushed and angry. 'Ye know I could not. And no more could I sit by and let her gang her ain gate. For she needed someone she could trust and by the grace of God she had chosen me. If I abandoned her the whole business would miscarry. So I promised her my help. And so ye see that your life or your dirty neck doesnae matter a pinch o' bad snuff to me. But her happiness does, and so does that of another that you've never thought on, and that's Woodes Rogers.'

He went over to his desk and sat down and picked up his quill and snapped it between his fingers. His voice sounded tired, as though his outburst had sapped his energy.

'Rogers took me out o' the gutter – ye didnae know that. He saved me from a life of pinch and peck at a clerk's stool where I'd have earned a few paltry shillings and a poor man's grave. He brought me out here, gave me this good life, honoured me wi' his trust, made me his friend, and I would put this hand in the fire for him. And now I must betray him.'

He turned the broken quill over in his hand and rubbed it between his fingers.

'But in betraying him I hope to serve him. He loves this lassie, and she's no' unkindly set towards him. If he should find out what she's done – well, folk don't die o' heart-break, but it would wound him as nothing else ever could. Even suppose she escaped the law, even suppose they were wed in spite of all – d'ye think he'd ever know a moment's ease for the rest of his days? He would wonder about you, and what ye meant to her: it would be his life spoiled as well as hers – and I love them both too dearly to let that happen. So that's why ye must live.

'If you fail to-day, there's an end to them. There's an end to Woodes Rogers' work, forbye. And for that reason alone I'd cheat him behind his back in this. Aye, so that he can go on doing what he started in the Bahamas two years ago. With her he'll go on to greater things: without her it's odds he'll go nowhere at all.'

Rackham took a long time to answer. Bitterness was a useless thing. It was enough that he was going free, and yet there was a tiny seed of misery and regret in his mind and he could see no way to rid himself of it.

From somewhere far off came the flat report of a cannon, muffled by the distance and the morning rain. Master Dickey cocked his head.

'There goes the first of your friends,' he said.

Rackham put down his glass. He felt suddenly sick. That gun, then, meant Bull, or Carty, or Malloy, or Dobbins: it could have meant Jack Rackham. He felt the sweat breaking out on his face. God, it might be Ben. Ben, the loyal companion and stout seaman, dying under a butcher's knife in front of a jeering crowd. Nausea seized him and he held on to the table for support.

Master Dickey was watching him gravely, and his face had lost something of its harshness.

'At all events, ye can console yourself that the Bonney

woman isnae hanging with them,' he said. 'Ye'll ken she had a reprieve, since when she's been paramour tae this Bernard that calls himself a chief justice. It's one of those guilty secrets that's a public scandal – everyone kens except the Governor and it's odds he wouldnae understand it if it was shouted in his ear. God help the Government! And it goes beyond sayin' that she'll no hang in the long run either.'

'Thank God,' said Rackham quietly.

Dickey looked at the clock. 'It's time you made ready. Put you on that jacket on the chest yonder, and the bonnet, and listen to me.'

As Rackham was fastening the jacket Dickey crossed the room to a side door near his desk. He threw it open revealing a flight of stairs going downwards.

'At the bottom of this flight ye'll find a passageway. Beyond is a wee closed court, wi' a door. It's unlocked and beyond lies the street ye can look down on from this window.' He beckoned Rackham and pointed. 'Not the first turn to your right but the second, where the handcart stands. D'ye see? Down yonder lie the quays and there ye'll find the *Willem Damman*. The master's name is Haas. Your name is Martin. There'll be nae questions asked, but ye'd best lie low once ye're aboard. By to-night ye'll be far from here.' He paused. 'Is all clear to you?'

'Yes.' Rackham was beginning to feel a tightening of his stomach muscles at the thought of that lonely walk to the unknown brig. 'Yes, I think so. Sir, for what ye've done, and . . . for your help . . . there's little I can say . . .'

'Ach, tut!' exclaimed Master Dickey. 'D'ye think I care for thanks. I've told ye why I do this, and it is not in your interest.'

'Even so,' said Rackham, 'I do thank you. I would thank her, too, if . . .'

'Not a word!' snapped Dickey. 'Not one word goes to Mistress Sampson, understand that! The thing's over and done wi'. Calico Jack Rackham's dead, and good riddance to him.'

They stood in silence for a few moments, and once again the gun sounded in the distance. Master Dickey referred again to the clock and turned away, his hands clasped behind him.

'It seems a long while since ye came in my window at Providence,' he remarked. 'Aye, a long while, and a queer way things have gone. Weel, it's no for me tae judge, God knows. We are what we are – and there it is.' He cleared his throat. 'What I said a minute since was true: my concern is for Mistress Sampson and my friend Woodes Rogers, but that doesnae mean I'm ill pleased at how things have fallen out. Ye see, as a man grows older he sees that there's no good folk or bad folk, but just . . . weel, just different ones in different conditions. A man has only a share in shaping his destiny – the rest is chance. That holds for most of us, for all except those that are strong enough to mould life to their own liking. And some are lucky, and some are not. I think you're one of the unlucky ones. And because I've been like that, too, until fortune served me, I can view mankind, I hope, wi' a tolerant eye. There's no' many perfect, and there's no justice at all. I see greater rogues about the street every day o' the week, like this greasy villain Coates, that I have to tak' my dinner wi'. Aye, and Kinsman, who's naught but a rascal-at-arms, when all's said. Or this other scoundrel Bernard, pervertin' justice for lust's sake. D'ye think you're worse than they? No, but ye're unluckier, and no sae clever, perhaps. I'm no justifyin' ye, for God knows the Archangel Gabriel couldnae do that, but there's others as bad that 'scape whipping. So I'll no lose sleep because ye cheat the rope, laddie, which is a maist un-Presbyterian thing tae say. Perhaps it's because I know Mistress Kate wouldnae risk what she's risked for just any man; whatever it is, I'm no sorry ye're going free.'

The distant gun boomed, and he stopped short as though aware that he was talking too much.

'Time for ye to start,' he said, and abruptly held out his hand. 'God speed.'

Rackham shook hands, and then the door closed, and Dickey was alone. He went over to the window and looked down into the street.

There were few folk about – a porter with his bale, a woman with a baby on her hip, a group of idlers at the first corner. Tobias heard the faint sound of a door closing somewhere beneath him, and then he saw Rackham in the street, striding swiftly forward with his collar turned up against the wind. No one so much as glanced at the tall man in the sailor's jacket who hurried past them without glancing to right or left; Tobias watched his figure grow gradually smaller until it reached the second turning. There he hesitated for a moment before turning quickly down the street that led to the quays.

Tobias shook his head, smiling gently to himself. He felt philosophic and strangely content. The work that awaited him on his desk seemed of little importance; he had much to think about, not least of the new chapter that must be added presently to his journal. But not for a while yet; it would be safer stored away in his mind until the time came when he could set it down without fear of consequences. That would be a long time, he reflected, years perhaps. But some points he could jot down at once in case they slipped his memory, wording them carefully so that none but himself could understand them. Then in time they could be combined and related in an ordered narrative. In the meantime there were other matters to attend to.

Master Dickey turned away from the window and went back to his desk, whistling.

Letters
from the
Archive

These letters from The Authors' Alliance were found with the manuscript of *Captain in Calico*. Their contents would have been enough to deject most would-be authors, but their preservation suggests that GMF was sufficiently confident of his talents to believe that they might one day be of interest. Despite the criticisms, one particular remark in the Reader's Report no doubt gave him heart, since it sums up everything he strove to be as a writer: 'He is exciting some of the time, and entertaining all of the time'.

Caro Fraser, 2015

TEL. ENTERPRISE 1041

J. HATHERLEY CLARKE, MANAGER
A. L. HAYDON, LITERARY ADVISER

The Authors' Alliance
LITERARY AGENTS FOR OVER 40 YEARS
44 PARK WAY, LONDON, N.20
AND AT NEW YORK, U.S.A., AND MELBOURNE, AUSTRALIA

Encls.

10th. January 1957

George Fraser Esq.,
58 Manchester Drive,
Glasgow, W.2.

Dear Sir,

I now send you a copy of the Report which I have received upon your adventure story entitled "Captain in Calico".

The Reader has dealt so fully with the merits and demerits of your work that there is really very little which I can usefully add to his comments. The main point is that this story is much too long and definitely overwritten. Before starting upon the drastic pruning which will be necessary in order to make the book a commercial proposition, I would strongly advise you to study a selection of the adventure stories of a similar type - you should find plenty of such books in any good public library - and notice the technique employed by established writers in this particular field. You must bear in mind all the time that it is the story proper which interests the reader and not the side-issues and unimportant details to which the Report draws attention.

Another point is that there is a limit to the price which can be charged for a book of this kind. The cost of printing and binding - apart from paper and, perhaps, illustrations - would be very heavy in the present case, and unless a publisher could visualise a sale of some thousands of copies he would not be justified in shouldering the financial risks.

If you are prepared to thoroughly revise your MS. it should then stand a reasonable chance of attracting attention; but you will appreciate that I cannot guarantee that it will meet with acceptance. I would suggest working on the present typescript and submitting the final version of the story to my Reader before you go to the expense of typing a clean copy for submission to publishers. Kindly let me know if you need any further assistance.

I return your MS. herewith.

Believe me to be,
Yours faithfully,

J Hatherley Clarke.

C A P T A I N C A L I C O

by

George Fraser.

The author states in his covering letter that this
is an historical novel; but it is not. It is a plain pirate
story of the good old kind and can only be regarded as 'historical' in so far as any pirate, or any highwayman story
must be.

This is uninhibited and unpretentious; just plain
blood and thunder, and it is very good. Although the modern
thriller covers the same market, publishers sometimes go in
for a thing of this sort for a change, and strangely enough,
such books get well noticed: the reviewer's cliche for them
is 'refreshing'.

Your Client writes very well and succeeds in holding
the reader's attention from the word 'go'. He is exciting some
of the time and entertaining all of the time. He creates a
convincing atmosphere and draws his characters boldly. That
they are book-characters rather than real-life characters is
undeniable, but the type of story demands intensively 'ficti-
tious' characters - they fit into the background and suit the
story. It is true that he changes a character's character to
suit the situation, but that does not matter in the least: a
book of this kind sells for the fun of it, and critics are apt
to be kindly, to praise it for what it is and refrain (for
once) from pointing to what it is not in order to underline
their own cleverness.

It is a pity, having regard to all that, that as it
stands, this story is quite useless and cannot be offered.
The author says he will have it retyped, if necessary - it
would be, seeing he has done it on half sheets of paper -
but what it needs is rewriting.

For this market, sixty to seventy thousand words is
the length required, and the MS. is all of a hundred and sixty
thousand.

/

2

Every scene, every incident is over-written. There
is not really more story than would go into 60,000 words, but
there is a wealth of minute detail at every turn. We do not
want careful calculation of each cut and thrust in each duel.
We do not want to study the wounds of every member of the crew
after every seafight. A number of minor characters could be
done away with and many smaller incidents dropped.

I think the very idea of getting rid of two-thirds of
the book will give the author colic, but it is quite out of
the question to offer the story as it is; while in a shrunken
state it will be very well worth trying.

I would advise your Client to read (or re-read)
R.L.S's. "Treasure Island" - which has, in fact, more story
than he has in "Captain in Calico" - but is so short that it
is usually printed with "Kidnapped", or else illustrated to
fill out the covers. I must strongly impress upon Mr. Fraser
the great importance of close writing. He must make his
motto MULTUM IN PARVO.

TEL.: ENTERPRISE 1041

J. HATHERLEY CLARKE, MANAGER
JULIAN FRANKLYN, LITERARY ADVISER

The Authors' Alliance

LITERARY AGENTS FOR OVER 40 YEARS

44 PARK WAY, LONDON, N.20

AND AT NEW YORK, U.S.A., AND MELBOURNE, AUSTRALIA

13th. May 1959

Encl.

George Fraser Esq.,
56 Manchester Drive,
Glasgow W.2.

Dear Mr. Fraser,

I quote below what the Reader has to say about
the new version of "Captain in Calico".

In view of the time which has elapsed since I read
the original script of this story, a sight of my first
report has enabled me to refresh my memory of the reasons
why I found it necessary to turn it down.

Mr. Fraser has revised and cut the MS. very considerably; but it is still much too long for the market at which
it is aimed. It is definitely light - very light - fiction.
In fact, I regard it as little more than a juvenile; hence
it must not exceed 60,000 words if it is to stand any chance
of publication.

Mr. Fraser has not written a classic to compare with,
say, "The Count of Monte Christo". I only mention this, because he did submit the MS. in the first instance, as an
historical novel.

It can be cut quite easily - whole chunks can come out
and no one will miss them. Mr. Fraser's experience of the
vital importance of close writing in the newspaper world will
have taught him how to make effective use of the blue pencil.
On p. 90 I have very gently, and in black lead only, indicated the kind of thing that must come out of a story of this
kind.

I must say quite frankly that there is nothing about this
MS. - either in the plot, the characters, the situations or
the literary style - to even suggest that it will find favour
with that strata of the reading public which is willing to
pay about 15/- for a novel. Its only chance is in the cheap
market for which the maximum length is 60,000 at the outside.

Finally, it should be made clear to Mr. Fraser that 'cut
price' publishers work on such a very close margin of profit
that the remuneration - a lump sum as a rule - they can afford
to offer their authors is so meagre that I am surprised that
anyone is prepared to produce creative work for what is little
more than a pittance.

I am wondering what will be your reactions after reading this lukewarm report. If you decide to set to work again with the pruning knife I will, of course, see what can be done with the story. I am not at all surprised that it was turned down by the publishers you mentioned, with all of whom I am in close contact.

Your MS. is returned herewith and I take this opportunity to enclose the correspondence you were good enough to forward. In conclusion, I can only express my regret that, in spite of the time and labour you have put into the story, it is still not a marketable proposition in the opinion of my Reader.

Believe me to be,
Yours sincerely,

J. Hatherley Clarke

J. Hatherley Clarke.

The FLASHMAN Papers
(In chronological order)

The FLASHMAN Papers
(In order of publication)

Also by George MacDonald Fraser

Mr American
The Pyrates
The Candlemass Road
Black Ajax
The Reavers

Short Stories
The General Danced at Dawn
McAuslan in the Rough
The Sheikh and the Dustbin

History
The Steel Bonnets:
The Story of the Anglo-Scottish Border Reivers

Autobiography
Quartered Safe Out Here
The Light's on at Signpost

*

The Hollywood History of the World